The Village House

SOULLA CHRISTODOULOU

KINGSLEY

PUBLISHERS

First published in South Africa by Kingsley Publishers, 2022
Copyright © Soulla Christodoulou, 2022

The right of Soulla Christodoulou to be identified as author of
this work has been asserted.

Kingsley Publishers
Pretoria, South Africa

www.kingsleypublishers.com
A catalogue copy of this book will be available from the National
Library of South Africa
Paperback ISBN: 978-0-6397-1466-0
eBook ISBN: 978-0-6397-1467-7

Also by Soulla Christodoulou

Broken Pieces of Tomorrow
The Summer Will Come
Alexander and Maria

To my sisters, Lia and Maria, with huge thanks and lots of love.

Chapter 1

The building, in the heart of London, screamed success. Katianna relished it. Her patent heels clipped across the marble flooring, the echo bouncing across the bright, open space. She took the green coded escalator to the double-decker lifts, leather laptop case in one hand and designer handbag in the other.

The glass doors pinged opened, closed immediately after her. She pressed the button for the twelfth floor, the location of her dating agency, *Under the Setting Sun*. She looked straight ahead at the control panel; the buttons lighting up the company names as the elevator whooshed past each floor: Investment Management PLC, Kew and Press Lawyers, ARC Project Management, Cyprus Property Portfolio… her eyes stayed locked with the word Cyprus… the letter she had recently received on her mind, still sitting on her desk, but she shook the niggling, invasive thought away, refocused.

In her office, she tucked her handbag under her desk and smoothed out her black pencil skirt. She plugged in and switched on her laptop. She sat facing the glass-walled partition which afforded her with a view of her team and the open-plan workspace beyond. At eight promptly she went through the day's key activities with her PA.

'That's great, thank you Angie.'

'I'll get your coffee,' Angie said, her tight ponytail and wide-legged culottes swinging in time with each long step. Her yellow flat pumps coordinated nicely with the mustard of her trousers and echoed the colours of an uncharacteristically warm July. At almost six-foot Angie didn't need any more height. She towered over Katianna, who at only five foot four considered her own heels necessary, especially at work.

Angie was in her early thirties, a few years younger than Katianna, but her mature attitude and commitment shone through from the moment she said "anything it takes" in her interview five years before. Katianna recognised a kindred spirit in her and despite Angie's patchy work history hired her instantly never regretting it.

A real asset to the company, Angie was efficient, productive, proactive and loyal. She had become a good friend over the years and with life very much tipped towards work, genuine friends were hard to come by for Katianna. The glitz and glamour of award nights and ceremonies were just that and Katianna snubbed her friends' comments.

'Slow down,' they urged. 'Not everything which shines is made of gold.'

But her circle shrunk as she rebuffed their comments telling them everything did in her world.

Katianna's sole purpose to be successful was all-consuming, her single-minded ambition her steed. Eight years before, she had won the court case against her business partner, also her ex-fiancé, to keep the business name. She had since spent every waking hour and every ounce of energy making the business a leader and had vowed never to be indebted to anyone ever again, especially in business. But in love too.

Judged by the UK and European Dating Awards' independent panel on reputation, success rate, approachability, and customer service, *Under the Setting Sun*, had been favoured many times over.

Framed awards hung in a perfect line across one wall and gave no room for doubt: UK Matchmaking Agency of the Year 2015 and 2018, International Matchmaker of the Year 2015, European Matchmaking Agency of the Year 2016 and 2018.

But achievement had come at a price; the ensuing months of working long hours and at weekends had pushed away the university friends Katianna had in her inner circle. The odd text or phone call was all she had time for now. She recognised a shift once they had husbands, wives, families of their own. She pushed aside the split-second prickle. She had her empire, didn't she?

She swiveled round in her seat to face the London vista laid out before her, the leather squeaking against the fabric of her skirt. This, all of it, she breathed, was worth every minute of working past midnight, waking at dawn, and missed lunches with friends. This is what made life worth living.

Every day she breathed in the success of the dating agency and her innovative approach had kept her ahead of the ever-growing competition and away from negative press increasingly associated with dating agencies and relationship apps.

Hers was different; clients plugged into a network of high-calibre, aspirational, professional singles. Supported by an assigned matchmaker, they worked towards the ultimate goal of a long-term relationship. Their sign-up package included professional photography, Myers Briggs-type indicator assessment which provided information on who each client really was and ID-checks on all members which ensured safety and security. Her matchmakers had backgrounds in psychology, counselling, and life coaching. Her newest recruit was a chartered psychologist and Associate Fellow of the British Psychological Society.

She took a call from John, her full-time accountant and finance manager. Running any business effectively relied on the owner's understanding of costs, money in and money out, and John handled that side of the agency for her; she preferred the company of people to figures and spreadsheets and she was instinctively yielding around him, trusting his knowledge and expertise implicitly.

John had been working with Katianna for almost seven years and he had been one of the first people she consulted with in terms of growing the business. It took off in its second year, more than tripling her forecasted income.

They rescheduled their monthly meeting around another appointment that had moved for John and said goodbye.

Katianna checked her emails and looked over the schedule of client photo shoots and website update meetings planned with her team; she kept a keen eye on the competition and read the main broadsheet newspapers and magazines every day. She followed trending hashtags, Instagram stories and LinkedIn news, including trends in the USA, Canada, and Europe.

She turned around, a knock-knock at her door.

'Come in,' she said, already gesturing to Warren, one of her advertising sales team.

'Have you got a minute?'

'Of course,' she said, nodding towards one of the black leather club chairs.

'I've got good news and bad news,' he said. 'The Mayfair Inn, Sherlock Mews and Devi Ahilya India have confirmed their online advertising for another year. I've increased the ad fee by 10%.'

'And the bad news?'

'One of the new restaurant accounts has paid for the key spot on our home page for twelve months.'

'Bad news because?'

'The Broadgate Hotel & Spa has already confirmed that spot for three months and paid-up front.'

'Use your negotiation skills to keep them holding on until then… offer them something else for the first three months and then the nine months, or even the year, on the home page.'

'I did that already. They're not biting.'

'Leave it with me. When did you last speak to them?'

'Day before yesterday.'

'Email across the details, your conversation notes, files.'

'I'll do it right now,' he said, making for the door. 'Thanks Katianna.'

She smiled at his retreating back. Warren was good at getting the advertising in but not so good with what she called "being cute"– keeping all sides happy when a pickle arose which thankfully wasn't often.

Her laptop pinged, Warren's email. She read the attachments, nothing to worry about. She was sure she could keep both accounts happy.

She pushed the laptop away and the letter caught her attention;

the letter that had been mailed three times to her previous address. It was quite by chance she had bumped into her old neighbour who mentioned she had been holding onto post for her.

Katianna had hated sharing a letter box with Nosy Rosy, as she not-so-affectionately nicknamed her, who never missed an opportunity to ask why Vodafone were sending so many letters or why she received discount offer cards when everyone did their shopping online; her own daughter and three nieces did. Katianna had forced a smile and tightened her lips holding back on what she had really thought of her nosiness even though it was cloaked as neighbourly concern and kindness.

She took the envelope in her hand, felt the weight of it, in more ways than one, ran her fingers over the perforated edges of the Cyprus stamp and slipped out the thick cream sheet. She read the three short paragraphs again. She needed to book a flight to Cyprus when all she wanted was to stay in London, enjoy the rare hot summer and get on with running her business. She didn't have the time to take the four-and-a-half-hour trip to a country she hadn't been back to for years and recalled a client, two years ago, who the agency had successfully paired with a French lawyer. She believed they now lived happily in Paphos.

'Look at it as a well-deserved break,' Angie had said, 'on the island of l-o-o-o-v-e.' Katianna smiled, remembering how Angie had drawled the word.

Katianna had tried dismissing the unexpected wave of wistful affection. Her *yiayia* Anna had been the only grandmother she had known in her life and memories filled her; *yiayia* hugging Katianna tight, pinching her cheeks each summer in exaggerated awe of how much she had grown, plucking juicy purple figs, and picking grapes together.

Was going back to claim her *yiayia's* house a good idea? Her grandmother's passing had been painful, a shock, yet Katianna had not returned for the funeral still reeling from the deaths of her own parents; a stab of guilt poked at her, even more so now that the village house had been bequeathed to her and her parents were no longer here to know it. For a moment, tears threatened to fall but she pushed them away. There was no time for silly sentimentality and regrets. Living in the moment was all she had, and this is what she had right now; a house in the village waiting for her to what? Breathe new life into it? Connect with a life and a culture she had negligible ties with?

Her cousin Savva, who had linked up with her, after more than twenty years, put on the pressure, begging her to fly out.

'You can stay with me,' he said. 'I'm all grown up now.'

She had to go. She could not get out of this. Savva wouldn't take no for an answer and, of course she had to sign the legal documents for the house. Cyprus, it appeared, didn't recognise technological advancements and the solicitor insisted she visit to sign the paperwork in person with her identification: 'We have to have the original documents in front of us,' he repeated, though she wondered whether Savva had anything to do with their lack of enthusiasm to do things online.

Saying goodbye to her team was bittersweet; part of her looked forward to a break, a change of routine, and she had solved Warren's issue, with charm, so she was leaving on a high. Her team was the closest she had to family, yet she held them at a distance, preferring not to blur the lines between her work and their private lives. But she was admittedly going to miss them all as well as the buzz of the day to day in the office. As she left shortly after seven, she quietly relished the idea of disappearing for a few days, remembering her mother's words: *Rest is not an indulgence, it is essential Katianna. How can you be your best self if you don't treat yourself well?* Cyprus was going to bring her the rest she needed, she reassured herself.

Chapter 2

Katianna arrived at Larnaca International Airport exhausted and crampy; the pains in her tummy twisting her intestines with anticipation but her exterior façade portrayed nothing of her inner anxiety. It was nearly midnight by the time she exited the airport even though passport control had been efficient, and the queues had moved quickly. She hoped Savva was still waiting for her.

The flight from Heathrow Terminal 5 had been delayed by two hours because of "mechanical issues". The announcement had left her uneasy and anxiety consumed her entire flight despite the luxury of flying first class. All the while the whiney antagonistic voice in her head said: "You should have stayed at home. Leaving your business and gallivanting to God knows where..."

Katianna marvelled at the modern, bright airport remembering how she used to arrive with her parents and have to queue on the tarmac; the airport building too small to accommodate a full plane of arrivals. She walked out of the air-conditioned building with a renewed bounce.

The muggy heat of the night enveloped her and conscious of a sheen of sweat she brushed her hand across her forehead and upper lip. August, the hottest month of the year. Her clammy hand slipped against the suitcase handle as she dragged the oversized luggage behind her. Trying to keep it upright, she crossed the tarmac, no longer riddled with potholes and cracks as it had been years before, though the intense summer heat was the same. Her ankle doubled over as she caught her red stilettos on the edge of the raised walkway and her designer jacket slipped off her arm. Looking down at the heel, the leather had been shredded. Damn, she thought and gathering the jacket draped it over her shoulders despite the heat.

'Katianna,' Savva called from where he leaned against the shuttered kiosk, the streetlamp casting a harsh light.

She carefully navigated her way between the rows of parked hire cars and minibuses. As Katianna neared him, she took in his dishevelled appearance, yet his stance oozed a quiet, sexy confidence which took her by surprise. He was unkempt yet surprisingly attractive. He seemed bolder, more mature, in real life, not the soft, baby-faced man she saw on their video calls.

He threw his unfinished cigarette to the ground, grinding the stub into the tarmac and leaned in to kiss Katianna's cheeks, exhaling smoke over her shoulder. Katianna, taken by surprise, felt a blush of colour fill her cheeks. She had forgotten how kisses and hugs were nothing to shy away from in Cyprus, especially when greeting friends and relatives.

'I thought you said you were quitting?' she grimaced and then smiled as she waved the tendrils of Savva's cigarette smoke away.

'I was, until a week ago when the thought of my English cousin visiting stressed me out.'

'Very funny. You can't blame me. What's the real reason?'

'Lack of will power.'

'That's it?'

'That's it. Now come here and give me a proper hug.' He pulled her close.

'You stink like an ashtray,' she said, pulling away and giggling, surprised and delighted with the familiarity between them.

She liked the way she was able to connect with him even though her Greek was inferior to his fluency in English. But the closeness between them, there since childhood, was evident and flooded back like a ribbon-like flow of water, comfortable moving with the force of gravity, unperturbed by any babbles or ripples. They were almost twins; their birthdays only three days apart and it didn't take long for Savva to tease her about being older and therefore demanded respect.

'You haven't really changed at all,' she said.

As children they had been thrown together every summer holiday; they danced together, swam out to the floating raft at Santa Barbara beach despite words of warning from their parents, and as a teenager Savva had escorted her to clubs, keeping a close eye on anyone who dared approach her, ready to pounce with the protectiveness of a lion over his pride.

***

The drive to the village from the airport took just shy of an hour and a half; Katianna took in the silhouetted view of tall buildings and huge lit billboards, almost unrecognisable to the landscape she remembered as a child.

The peaks of the Troodos Mountains loomed darker still behind the buildings, with the stars twinkling like Van Gogh's *The Starry Night*. She recalled a specific camping trip to the Kykko Monastery, a royal, Patriarchal Stavropygian Monastery located in the western part of the mountain range, twelve miles from the highest peak of Cyprus' Mount Olympus.

All those years ago, lying side by side with Savva, sharing the same sleeping bag, the same splintered stars had dotted the inkiest blue expanse which felt so close it was as if she could pluck one from its blanket. Savva had tried to grab one for her, huffing and puffing, exaggerating his efforts. The other campers had been woken by her laughter followed by the smack of the thrashing slaps from their parents; both had hidden inside the lumpy sleeping bag till they almost couldn't breathe, holding hands, their bodies squashed against each other's in innocence, as any brother or sister.

'Almost there already,' she said, disappointed when the car indicated at the final E-road exit for Omodos. Omodos, she thought, coming from the Cypriot word "modos," meaning "taking your time," with tact, carefully. She had found the snippet of information on the in-flight magazine. She hadn't realised how popular a destination her ancestral village had become and felt a sense of pride shadowed by a sting of guilt at not having known it.

As a child, the drive from the airport seemed to take forever, the journey made almost in complete darkness with no lighting along the poorly tarmacked roads, pot-holed and rutted–dirt tracks–unlike the roads now, the majority brightly lit and well-maintained.

They arrived in the village, built at the slope of the mountains, the winding roads narrower than she remembered and the pretty stone village houses, with their tiled roofs and terraces and picturesque upper floors, glowing in the amber light of the streetlamps; those replaced at intervals with brighter bulbs shone at a sharp downward angle and she scrunched her tired eyes against their harshness. The sweet smell of grapes carried on the mid-night breeze as it swept over the vineyards towards the village. A stray cat, not straggly or emaciated like the strays used to be, ran out in front of the car, her shiny coat glinting in the headlights. Savva slowed down and the cat's eyes seemed to stare at Katianna.

Katianna shivered against a little tremor running through her, but she looked upon the cat crossing their path as a good omen and her black fur even more so. She slinked away and disappeared under a parked pick-up truck; battered and missing a back bumper.

***

So where do you want to start today? I've taken three days off work to be your translator, chauffeur, whatever you need.'

'You're a real good sort. How comes you haven't been snapped up?' Katianna wiped her brow, already sweaty from the rising temperature.

'Who says I haven't?'

'Because your house is still a house, not a home,' said Katianna, pointing to the stark walls and clutter-free surfaces of the open-plan kitchen and sitting room.

'How is that observation going to help you sort out your *yiayia's* house?'

'Sorry. It isn't. It's a habit of mine… comes with the job.' She smiled, hoping to take the sting out of her comment. 'Let's start with breakfast and then you can accompany me to the house.'

'Sounds good. I want to know everything that's been happening. There's something different about you I didn't catch on our video calls. I can't put my finger on it.'

Chapter 3

'Black tea with cinnamon sticks and cloves, and a halloumi and mortadella toastie for me, thank you.' Katianna placed her order after Savva introduced her to Sofia.

Katianna had spotted the little café *stafilia kai meli* which translated as "grapes and honey" as they walked arm in arm across the village square and though Savva had tried to persuade her to walk further, Katianna's puppy-dog eyes had won him over.

'How delightful. I haven't been asked for a cinnamon and clove tea in years.'

'It's how my *yiayia* Anna made it. It seems right I should drink it now I'm back,' said Katianna.

'She was a wonderful old lady, so kind,' said Sofia.

'You knew her?'

'She was a grandmother to all of us growing up in the village,' said Sofia.

'I guess she would have been, yes. I wish I'd known her better, especially these last few years.'

'Well, there are many around here who can tell you about her,' said Sofia.

'Just a coffee for me, Sofia,' said Savva, interrupting them.

Katianna gave him a look; one she had perfected in the days of child minding to pay her university fees. Memories flooded her: piles of ironing, scrubbing shower doors until they gleamed, tidying endless toys, sleeping on her side on the edge of a single bed until her arm went numb while Jessica and James fell asleep, working with her laptop balanced on crossed legs on the sofa until after midnight, reading Eric Carle's *The Very Hungry Caterpillar* and Michael Bond's *Paddington Bear* Books over and over until she almost knew the stories word for word.   She sighed, and then recalled the heavy hardbacks of J.K. Rowling which the family gifted her when she finished working with them two years later together with a generous bank transfer which put her in the black for the first time in four years.

'What?' he asked, cutting across her thoughts.

'You've taken me back to my nannying days... and not the good ones.'

'What d'you mean?'

'No smile. No please. No thank you.' She paused. 'You could at least acknowledge her. She's lovely and no wedding ring.'

'That's because she's not married,' he said, folding his arms across his chest.

'How come?' teased Katianna. Her lighter tone eased the tension she picked up on and Savva gave her a half smile.

'I don't know. She's always lived in the village, never left. Opened the coffee shop when her parents died,' he said, avoiding eye contact.

'She looks happy.'

'They say happiness can come from the deepest sorrows, don't they?' said Savva.

'You're right. Kahil Gibran said something like, *when you feel joy, look to your heart and you'll find it's only that which has given you sorrow that is now giving you joy.*'

'I guess that's kind of true.'

'And she owns this place?'

'She spent all her inheritance breathing new life into the once derelict building abandoned by the previous owners. She's always here. Working.'

'Working but happy,' said Katianna, Sofia's situation closely mirroring her own.

Katianna sat a while, didn't say anything but her mind was already ticking with anticipation, an idea forming. Back in London and across the industry she was inevitably known as *The Matchmaker* and even though she was single herself she had this knack of pairing single hearts together and matching them fruitfully. With a first in psychology, she knew what made people tick and *Under the Setting Sun* had become more than a simple dating agency. It attracted clients serious about partnering and with a view to getting married, finding a life-long partner and it worked.

Sofia returned with their order served in a mishmash of crockery.

'So pretty,' said Katianna, fingering the pretty floral teacup and saucer.

'Thank you, it meant a lot to my mother who received it as part of her dowry when she married. My intention was to use it temporarily and replace it once the business began making a profit but I'm glad I didn't,' she said, with a faraway look in her eye.

'I'm here refurbishing my grandmother's house and when it's done, I'm hoping to have a little celebration in memory of her life. I wonder...' she said, turning an idea around in her head. 'Would you cater for it and, of course, join me as a guest.'

'I'd be happy to arrange anything you need food-wise, but this place takes up all my time. But thank you for the invitation, that's sweet of you.'

'Don't say no to joining us just yet. Let me get sorted and once I have a date you can decide then.'

'She said, no, Katianna. Leave it,' said Savva.

Sofia's cheeks turned a fiery red. She grabbed the empty plates from the next table and scuttled off towards the serving hatch where Petros, her part-time chef, was already lining up the next round of breakfast orders.

'You embarrassed her,' said Katianna and slurping her tea she focused on its sweet, spicy fragrance to take away the sourness in the air.

'Me? You're the one going on about the catering and the invite,' he said and pulling his mouth with both fingers, stretched it wide, and waggled his tongue at her.

'You're not ten anymore,' she tutted, 'but I guess that's what so loveable about you.'

'Enough of me and how immature I am. Let's talk about you. What are your plans with the house?'

'Spruce it up and sell it. It's not convenient to keep it. I'm like Sofia with work leaching my time. And my life's in London.'

'The house is in pretty bad shape so sprucing may realistically need to be translated as refurbishing and even rebuilding in places.'

'It's been old and run down for as long as I remember,' she said, taking a bite of her toasted sandwich. The nutty aroma of the toasted, sesame-seed bread filled her nostrils. 'This is so good. The bread I buy from the bakery back home is good, Polish bread, but this is just heaven.'

'I'll tell George when I next see him. He's very proud of his baking skills.'

'And so he should be,' Katianna said.

'Eat and then let's get the solicitor out of the way.' Savva took the last swig of his Greek coffee as Katianna picked at the errant crumbs on her plate.

She wondered what the story was between Savva and Sofia, and she knew there was one; she felt it.

Chapter 4

'I can't believe that meeting went as smoothly as it did,' said Katianna, holding the deeds to the village house in her hand.

'It's not all slow and laborious over here. We've come a long way since the 90s.'

'But I still had to come over to sign for it,' said Katianna. 'I'm glad I came though'

Katianna surveyed the house from the street; the gaps in the roof where tiles had slipped looked like the gaping toothless grin of an old hag, reminding her of the stories her *yiayia* used to tell her. She felt Savva evaluating her and she shook off an urge to lean into him with a hug. The entrance, a blue wooden door set in the thick, stone wall, looked sturdy despite its obvious age. It was locked. She leaned against the door, shoving all her weight into it. Just as she was about to give up, Savva gave it a push behind her; it loosened and swung open with a creak.

She took a tentative but excited step into the courtyard; a warm feeling like honey against a sore throat enveloped her and she felt instantly at home despite the overgrown, unkempt derelict outlook of what peered back at her through glazed eyes.

'Told you I'd get in,' she said, marking a one in the air with her index finger, before regaining her posture. Katianna flicked peeling paint flecks from her shoulder, and they fell in a flurry like confetti at her feet. She dusted down her skirt, taking in the surroundings. A prickle of emotion electrified her senses, a magical aura enveloping her, like an eager embrace.

She caught sight of a nest of starlings tucked under the decrepit guttering; the fledglings let out a medley of whistles and clicks as a mother, black with buff-edged wing feathers and reddish-brown legs, flew back and forth with food in her pink bill. She wondered how they survived in the furnace of the mid-morning sun.

The house was typical of the older village houses with its low sloping roof and two huge chimneys; each room's door opened into the courtyard. In the garden's centre, the ancient olive tree silvery green and full of life so many years ago appeared dry and dusty; many of its branches hacked and out of shape, the narrow top of the tree seemed disproportionate to the wide, gnarled trunk which rose out of the cracked slabs of the outdoor space. A sadness encroached her previous moment of joy; the tree had been so magical, the life of the garden. Her *yiayia* used to sing nursery rhymes and tie rainbow-coloured ribbons on its branches.

'Do you remember that little verse *biri to bervoli*?' she asked. Savva shook his head. 'And that other one '*Sousa, mbela, omorfa* something, something?' she said, imagining being pushed once again higher and higher, in the old swing which had hung from the boughs of a fig tree.

'Now that one I do remember. *Omorfa kobelia*,' finished Savva.

In another corner, against a dry-stone wall showered in a rich waterfall of bougainvillea, the moss-covered terracotta pot she had hidden in one summer looked like it had shrunk.

'How did I ever fit in there?' she said, taking shots from every angle with her mobile.

'That was your go-to hiding place,' said Savva. He remembered too.

Inside, darkness engulfed Katianna. It took her a few seconds to adjust to the dullness. The kitchen was bare; a simple stone sink propped up by two huge wooden supports and a free-standing cooker dominated one wall. A Formica topped table with four mismatched chairs took centre stage in the square room. Pots of herbs, withered long ago, lined the window sill and a pale blue-painted larder leaned against the adjacent wall, one of the upper doors hanging open like a gaping mouth waiting to be fed. Memories flooded back; her *yiayia* standing at the stove and frying chips, patiently turning them with a fork until they were just crisp enough before she scooped them out onto a plate, rolling out pastry to make *anari*-filled *bourekia*, Katianna dusting the little moon-shaped parcels with icing sugar from a metal shaker. A warm shiver ran through her, instantly love and comfort enveloped her.

The overwhelming familiarity of the damp in the air, which her grandmother always told her rose from the depths of the "magical" well hidden under the house, came flooding back. For a few moments, her *yiayia's* mythical stories, bursting with *kallikantzaroi,* wild imps, mountain hideouts and talking snails, filled her thoughts. Juxtaposing warmth and painful regret she hadn't kept in touch more over the years filled her.

She wandered from room to room. The kitchen smelt of musty, dried herbs but also of a feint cinnamon smell which filled her nostrils. Flaking paintwork, damp wall patches and abandoned furniture portrayed the ghostly shell of a once loved home.

The bedstead in the largest room, which was once adorned with a beautifully embroidered bedspread and crocheted, patchwork blankets, called out to her for tenderness. She reached out and touched it, the bedstead cool to the touch, her fingers moving over a now tarnished silver-filigree photo frame propped on the dresser. The faded-sepia image of her grandparents on their wedding day pulled at her heart and she smiled; their faces held expressions not of open joy but of a stoic seriousness.

Love was a serious thing. Matrimony for life. Commitment a hard slog back in the days of arranged marriages. The word *proxenia* crept into her mind and she wondered how men and women introduced to each other for the purpose of marriage with no previous courtship sustained long and loving relationships to the end.

She wiped away the coating of white dust. Her heart melted and, for a second, she wanted to cry. Here she was in Cyprus but had no boyfriend or husband to share this moment with; no one to build a future with. Her feelings surprised her.

She missed her parents. Missed their tales of falling in love, drinking red wine straight from the bottle in the shade of the lemon trees and sneaking off for secret midnight swims in the Mediterranean Sea, her dad's uniform folded neatly and placed on a rock, her mum's clothes strewn haphazardly across the sandy beach, but they were made to be together, despite their differences. Mirror images of each other, they had always said.

Inside a drawer she found a stash of yellowed-crayoned pictures staring back at her under a film of grey dust. She took a closer look, wiping away the debris, coughing with the dust in the air. One was of two people holding hands: Katianna and her grandmother. The other was of the ocean – the sea a strip of blue, the sand a horizontal line of yellow and the sky a paler blue stripe with the sun, a yellow circle, in the top right-hand corner.

This was Katianna's picture of the seaside at *Ayia Varvara* where she had spent many happy days on the water's edge with her grandmother and her parents. Splashing waves delighted her, spraying her with their salty drops. The sand squelched between her toes as she sank into its softness pretending to be eaten alive by Savva, the sand monster of Cyprus, buried with only his head exposed. They were happy days when even scorched shoulders and sun-burnt cheeks had not spoilt their fun.

She hadn't really appreciated those days but looking back she had cherished them; meatballs and big chunks of cucumber for lunch followed by a cornet of pistachio ice cream. Her grandmother always insisted on "proper" food even at the sandy beach; slabs of oven macaroni or stuffed vine leaves tightly wrapped into soft bite size fingers. She tried to recall the names of all the food and felt a stab of annoyance at not remembering.

She slipped the drawings back into the drawer and forced it shut with a scrape. She went out into the courtyard, her heels click-clacking against the stone flooring.

The door jamb stooped crooked out of its ninety-degree angle preventing the door, left warped with age over the years, from closing properly.

Chapter 5

Later that same day, Katianna shared the photos on her mobile with Polis, the local builder Savva recommended. After drinking their coffee, they walked from Savva's house for Polis to assess first-hand what the job entailed.

The side streets and main square buzzed with tourists taking photographs and posing for selfies, and the shop owners and stall holders chatted to customers showing them their wares. Crocheted tablecloths, delicate scarves and pretty aprons fluttered in the breeze as they hung from the striped awnings above, jewellery with the bright blue evil eye sparkled in the sunlight and handmade pottery depicted the pressed imprints of local flora and fauna. Eager artisans offered taster-bites of *arkatena koulourka, siousioukos* and *palouze,* crunchy rusks made with yeast, grape-must stick with almonds and fresh grape-juice jelly.

In contrast, her yiayia's house, tucked away from the hustle and bustle, was quiet, the creaking of old doors and windows the only sounds. With much relief to Katianna, Polis understood what would be required to make the house habitable again and what she envisaged. He made thoughtful, sensitive suggestions regarding the proposed building work, all the while nodding. For a Cypriot, she ascertained, Polis had the patience of all the saints in Cyprus. Despite his heavy Greek accent his English saved Katianna from having to pigeon-talk in Greek and any ensuing embarrassing moments.

Katianna made notes and Polis intermittently grabbed the pen out of her hand and drew sketches of walls and rooms. He explained what the work would entail and made suggestions on how to make the best use out of the space and odd angles.

'I'm not going to be living in it,' she said.

Polis nodded, his wide smile revealing a row of slightly crooked but bright white teeth. 'That's what they all say until they fall in love here.'

Katianna blushed at the mention of the word love and wiped a tiny trickle of sweat from her décolletage. The grip of a fist twisted inside her unexpectedly. She shook off the feeling and laughed, a little too loudly.

'Her parents fell in love here,' said Savva.

'Dad whisked Mum off to England. They were still as rapt in each other after sixty years as they were that first day they met.'

'Her dad was stationed here at the English base,' said Savva.

'They met in a bar. The rest, as they say, is history,' said Katianna, finishing off the story as if a love-story of ages. But there was so much more she could have said. How they had loved each other desperately to the end. How they had done everything together and in harmony. How their love had been a lot to live up to.

***

The following morning, Polis and his young protégé, Tasos, arrived at the village house, only seconds after Katianna. She had swept her hair into a top-knot and loose tendrils framed her face, unusually devoid of make-up.

'Thank you for prioritising this,' Katianna said.

'We'll get as much of the preparatory work done as possible,' said Polis, visibly puffing out his chest, despite struggling momentarily under the weight of a cement mixer he heaved across the little garden with Tasos.

Katianna surveyed them as they unloaded their tools, time not a concern, Polis stopping every few minutes to wipe his sweaty brow with the back of his hand. After almost half an hour, an amorphous mountain of steel and wood and electric drills and dustsheets filled the far corner of the courtyard. The modern heavy-duty machinery and equipment lay incongruent against the dry-stone wall and silver olive tree. The work had begun. There was no turning back. She breathed a sigh of relief pleased she could get back to London and normal life again in a couple of days.

'You look thoughtful,' said Polis, wiping his sweaty brow with a rag.

'I'm just thinking the garden not only reflects my *yiayia, but it* also reflects an understanding of its own history. My family's history and mine too.'

Chapter 6

On her second day, Katianna was semi-roused from sleep by the braying donkey in the derelict field opposite Savva's house, but then the insistent barking of the dogs, left to prowl untethered in the streets, forced her eyes open. Rubbing them fiercely, she threw back the cotton sheet and swung her feet onto the cool tiles.

She took in the décor; dark stained wooden shutters, white walls, a modern chest of drawers and a tall cupboard she thought she recognised from long-ago visits to her aunt's house. The eclectic mix of old and new worked well and she wondered whether someone else, a female, had indeed helped Savva with his interior furnishing and design or whether he just could not be bothered to stamp his own identity onto it.

In the galley kitchen, she found a scribbled note from Savva on the marble countertop: *"Kalimera.* Buying bread and milk."

She unlocked the sliding patio doors and stepped out onto the square verandah. It was already hot, and she wondered what the temperature was like in London. She checked her phone: "11 degrees and cloudy". Nothing new there then, she thought. She sunk back into the padded cushion of the lounger and checked her emails. Nothing required her immediate attention. She took in a deep breath, the geraniums, cascading over one of the low, white-washed walls from the multitude of terracotta pots, filled every available space along the far side of the crowded garden.

Her cousin was not green-fingered; these flowers bloomed everywhere, tolerant of drought and needed little care during the long hot summer months. A little water and the reward was a riot of season-long colour. Her mind turned to dating and wondered again why Savva hadn't met anyone or at least mentioned anyone special to her. She would have to persevere and dig deeper.

The roll of a motorbike pulling up on the other side of the garden wall interrupted her thoughts and within seconds Savva was pushing through the gate.

He smiled as he dropped two brown paper bags and a carton of milk onto the plastic garden table. 'Did Nino wake you?'

'Nino?'

'The donkey... you'll get used to him.'

'I don't know that I want to. And anyway, I think it was the dogs.'

'Nino complains too, believe me. But when Nino hee-haws it means he's happy.'

'Braying's good, but barking before 8am is best silenced,' she laughed. 'You need barking sound proofing.'

'You're funny Katianna. You've lived in the city for too long.'

'And you've lived in the village for too long,' she said, recognising her suppressed yearning for more peace.

As if interpreting her thoughts, Savva said, 'This will give you the chance to have some peace, a chance to escape the intensity of living in a city.'

'Maybe. Anyway, when are you going to get married?'

'When you do.' He winked at her and disappeared into the kitchen. She heard the flick of the kettle and the clatter of mugs on the worktop. He came out with plates and a tea towel which he laid out on the plastic table before arranging the crockery and two knives.

He opened the bags. The smell of the fresh olive bread and feta cheese parcels filled her nostrils and the hollowness of hunger rumbled in her stomach. She tore the soft dough, still warm from the bakery, with her hands and savoured her first mouthful. The saltiness of the black olives and the fresh mint flooded her with childhood memories; her *yiayia* stooped over the kitchen table pitting the olives deftly with her nimble fingers, harvested from the olive groves on the mountainside above the village, rolling out the soft buttery pastry, pulling out the baked loaves from the outside stone oven with the huge wooden paddle, the baskets filled with the hot breads of all shapes and sizes, bursting with olives, scattered with sesame.

'This is so good. There's no one back home who can bake olive bread like this,' she muttered while still chewing.

'Not the only good thing about Cyprus,' said Savva.

'I'm sure but my life's in England. And London is one of the best cities in the world to live in.'

'Who are you trying to convince? Me or yourself?'

'Oh, shut up,' she said playfully. 'Go and make me a tea.'

'Of course, whatever your English highness likes,' he said, teasing.

Sipping the tea from the China mug Katianna felt content even though she already knew in two days' time she would be back at her desk dealing with lonely hearts and broken hearts, desperate hearts, and hopeful hearts. The open space, the fresh, clean air… somehow it worked its magic and set her free from the unusually felt burden; she shook off the unfamiliar strain bearing down on her.

She read through the neatly written list of notes and reminders on the pad in front of her. She carried a notebook in her bag wherever she went, despite being tech savvy she preferred paper and pen. Even when interviewing new clients at the office she scribbled by hand and then Angie transferred everything over.

'So today… we'll head off to the building merchants and choose tiles for the kitchen and bathroom,' she said, taking a gulp of her tea.

'You can also select the bathroom suite and taps, kitchen sink, worktops… we can get most of that done today. That way it will all be ordered, and you can leave for London certain delivery has been organised.'

'It's a lot to do in one morning but it makes sense to get everything ordered so that Polis can get on while I'm back in London.'

'We think alike, don't we? At least on this one thing.'

'We're like two peas split from the same pod at birth,' she laughed, taking the last bite of her olive bread, and picking at the

errant crumbs off the plate. Savva smiled at her. 'What?' she asked.
    'You, doing that... reminds me of ...'
    'Who?'
    'I don't know... it looks so familiar, déjà vu.'

Chapter 7

Limassol heaved with tourists and locals alike. The only difference was their outlook; the tourists looked hot and bothered, hidden under floppy sunhats and peaked caps, their sun-burnt shoulders and cheeks proving they had overzealously soaked up the sun's rays. The locals, in contrast, moved slowly and spoke loudly: two old women, clothed in black, rested on the cool stone steps of a shaded doorway and two teenagers hung over their balconies chatting to passers-by. Further along, an old man played with his worry beads leaning against a huge door with peeling paint and an iron door knocker, hinting at a past of wealth and luxury and two neighbours chatted as they idled in chairs that had seen better days but which provided the authentic Mediterranean look so many tourists sought. Such a different outlook to that back home.

A short drive out of the village, they stopped at a building merchant.

'How old are these?' asked Katianna, as the store owner offered her a seat from a row of chairs.

'Not as old as you imagine. There's a Phini chair project dedicated to keeping Cyprus' cultural identity and ethics thriving through workshops,' he said, pointing to a poster pinned to the wall.

'That's wonderful. A way of moving forward yet still holding onto the past.'

'These craft skills are dying fast, some almost extinct.'

'And where does the name Phini come from?'

'A village near the springs of Diarizos river in the Troodos Mountains. They are keeping the craftsmanship alive.'

'I love that… creating something new for today.'

'You're a traditional girl at heart.'

'I think I must be, and I want to capture more of an authentic look,' said Katianna, flicking nonchalantly through the thick, dog-eared catalogue which rested on her lap.

'If you're planning on selling the house, why bother with the expense of original fittings? Go new, it's cheaper,' said Savva.

'It doesn't feel right. I want to honour *yiayia* Anna's house, create something that will attract buyers who'll appreciate its history, the solidity of its past.'

Savva explained what Katianna wanted and the store owner stared back vacantly before saying, 'That's what all these foreigners want until they see the price of salvaged items. But she can go to my cousin's place on the road towards Limassol. It's a bit far to go but he has one of the biggest hoards of salvage and reclaimed items. He's been rescuing stuff for years.'

***

Finally, Katianna spotted the sign to "Dimitri's Salvage" painted in bold black letters on a metre-high piece of wood staked into the dry ground.

'How did we miss that?' sighed Savva as he took the dirt track off the main road, sweat dripping into his sideburns.

'We're here now,' said Katianna. She coughed on the billowing dust, closed the car window.

Dimitri's Salvage was a paradise of every item you could want in wood, metal, iron, clay, glass, porcelain, and a complete explosion of colours, textures and shapes.

As Katianna browsed the spread of items piled high on trestle tables, stacked on the floor, or leaning against the metal frame of the huge outbuilding, a man in overalls with a cigarette hanging from his mouth appeared from behind a stack of old doors.

'*Kalimera*, my friends,' he called out, waving his arm.

'*Kalimera*,' Katianna and Savva responded in unison.

'My cousin's renovating her *yiayia's* house.'

'I've been expecting you.'

'I'm sure you have,' said Savva and then in a lower tone to Katianna. 'You can't do anything in Cyprus without everyone knowing your business.'

'We're looking for original bathroom and kitchen salvage and possibly some items for the bedrooms and sitting room.'

'You've come to the right place. Building and renovating is at a high and the economy is booming. The Russians don't want old, they want new; new reflects status, wealth, and position. My yard is bursting at the seams. Follow me and I'll show you what I have.'

Taking a narrow path between two huge mirrors and what looked like the doors of an old church, they followed Dimitri to another space, equally overflowing.

Katianna took out her notepad with measurements and sizes and room plans. The salvaged items looked overwhelmingly beautiful, and she wondered how she would be able to choose one piece from the other. She wanted to be practical as well as honour the age of the house and her *yiayia's* memory.

After sharing room dimensions with Dimitri, Katianna chose an old ceramic sink with two tap holes and a set of brass taps. Dimitri promised to descale and polish them at no extra charge. She chose an old high-rise cistern for the toilet which needed a clean-up but nothing too major and an old low-lipped square stone tray for the shower.

'You're certainly not looking for the modern luxury of your London flat,' said Savva.

'London is different. Life is different there,' she said. *I'm different there. My life is different there.*

'I might try one of the online sales sites back home for a brass shower attachment and send it over.'

'I'll look too. This will not be so old and if you can't find one, we can age it,' Dimitri winked at her as they bid each other farewell.

'I think Dimitri took a shine to you,' said Savva as they drove back towards the village.

'Don't be ridiculous. That was his salesman's patter. His only interest was in making a sale.'

'He certainly did that.'

'The mirror was gorgeous.'

'It's going to cost you twice that much to send it back to London.'

'I can afford it,' Katianna said, stubborn pride in her voice.

'I'm glad for you. But I still think he'll try to cross paths with you again. Mark my word. I know about these things.'

'Maybe you should be the matchmaker, Savva.' She giggled and looked out of the window in an effort to hide the flush across her cheeks. She hadn't had the time or had the inclination to think about men and love in her life for a long time. She had to get back to her life in London, yet she felt a tinge of sadness too at having to leave Cyprus so soon when she had only just reignited her love for this beautiful country which held so many happy memories.

She forced herself to think about home. Home was comfortable; a modern two bedroom open-plan living show flat overlooking Camden Lock. It had every amenity she needed, and her luxurious lifestyle suited not only her work but her need to be pampered, to be recognisably successful in what she did. The need to prove to her ex that the business was a success with Katianna at its helm drove her. Every decision she made was driven by her intense, all-consuming need to be winning and she was. Owning a little village house did not fit into her game plan or the image of success paraded in the pages of the top young entrepreneur pages of magazines and newspapers.

She had everything she needed in London; her home, her business, a good standard of living and her friends, though she had not spent any time with them in months.

She thought about the questionnaire she asked new clients to fill in and suddenly realised that she wanted all of those things too; security, the company of another, someone to laugh with, to share dinner with, to sit in front of the TV with and eat ice cream or take-away Chinese food or to snuggle in bed with and wake up to a cup of tea with.

'You, okay?' asked Savva.

'Shaking away some silly thoughts. Thoughts I have no time for.'

'Sometimes it's those silly thoughts that speak to us the loudest. They're your instinct trying to get through to you.'

Katianna didn't answer but pondered on her cousin's surprisingly philosophical opinion on the matter of silly thoughts. Perhaps her inner voice was whispering to her, but before she could think about it anymore, they were back in the village.

Polis looked stressed; his hand gestures implied he was shouting at Tasos. Tasos in turn shook his head, hurled a trowel to the ground. Katianna watched the younger man stomp off beyond the open gate, disappearing into the courtyard.

'What's happened? Why is Tasos upset?' asked Katianna as she jumped out of the car before it was properly parked.

'Because he's a fool. He never listens and I can't get him to understand that when love comes it cannot be stopped. It's a force more powerful than a storm,' he said with passion, and then more quietly, 'Love is love.'

His answer, incongruent with his gruff voice, and three-day shadow across his chin, surprised Katianna and she stifled a giggle as it bubbled from somewhere inside. Love is love... she knew that perfectly. She knew it from every angle, every level and in all its intensity and she yearned for it, though she had not realised that until now, this second.

She'd witnessed it so many times between so many people. It was her own passion to achieve and belief in love, despite her own miserable experience, which pushed her business to be more than a dating agency. She was like the Goddess of Love for so many couples, the Aphrodite of England. And for the second time that day a man had surprised her with his view on life and love.

Chapter 8

The small taverna, *E Petaloutha,* located on the north boundary of the village, was owned, and run by Mihalis. From November to March, he did the cooking and serving himself with the help of his wife and youngest son; his patrons consisted mainly of locals who otherwise dined at home in the colder months unless celebrating. Those who frequented *The Butterfly,* during the off-peak season, either lived in the village or surrounding villages dotted along the mountain roads or snuggled in the valley at the bottom of the pine-peppered mountains and fields of watermelons, tomatoes and of course the beautiful vineyards.

At the weekends, during the high season, he employed a chef and two more serving staff from local families. Tourists flocked to the traditional restaurant changing the atmosphere from one of the familiar Greek Cypriot chit-chat about local church activities, the catch of the day and whose son was dating a Russian girl to one of buzzing excitement, the smell of after sun lotion, tales of getting lost in the mountains and silly laughter after one too many shots of *zivania* or a glass too many of the locally-produced wine.

The local vineyard, Savva had taken great pride in telling her, *Oenou Yi,* enticed visitors to taste and explore the wines produced with high-technology equipment but historically honoured practices. He had talked with confidence and sound knowledge about the special Omodos wine-making culture. Wines, named after local customs and places of interest included *Thalero, Oikade, Xinisteri-Malaga* and *Playia*.

Mihalis had invited Katianna and Savva for a meal on the house. Pleased to see her *yiayia's* house being so thoughtfully and authentically renovated instead of being sold to the highest Russian bidder, Mihalis wanted to express his thanks that he would not be forced to live next to a property which was inhabited for a mere eight weeks of the year by those whose only priorities, it seemed, were money and prestige.

Having spent the past forty-eight hours rushing around Katianna wanted to make a special effort for her last evening in the village. A stone-ribbed tube skirt hugged her narrow hips and a blouse with tiny mother of pearl buttons down the front nipped her waist; the capped sleeves skimmed the tops of her sun-burnt shoulders. She slipped her pedicured feet into a pair of sling backs she'd grabbed at the last minute from the back of her walk-in wardrobe in London and slung her handbag over her shoulder.

'You look lovely,' said Savva from the kitchen. He stood puffing on a cigarette. 'Lipstick too, eh?'

'Aren't you getting changed?' she asked, walking towards him.

'We're only going to *E Petaloutha*. It's hardly a five-star experience.'

'It's my last night. I want it to be special.'

Savva, pulling a face, reluctantly disappeared. 'Okay, okay...' Fifteen minutes later he emerged from his bedroom looking handsome indeed.

'Amazing what a bit of hair gel and a white shirt can do for a man,' teased Katianna.

'Is that all you can say? What about my trousers?'

'They're great too' she said, but secretly she hated his trousers with the fold pressed into the front of each leg. 'Now come on, stop messing about. I'm starving.'

They took the ten-minute walk to the village plaza, the click of Katianna's shoes bouncing off the cobblestones. Fig trees bowed, their branches sagging with the weight of the overripe pear-shaped pods, green and purple, hidden amongst shiny fat leaves, their grassy, syrupy perfume permeating the air.

But it was not the idyllic stroll Katianna imagined. The calmness reigning over the humid night was broken by the dogs' all-too familiar and persistent barking. She swatted wildly at the night insects and wiped her sweaty brow while bunching her hair up to cool the back of her neck. *She should have tied her hair up.*

Not concentrating on the cobbles, Katianna lost her footing and fell. Savva swept in and clumsily pulled her up. Fighting back the tears, mainly of embarrassment, Katianna leaned into him for support and limped the rest of the way until finally they arrived at *E Petaloutha*, both cousins hot and out of breath.

'Welcome,' said Mihalis, standing at the entrance of the restaurant. 'You look just like your *yiayia.* God rest her soul.'

Katianna's face twisted in pain as she hobbled towards him. 'Hello,' she said, through gritted teeth as she fought the agony.

'Oh, my dear, what happened?' he asked.

She hobbled up three little steps, holding onto the wooden handrail and ducked under an arch of tangled vines which opened onto the most beautiful outdoor dining setting within a stone-flagged courtyard.

Katianna, relaxed instantly, forgetting about the insects and her throbbing ankle which had thwarted the enjoyment of her walk. Her breath caught as she took in the beautiful sight before her; tables covered in pristine white cloths and tea lights glowing on each. The most wonderful scent carried on the light breeze; fresh herbs filled ribbon-trimmed jam jars at the centre of each table setting. Rusty fisherman's lamps, hanging from the vine-clustered arbour, cast golden halos of light above each table.

Mihalis ushered them to a table for two, three tables in from the entrance. He pulled out a chair for Katianna and swiftly produced a wooden stool for her to rest her ankle; red and visibly swollen. Katianna caught Savva's mocking eye and cheeky grin and looked away not wanting to spoil Mihalis' attention. Moments later Mihalis returned gripping a blue-checked tea towel bulging with crushed ice, packing it gently around her ankle, making calming humming noises as he did so. Katianna reddened, uncomfortable with the stranger's attention.

A couple in faded ripped jeans walked in and Mihalis showed them to the table opposite; another long table, made up of three-square ones pushed together, accommodated a group of six older people carrying a birthday cake. The three women sat facing into the restaurant, facing their male partners, the fan against the back wall billowing the delicate Chantilly-lace curtain at the open window. Katianna recognised the lace hand-made by the women in the village.

Savva pushed his seat back, stretched his legs out and in so doing knocked into the woman sitting behind him. 'I'm so sorr–Sofia.'

'Savva, hello. How are you?'

'All good apart from my clumsy cousin here.'

'Hello again,' she said to Katianna. 'What happened?'

'Nothing a glass of wine won't cure,' said Katianna.

'She's in more pain than she's letting on,' said Savva.

'Stop fussing,' said Katianna and then noticing Sofia was alone said, 'Please join us. You'll save me from listening to Savva's fussing all night.' Katianna was secretly pleased to have the opportunity to play Cupid for the night and avert the attention from herself.

'Thank you. I'd like that.'

Mihalis indicated to the waiter to bring another chair to the table. Sofia sat and twirled her long auburn hair around her slim fingers, a flush tinging her cheeks pink, her long thick lashes sweeping across her eyes a sight to behold.

Savva gave Katianna a look, but she ignored it.

The waiter brought a raffia-decorated carafe of already decanted wine, a flat basket of cut bread and a tiny plate of olives dressed in olive oil, smashed coriander seeds and garlic. He generously filled their wine glasses expertly twisting the bottle with each pour to avoid any spillage.

'Smells deliciously fruity,' said Katianna.

'I chose this specially,' said Savva. 'It's *Oikade* which means "return to the house" or "to the homeland".' Katianna swallowed, a lump forming in her throat moved by his sentimentality, and she squeezed his arm.

'To friends,' toasted Sofia.

'To friends,' echoed Katianna and Savva, raising their glasses, and though Savva seemed buoyant and happy Katianna detected an edge to his voice too and wondered why.

For the first time, Katianna noticed the mottled burn scars on Sofia's left hand. They ran up her arm, smooth and shiny and pale with time. They happened as a child, she thought, but didn't like to ask. Sofia caught her looking and a lick of shame swept over Katianna. She made a note to ask Savva about them. As Sofia seemed to relax in their company Katianna noticed how she ran her fingers gently over her arm. Katianna pondered. *We all have scars to bear some visible to the eye and others only visible to our hearts.*

They filled their plates with crispy deep fried white bait and heaps of salad drenched in local olive oil. They shamelessly scooped *houmous* and *tzatziki* dips with their bread and talked with their mouths full as Sofia shared out the smoky sea bass cooked on the charcoal. Katianna divided the potato salad between their plates.

'You have the last spoon,' Savva urged Sofia, pointing to the freshly pickled beetroot.

'I can bring more,' laughed the waiter and he returned with another dish heaped high with

thick red slices. 'From Mihalis' own personal supply,' he said with a wide grin.

Mihalis topped their wine glasses and Katianna made another toast impressed at how he seemed to appear at just the right moment. Some of the finest restaurants in Mayfair didn't come even close to offering such unobtrusive service.

'To friendship,' they toasted.

The red wine loosened their tongues and their full stomachs stripped them of their inhibitions, they talked companionably about life in the village and how Cyprus offered a luxury lifestyle to those who could afford it. Katianna's life in London mirrored the success stories of millennials in Cyprus. Nicosia, despite being the world's last divided capital, offered as much in café culture, museums, shopping, and history as London did; Katianna felt the strength of pulling and pushing.

'And new beginnings,' said Katianna.

'And here you are,' said Savva.

'The universe, once in a while, likes to throw a firecracker to shake things up a bit,' laughed Katianna.

'And to love,' toasted Sofia, clinking her glass against Savva's.

Katianna noticed Sofia's dreamy look and scarlet cheeks. *Was it all the wine? Or the warmth of Savva's comradery?*

'I can tell you a lot about love,' said Katianna.

'You're the expert,' said Savva, averting his eyes.

'Tell me... what do you know about the four-letter word?' giggled Sofia, licking the wine from her lips.

'She runs a highly successful dating company in London. To do that, you must know a thing or two about love.'

'You do?'

'Love gives you strength and courage... it's madness and laughter... it's two people who are completely and totally in tune with each other's differences yet recognise the strength in that. I've seen people fall in love... love mirrors their actions and behaviour, thoughts and even their words... it's like singing together free one moment and tied together for all eternity the next.'

'That's beautiful,' said Sofia.

'The wine has loosened your tongue,' said Savva.

'Not just the wine, Savva mou. Being here. In Cyprus. It's caught me unawares,' Katianna whispered to herself. 'Love is beautiful,' she said, boozy and sentimental, and a small pang of regret she was leaving the following morning momentarily dented her mood.

'Do you have someone special at home?'

'I don't have the time. I'm too busy matchmaking everyone else.'

'Your time will come. Maybe Cyprus has kept someone for you all this time and you don't even know it,' said Sofia, her eyes sparkling. It was Katianna's turn to blush, the idea of a fairy tale romance warming her.

'Come on, you've a plane to catch in the morning,' said Savva, scrunching his napkin and discarding it as he pulled Katianna from her seat.

The bells rang, from the tower of the monastery; they would once have announced midnight prayers to the monks, but now only an end to the evening. Katianna kissed Mihalis on both cheeks promising to return soon.

'Next time with a husband. You're too beautiful to be alone,' said Mihalis.

'Perhaps,' said Katianna, the red wine making her tongue run away with her. 'You walk Sofia back. I'll go and pack the rest of my things. It's already after midnight,' Katianna said, playfully nudging him towards her.

'I can walk you home first... your ankle.'

'I'm fine. The ice did wonders. You go.'

'Thank you for a lovely evening, Katianna. I had a lot of fun. And safe flight back to London. I wish you well.' The women kissed each other on both cheeks and hugged each other with warm affection. Katianna felt the aftermath of Sofia's warm embrace, genuine and kind.

'I'll be back,' Katianna called, her sling backs in one hand and clutch in the other. Mihalis' smile danced in front of her; she had enjoyed his attention just as much as Sofia had enjoyed Savva's.

Katianna looked back at Sofia and Savva as they took the narrow lane leading back towards the square and the majestic monastery of the Holy Cross and on to Sofia's house, noting how they moved in tandem, their hips nudging each other's, and she made a special wish on the single bright star which hung in the clear blue-black sky.

Chapter 9

Katianna woke with a fuzzy head. She flopped back onto the bed, her vision, unfocused. She cursed herself for having drunk so excessively. If that's what being relaxed did to her, then she would have to steer clear. She winced in pain, her ankle throbbing.

In the shower she tried to wake herself up, humming one of the traditional tunes played in the restaurant the night before, but the cool water did nothing to alleviate her headache or foul mood. She wasn't looking forward to the four-and-a-half-hour flight home and even the assured comfort of her first-class seat didn't abate her irritability.

'You're cutting it fine.'

'I can do without the sarcasm.'

'Good morning to you too,' said Savva, pushing a glass of water and two tablets across the kitchen counter.

'My head's pounding.' She washed the tablets down with the water.

'And you have to get to the airport.'

'Why didn't you wake me?'

'I thought Nino would have done that,' he said.

'Well, he didn't.'

'I called you twice…'

'Thank goodness my PA's checked me in already.'

'This is Cyprus. It doesn't make that much difference,' he laughed and disappearing into the spare room returned with her luggage.

Katianna grabbed her handbag, checked she had her passport and mobile phone. She took a swig of black coffee from the travel mug Savva thrust at her.

***

The airport heaved; the air-conditioning did nothing to alleviate the oppressive heat which still clung to Katianna despite driving with the windows open. It seemed every single holidaymaker had chosen this same morning to depart; sun-burnt children skipped and hopped across the polished floor while stressed parents queued along the roped walkway dragging their luggage and balancing babies on their hips while calming shrieky-teared toddlers with strained patience.

Katianna made her way to the British Airways Priority check-in desk. Nothing like British Airways' First Wing experience at Heathrow but at least she was front of the queue.

'I'm sorry but Flight BA0645 departed last night. Are you wishing to take the next available flight?' asked the ground steward.

'What do you mean left? My PA checked me in online,' answered Katianna, leaning on the counter, taking the weight off her ankle.

'The flight was yesterday. It is out of my hands.'

'Please don't say that to me…'

'What's the problem?' asked Savva, pushing past a family of four with a buggy and a pile of open suitcases; their belongings strewn all over the floor.

'I've missed my flight. Apparently, it was yesterday.'

'Looks like the laid-back attitude of us Cypriots got to you,' said Savva unfazed by her obvious frustration.

'Next available seat is in… five days' time, 17th of August at… 08.45, an economy seat. You can book now or call us on this number after 5pm when our systems are updated. There may be earlier availability then if there's a cancellation.'

'Please, Yiannis,' said Katianna, reading his name badge, 'is there nothing earlier? I'm due back in London today.'

Yiannis shook his head and repeated what he had already said, robot like, with no inflection in his voice or expression.

Chapter 10

After calling Angie, the ride back to Savva's was subdued. Something was bothering Angie. She would usually go into action mode, be vocal about stepping into her "big boss" shoes, be unfazed by a change in schedule, but instead had been quiet learning Katianna wouldn't be back in the office for another few days.

Savva, daring to break the silence, mentioned paying attention to the signs of the universe.

'You are seriously going to get it cousin,' she said.

'You're here for a few more days. So what? You have your room at mine although I'm back at work this afternoon, but you know your way around now. You can keep an eye on Polis and Tasos, make sure they don't cut any corners. You can be here for the delivery from the reclamation yard and… you'll be here for the August 15th celebrations.'

'That date rings a bell somewhere in the recess of my mind.'

'It's the Assumption of Mary. One of the most celebrated days on our Orthodox calendar. Don't you remember our big family celebrations?'

'Every day here was a big family celebration,' said Katianna, smiling.

'This is the biggest. The whole country grinds to a standstill.'

'Not the north.'

'Not the north, though it did once, but you get the picture.'

'What else will I do?'

'You can learn to cook so that one day you can be a proper Greek-Cypriot Anglo-British homemaker extraordinaire,' he said, bursting into laughter.

'I knew that would come up,' she said, playfully punching him in the side.

'I'm being serious. Is it so bad?'

'Where do you get your positivity?'

'From you. Now cheer up.'

Katianna looked at her phone and checked her flight details again. 'How could I have got the departure time so wrong? Maybe there is something conspiring against me or for me, either way, you're right, I have to make the most of being here.'

As she uttered the words out loud, she felt a calm, happier vibe fill her. She was staying in Cyprus for another five days. How can that be a bad thing, she asked herself.

***

At Savva's, she lay across the bed leaning on her elbows, the sunshine poured in from the open window and kissed the backs of her legs and within minutes she felt the sting of scald burns on the pits of her knees.

She unpacked her laptop and prioritised her emails and, with some hesitation, delegated the majority to Angie. She couldn't face looking at spreadsheet after spreadsheet of figures while absent, so she flagged the two from John to look at when she was back in the office.

She checked the new member subscriptions; twenty-two since yesterday morning; nine of those had already created a profile page and one had already arranged a date. She checked matches made; six since yesterday morning.

She struggled to focus in the growing temperature−touching on 32 degrees−and her concentration quickly waivered. After another fifteen minutes she closed the laptop. Relieved to be away from the screen's blue glare she flipped onto her back and squeezed her eyes shut.

She wondered when Savva would be back; he had disappeared to the gym. She tapped out a message and invited him to join her for some lunch. That organised she took a leisurely unsteady walk to *stafilia kai meli* stopping at one of the over-filled, eclectic tourist shops along the way to buy a pair of flip flops in the most shocking pink, and a straw sun hat with a faded orange ribbon.

'Katianna,' Sofia gave her a big squeeze. 'I thought you were leaving this morning.'

'Don't ask… it's an embarrassingly boring story.' She took the hat off and raking her fingers through her hair shook her head to cool the back of her neck.

'How will you spend your time?' asked Sofia and she handed Katianna a floral scrunchie from her apron pocket.

'Thanks. I've got five days to fill,' she said, pulling her hair back into a bun on the top of her head.

'The house will keep you busy, no?'

'Maybe, but I wonder, will you have time to teach me a few basic recipes? I am in awe of your culinary expertise, and I'd like to give cooking a go.'

'I'd be honoured.'

'Really?'

'I'm starting at five tomorrow, Petros is on leave for a week. What about your ankle?'

Katianna bit her lip. 'It's getting better already,' she said.

Katianna slipped her mobile phone out of her handbag and moved into the shade of the huge umbrella; the last thing she needed was a face as red angry as she had felt this morning… she kicked out her leg and surveyed her ankle. It looked slightly less swollen now that she wasn't squeezing it into a pair of high heels.

She sipped from the tiny white cup Sofia deposited on the table. She liked the sweetened black coffee and wondered why she rarely drank it in London. The only time she had ever had it was at an aunt's house and since her mother's passing Katianna had distanced herself from family; it had been too painful to be around her aunt or cousins, but she felt guilty now. Freezing them out of her life had been unkind.

In a bubble of nostalgia Katianna remembered the coffee was simple enough to make. Her mother used to make it in a tiny copper saucepan on the stove, waiting patiently for the coffee to froth round the edges as it heated and came to the boil slowly. Then at just the right moment, not a second too soon or too late, she removed it from the heat as the *kaimaki,* a frothy foam, folded in on itself creating a sea of floating "love bubbles" on the coffee's surface when poured into the demi-tasse.

She automatically checked her phone; no messages from the office… hopefully that was a good thing. She was about to take another sip when she heard her name being called. She turned to see Polis walking towards the café.

'Katianna?'

The sun highlighted his golden hair and Katianna fought against a flutter dancing in her stomach. She liked the way he enunciated her name, drew out the "aa…nna." She liked the way it sounded in Greek. The way it formed on his lips and sang to her softly, like an echoing love note.

Both her parents had always pronounced it in English despite it being a name made up of her two grandmothers' names: Katherine, Katie for short, and Anna. Her father, English through and through, liked the idea of creating a new name from two others. But it didn't work out quite like that once Katianna was at school…in primary school she was called Katie and in secondary school she was called Kat and Kat stuck until she established her own business and wanted more formality with her clients; she added her mother's birth name and became Katianna Joannou-Shepherd overnight.

The double-barreled surname suited her; men assumed she was married, and it kept them at bay which, in turn, kept her focused on her empire. The dating agency was last valued at several million pounds. She had a social media consultant, website designer and a personal assistant. HR and accounting were outsourced but she had used the same contacts since the start. The rest she managed herself and conducted meetings for sponsorships and promotions face-to-face. Anything else went through Angie first but Katianna made it her business to know what was going on with her team. Her team was the closest thing she had to family now.

Polis pulled out the seat next to her. 'I heard you didn't fly back,' and then he exclaimed when he saw her foot. 'That looks sore. You need to massage it with distilled alcohol. In the old days, your *yiayia* would have told you to bathe it with healing water from a well.'

Katianna gave him a weak smile. '*Yiayia* often told me long, meandering stories of a magical well but I can't remember ever seeing it and as for healing properties, I doubt that very much.'

Sofia brought out a tray with a Greek coffee and a glass of water for Polis and winked at Katianna, before turning her attention to two youngsters counting out the change from their pockets.

'Pay me tomorrow,' she said, returning with two vanilla milkshakes in fluted glasses and paper candy-striped straws. Both mumbled a thank you and slurped the thick milky drink taking their glasses to half full within seconds.

Polis sat deep in thought and Katianna broke the silence. 'What do you do when you're not working?'

'I read... poetry, Montis, Charalambides, Pasiardis, some of the old Greek poets.'

'They all sound wonderful. I can't say I know very much poetry outside of the standard Keats and Shakespeare we studied at school.'

'There's a lot we can learn from the great poets,' he said, and Katianna noticed a wistful sadness cross his features for a second and then, as if recovering himself, went on to say, 'I also play the bouzouki at a taverna in Old Limassol. You should come with Savva. Do you like dancing?'

'I liked dancing as a teenager, but now I can't even walk across the village without showing my clumsiness,' she said, nodding towards her ankle. Her phone beeped; Savva was delayed.

'Come tomorrow night if you're still here. If you can't dance, you can eat. I'll reserve a table for two. You and Savva.' His eyes twinkled, revealing his joy.

'Make it a table for three,' she said, looking in Sofia's direction, 'and I will make sure we are there to at least enjoy your bouzouki if not dance Saturday night away with you.' Her mind was already working on a plan to lure Sofia from the café and her mood lifted.

They sat in companionable silence for a few more minutes and the café filled with a group of tourists; cameras around their necks, hats and caps protecting their sun-deprived faces from the midday sun and a level of merriment which bounced around the café like that of a *panigiri,* a traditional village festival.

She peered up, startled by a leaf which had floated down, and wondered what the tree above her was. She didn't recognise it and Polis must have seen her confusion.

'That's a mulberry,' he said. 'It symbolises growth, wisdom, and patience. You should see the berries ripen in April. Such a wonderful deep red.'

'I imagine that's beautiful,' she said.

'Their buds appear quickly, sometimes overnight and the ancient Greeks dedicated the plant to Athena, the goddess of wisdom.'

She looked across at the horizontal brown-orange trunks, gnarled with large burrs and fissures, and the branches densely filled with thin, bendy twigs at the ends. It certainly was a beautiful old tree.

'The silkworm will only feed off the mulberry's leaves. Did you know that?'

'I'm learning a lot of new things. Omodos is my new teacher.'

'I'm happy to be your teacher, too,' he said. Katianna looked at him and their eyes locked. Was he trying to tell her something?

Sofia came over with two plates of pastry cases filled with soft *anari* cheese, sweetened with sugar and cinnamon.

'On the house,' she said, placing a dessert fork by each plate in front of them.

Katianna bit into the light pastry. 'Absolutely delicious. You made these?' she asked, licking the dusting of icing off her lips.

'Fresh this morning.'

'You really are incredibly talented,' said Katianna.

Polis nodded, unable to speak, his mouth full.

'I think that's a yes from Polis too,' giggled Katianna, feeling happy. Feeling the happiest she had been in a long time.

'When you're finished here, come to the house. There's something I'd like you to see.'

He got up, left five euros on the table and thanked Sofia with a tip of his faded cap. Katianna watched him amble away. No one was in a hurry in Cyprus.

Twenty minutes later Katianna pushed open the gate to her *yiayia's* house. She stepped around a pile of rubble and a long hose and found Polis and Tasos standing over a channel which led from the sitting room, with its stone fireplace and deep hearth, and out into the courtyard.

'Listen,' said Polis. Katianna watched as he took a coin out of his wallet and dropped it down the hole. Seconds later a tiny plop bounced off the sides and top of the crevice.

'Water?'

'A well… a natural spring.'

'My *yiayia* wasn't making up stories.'

'The only story here is that we have to get the district officer to come and do some investigations before we carry on with any other work. It means your inheritance may be sitting on golden treasure, a golden opportunity.'

'You make it sound magical,' said Katianna.

'It could be,' said Polis. 'It could heal your ankle.'

'In the meantime?' she asked as she recalled a game, she used to play with her *yiayia* where one coin thrown into the well would appear as two coins tucked under her pillow the following morning. But Katianna's mother would reprimand the old lady for her generosity and filling her little granddaughter's head with silly stories.

'We continue with the rest of the work but leave this untouched until we have permission to carry on or otherwise. They may ask for permits relating to the well's use.'

'I wouldn't know where to look,' said Katianna.

'One step at a time.'

'How long will all this take?'

'How long do you have?' He reached out and gave her a reassuring squeeze on the shoulder. Katianna felt the tiniest electric spark run down and back up her arm giving her heart a little jolt. She took a step back from Polis wondering whether he felt it too, but he was already eyeing the scrunched plan he'd taken out of his back pocket;

too engrossed in work mode to notice the high colour spreading across Katianna's cheeks.

'If you need me for anything else let me know. I'll be at Savva's,' she said.

'I'll call the board now. Have a good evening and I can fill you in on what they say tomorrow.'

Chapter 11

Back at Savva's she kicked off her flip flops, threw her sunhat onto the couch. She slid open the patio doors; the heat rushed in sucking out the cool of the kitchen.

Lying back on the lounger she squinted against the mid-afternoon sun and thought about what was happening. Correction. What she thought might be happening. She had not spent much time in Polis' company but kept imagining herself with him, spending time talking and laughing, spending time together, intimately even. She wondered what life would be like with a man in her life again.

'You're as red as a cherry tomato,' said Savva, standing over her.

'I must have fallen asleep. Oh no.' She touched her face; it felt taut and totally sun burnt.

'I'm such an idiot.'

'Put some of this on… it's antiseptic.'

'It's out of date… you're going to kill me,' she said, examining the tube.

'Dates are overrated… you'll be fine. What did Polis want to show you?'

'How do you know about that?'

'Sofia said she heard you talking in the café.'

'You made it, in the end?'

'Sorry. I picked up some food for tonight while I was there… because I didn't think you'd be in the kitchen cooking… and I was right,' said Savva.

Katianna ignored his jibe and instead said, 'So you had a chat with Sofia?'

'Not a chat as such… just the usual, hello, how are you kind of conversation.'

She gave him one of her lop-sided assessment looks and then, picking up on his earlier assessment of her, said, 'I can't be a businesswoman and a domestic goddess.'

'You can be any combination of things you want to be,' he said, with a fervour which surprised her, and she wondered whether he was going to take his own advice and work out a way to ask Sofia out.

Katianna bit down on her tongue knowing it was better to stop while she was ahead than to get pulled into a conversation about her cooking, or worse still, about Polis. At the thought of his name, she shivered and turned away from Savva. She rubbed cream into her face, relieved the sunburn hid her embarrassment. She mulled over Savva's words… *she could be anything she wanted to be.*

She shook off a little shiver and got busy, laid the table for their dinner while Savva opened the foil containers of roasted rosemary and garlic chicken, cinnamon potatoes, *houmous*

and a salad with crumbled chunks of feta. He discovered a long-forgotten bottle of red in the cupboard, the deep-red liquid synonymous with passion and Katianna, despite being on painkillers, indulged in a generous measure.

Katianna pushed her plate away and rubbed her tummy in appreciation of the meal. She would need to watch her food intake back in London. Loose summer dresses were a Godsend here but not acceptable items of clothing for the office and she pulled in her stomach at the thought of fitting into her figure-hugging, tailored business suits. A voice called out to them from the side of the house, and she released her belly.

Savva opened the side gate. It was Polis.

Katianna remained seated not wanting to look too eager at his arrival. What was wrong with her? She had forgotten how to behave around him.

'The water board said they will send an official to conduct some tests. They wanted a fee to make it a priority, so I paid it guessing you didn't want any further delays.'

Part of Katianna wondered why he hadn't taken advantage of a possible delay but then realised he was a businessman; if this job was set back then his payment would be too, and she was certain he had other jobs in line. It wasn't about her spending more time here. A stab of nostalgia, of regret poked at her and she felt suddenly emotional.

'That's great, thanks,' she said.

'How much will it cost?' asked Savva.

'Two hundred euros.'

'You are joking,' said Savva, running his fingers through his thick dark hair.

'You did the right thing. Thank you again Polis and I'll see you tomorrow morning.' Polis nodded and left.

'You're thanking him for what exactly?'

'Savva, keep your voice down. He knows I don't have time on my side.'

'Why haven't you? Your empire almost runs itself and you can just as easily work from here as you can from your flat in London. Stay here. Make a commitment to getting the house renovated properly over however long a period it takes and then go back in the knowledge that the house is ready to be put on the market.'

'I can't talk to you when you're like this. Leave it. I need to get back.'

'Why?'

'Because the longer I stay here the more complicated things will get.' But she felt a shift, like once invisible sound waves, the repercussions of a watery ripple just visible on the surface of the water, and she knew Savva had a point, a valid one.

'How complicated?'

'Complicated,' she said automatically but already her head and her heart were at odds as she toyed with the strong possibility of balancing work with spending more time in Cyprus. She needed to put her cool strategic planning skills into organising her personal life in the same way she managed those of her clients.

Chapter 12

The quiet village streets dappled in the glow of the old-fashioned streetlamps and a lone cockerel pecking at the dry earth in someone's front yard announced morning had broken; its crowing punctuating the morning's state of peaceful serenity.

Katianna passed the patch of land where Nino, still asleep, stood tethered to a fence post. The sight of him inexplicably pulled at her and she had the urge to cover him with a blanket; it was surprisingly chilly this early even in the height of summer. She picked up her pace. She brushed past a showering bougainvillea; its bright pink overshadowing the grey of the crumbling stone wall behind it and its sweet note caught her breath.

From a distance she glimpsed Sofia unloading paper bags and a couple of boxes from the side cart of her little scooter; the quirky logo shone in a pool of golden light coming from the open side door of the little café building.

Katianna's mind leapt into business mode. She marveled at how creative Sofia was and how she enjoyed running her business, was committed, and driven. Katianna already had some ideas of her own; Sofia's market could be increased: office catering, baking for other coffee shops or even the main towns' hotel lounges which served traditional afternoon tea in luxurious surroundings which warranted charging excessively soaring prices to holidaymakers.

Katianna hugged Sofia good morning and grabbed the last two

packages from the top box of the scooter. She walked ahead of Sofia, into the compact kitchen, noticing a pile of wooden crates propped open the door. The cramped space seemed to shrink further with both side by side. Katianna surveyed the wooden shelf stacked with jam jars of assorted sizes filled with herbs and spices, the peeling labels scribbled with the name of the most recent contents in black marker pen. Katianna recognised the Greek letters and remembered writing them each summer under her yiayia's patient instruction.

A stack of wooden bowls, chopping boards and a long slim rolling pin filled one corner of the kitchenette. The gleaming double oven, the only modern, industrial-looking piece of equipment dominated one side of the room.

Another deep shelf, painted sea blue, housed white China, a pile of paper napkins and salt and pepper shakers. A glass fronted cabinet, between the fridge and a thick trail of pipes, housed glassware and coffee cups piled haphazardly inside each other.

The smell of lemon rose from the deep stainless-steel sink; a disinfectant pad wedged next to the plughole. On the wall, hanging a little lopsidedly, an icon peaked out from behind a net curtain which hung loosely at the small window above the sink.

'Hope you're ready for some fun.' Sofia's light mood was refreshing. 'That's my Saint Euphrosynus the Cook, of Alexandria. My school friend gave it to me when I officially opened the business,' she said, following Katianna's eyes.

'I didn't know such a saint even existed.'

'There's a saint for everything,' said Sofia.

'I hope he helps me today. I'm up for learning how to cook something, and if I have fun along the way that's a bonus,' laughed Katianna. 'Thank you. I really appreciate it.'

'I believe everyone should know how to cook at least one main dish and one dessert to perfection. Even if you don't come back tomorrow, you'll at least have that,' she said, handing Katianna an apron. 'Put this on and then we'll get started but first hands.' She pumped some hand soap into her open palm and then into Katianna's. They both rubbed their hands together vigorously before rinsing them.

'We're making two trays of *makaronia* today. People have less and less time to prepare their own so I'm selling more take-home portions which is great for me because making a larger quantity is more cost efficient in terms of both ingredients and fuel.'

'And your time,' Katianna said. 'In business, time management is everything.'

Katianna listened, impressed with Sofia's understanding of costs and overheads. Katianna refocused and followed Sofia's instructions for making the oven macaroni; she boiled the long, thick pasta until just *al dente,* poured it out into a colander and ran the expanded tubes under cold running water before lining the bases of the deep trays with them. She chopped fresh parsley and mint picked from Sofia's tiny but abundant herb garden. Sofia demonstrated how to skin an over-ripe tomato by immersing it in boiling water and then peeling off the skin. Katianna then repeated the process, peeling and chopping twenty-five more tomatoes and grating two village *halloumia,* goat's cheese, for the white sauce. She cracked and beat eight eggs, laughing as she tried to fish out two bits of eggshell with her finger. Sofia melted butter and flour in a saucepan and mixed into a paste. Katianna slowly poured six pints of milk over it while Sofia continued to mix it into a thick sauce.

'Watch the temperature,' warned Sofia, lowering the gas just in time to avoid the sauce boiling over. 'Burnt milk not only smells awful it's a nightmare to clean.'

'I need a lot more practise. There's so much to think about.'

'You're doing great. Pour the beaten egg into the milk but wait a couple of minutes to let it cool slightly or you'll have scrambled egg soup instead.'

Sofia stirred continuously as Katianna poured in the mixture and added salt and pepper and two thirds of the grated cheese.

'Once the sauce begins to thicken turn off the gas,' said Sofia, 'and leave the pot on the side to cool.'

That done, Katianna watched as Sofia swiftly scraped chopped onions off the chopping board and into sizzling olive oil.

'Wow. That fried onion smell is so homey... takes me right back to my *yiayia's* cooking and my mum's too. She added finely chopped onions to everything,' said Katianna, her eyes watering, more from a rush of emotion than the chemical irritant of the chopped bulbs. Sofia tossed them gently with a wooden spatula. Next, she added minced pork to the caramelised onions. She turned the mince continually until it browned and scooped in the fresh parsley.

'Everything cooks together and then we begin layering the ingredients in the trays.'

'I've never thought about it before but it's like the Greek Cypriot version of lasagne.'

'Or lasagne is like the Italian version of our oven macaroni.'

'I read once that the word is derived from the Greek word *lasana*; a trivet or stand for a pot which the Italians cook their pasta dish in.' They both laughed. Katianna brushed the flour from the front of her apron. Katianna thought how she would feel doing this daily and peace settled within her; she wasn't missing her laptop or the constant ping of her inbox.

They filled the oven trays to the top with alternating layers of pork mixture and sauce and topped with one last layer of sauce. They sprinkled the rest of the grated cheese over the sauce and fitted the dishes snuggly into the top and middle shelves of the industrial oven.

'Quick break before we clean up?'

'Yes, please,' she said and checking her watch wondered how the hours had seemed to pass in seconds.

'There's fresh bread, olives, tomatoes there and some *lounza,* in the fridge too. Help yourself.'

'The smoked pork is delicious. I've seen something similar in the local delis back home.' Katianna cut into the loaf and a memory invaded her thoughts; her *yiayia* kneading bread, a tiny brass pot on the stove, the smell of coffee, a terracotta milk jug, creamy *halloumi*...

The women sat under the dawn's first rays and talked and the more they talked the more they opened up to each other. Katianna, quietly relieved she wasn't the only one putting her all into her business in an effort to hide from her one big relationship, felt a closeness to Sofia she hadn't allowed to develop with anyone in a long time. She listened intently.

'When he didn't show for the dress rehearsal using work as an excuse something flipped in me and I knew that my whole married life would be like that. Me waiting... waiting and wondering whether he would turn up... whether I was important enough for him to come home to, so I ended it,' said Sofia and Katianna saw the tears welling behind the young woman's eyes.

'I'm so sorry. That was a brave thing to do.'

'Brave or stupid. I don't know. But I'm okay and this place makes up for it. My customers have become my friends and people from as far as Limassol come to eat here so I'm happy.'

'We have more in common than I thought,' said Katianna.

'I suppose we do. Though I can see you're far more successful than I am or ever could be in this little part of the world.'

'Don't say that. You can grow. You can do so much more.'

'I dare say. There's still a lot to do.'

'I could help you.'

'Aren't you going back to London?'

'I can plant the seeds before I go... then keep in touch. And anyway, I'll be back to put the house on the market and oversee the sale so I will be back and forth.'

'You're selling then?'

'That's been the plan all along. Why do you ask?'

'I thought you might have felt the pull of your homeland, your roots... decided to hold back before making a final decision.'

Katianna took a sip of coffee. She stretched her arms above her head. The green mountains loomed in the distance; shimmering under the glowing sky, the north to south orientation of the rows perfectly formed. She remembered the green patchwork blanket her *yiayia* spread across the foot of the bed. Katianna used to line up her plastic farm animals on it pretending each square was a different field.

She wondered where it was and made a mental note to look for it. The mahogany wardrobe, still at the house, was now hidden under a huge dust sheet. It could be in there. Polis won't mind uncovering it for me, she thought.

'Ready for round two?' asked Sofia, pushing her chair back. She stretched her back, shaking and rolling her shoulders.

'I am.'

Back in the kitchen they worked in tandem, occasionally bumping into each other and within ten minutes the utensils used to prepare the oven macaroni were washed, dried, and put away.

'To make the *galatoboureka,* we need all the ingredients here.' Sofia pointed to a faded piece of paper with faint, loopy cursive handwriting, not too dissimilar to that of a child learning to form their letters correctly at preschool. It was on the fridge; a buxom Aphrodite bursting-out-of-the-sea magnet held it in place. 'That's a recipe your *yiayia* wrote out for me a few years ago,' said Sofia, catching Katianna's gaze. 'I still use it though I've added my own secret ingredient.'

'That's amazing.'

'She taught herself to read and write. Did you know that?'

'I didn't. I wish I could have known her better than I did.'

They stirred milk and eggs together and ground cinnamon sticks and nutmeg and took it in turns to thicken the custard to make a beautifully smooth, creamy filling for the filo pastry parcels.

Sofia expertly made the filo pastry and showed Katianna how to roll it out using a long, slim rolling pin.

'This rolling pin has been passed down through many generations of women in your family; your grandmother gave it to me when she wrote out that recipe.'

'That's so lovely. I sense her presence, as if she's trying to tell me something.'

'She was a wonderful woman. Always kind and so wise; always sharing her wisdom… right to the end.'

'I'm glad to hear that. To know she was loved.'

Katianna enjoyed making the pastry. Knowing she was using her grandmother's rolling pin seemed to push her forward to do her best. She didn't want to let her down. She marvelled at how she was able to make sheets of pastry as thin as paper. The melted butter smelt delicious. She brushed the sheets and her mouth watered making her stomach rumble. The golden lard glistened. They spooned the custard, now adequately cooled, onto the filo pastry sheets and then folded them into long finger-shaped parcels. Once arranged in rows, on the oiled baking racks, each roll was generously glazed with a beaten egg and milk mixture.

'This will add a shine to them,' said Sofia, smiling.

Happy that these were ready to go into the oven, Sofia took out the oven macaroni, golden and crispy on top, the thick cream bubbling round the edges.

'My stomach's somersaulting in anticipation of tasting *macaronia* made by me,' said Katianna.

'We won't cut into it yet. It's too hot and the layers will fall sloppily into each other,' said Sofia. 'When it's cooled slightly, we can mark the pieces like this,' Sofia said, scoring the crisp topping of the *macaronia* with a knife, marking out the portions, 'until we're ready to serve.'

'Sorry... looks like I've made a mess of it,' said Katianna, scooping out the layers now a mishmash on her saucer.

'I can see that,' laughed Sofia. 'Don't worry. You won't forget next time.' Katianna wiped the work tops and washed all the utensils and bowls. She cleaned the sink and put the dish cloths and dusters in the bag Sofia indicated for washing.

By the end of three hours, the women chatted like best friends; Katianna realised how much she had missed the close company of another woman. Most of her meetings were dominated by men; driven, dominant and demanding. Like her, she thought.

'What happened to you?' Sofia said. 'You run a dating agency. You should have men falling at your feet.'

'You'd think, eh?'

'What's your story?'

'Long story short, I met someone when I was at university. We founded the agency together once we graduated. Got engaged, had the party. It was amazing... and then he met someone else through the business. They "fell in love" and got married last year. We tried to keep things going professionally but it was impossible, seeing him every day. It was like a picking at a scab yet hoping it would heal. Eventually, I told him I wanted him out of the business. I had to fight him to keep the business name. A long and painful court battle. And expensive.'

'And you've never got over him?'

'Never got over what he did. Tried to destroy the business. Take the name.'

'And now?'

'I don't know. I find myself wondering what if we'd found a way to work together?'

'Would he have had influence on its success?'

'Maybe not. But just having someone to bounce ideas off, to talk at the end of a hectic day...' Katianna's voice trailed off, her eyes misted over.

'Do you still love him?'

'I don't know that either. But I suppose I've created this fairytale memory board of how we were. It's possible. That's why I'm so committed to helping others find love.'

'It takes the pressure off you but at the same time has prevented you from moving on. You can't let go. You've realised what you had despite the pain, and distrust takes up the space in your heart where there should be love.'

'I suppose, but only for myself, not for others,' said Katianna and she realised how more grown up in years Sofia seemed talking like this.

'So, there's no room for romance in your life. No man stands a chance of even getting close to you with your ex taking up the biggest part of you.'

'I've never thought of it like that before but you're right. I'm still that twenty-three-year-old madly-in-love girl stuck in a memory time-warp.'

'Time to shake yourself up a bit, don't you think?'

'I'd say more than a bit. Perhaps we can do it together,' said Katianna. 'Now, I can't wait a moment longer.'

She cut a square of macaroni, lifted it out of the baking tray and stabbed it with her fork. 'Oh my God,' she said, devouring it, savouring every mouthful. 'This is so good.'

Chapter 13

Katianna surprised herself; she began to feel more comfortable in Cyprus than she ever imagined or thought her lifestyle would allow. She had few belongings with her; at home she was a stickler for her beauty regime and her conveniences from her coffee maker to her tap with instant boiling water to her cleaner who ensured everything was topped, spruced, and plumped up how she liked it.

Village life, with its much slower pace and friendly folk, drew her in and settled in her, warm and familiar, like the love of an old friend. She enjoyed interacting with the locals who talked fondly about her *yiayia,* her mum's childhood and of course the village house. She even began to enjoy the inquisitiveness of the old ladies.

Wrapped in their black headscarves, dressed in the dark hues of their mourning clothes, having lost fathers, mothers, brothers, sisters, Katianna looked forward to their questions when she passed one of them in the street. They were kind, wise souls and looked Katianna in the eye when holding a conversation. Something too few people back in London did, too busy, hurried, or multi-tasking. *How's that house coming along? Your yiayia would be so proud of you... Just like your mother, you are... You're not going to miss upcoming celebrations, are you? If you need new roof tiles my son's boy is a supplier...*

While cooking with Sofia, Katianna, had enjoyed a couple of hours surrounded by flour and fun, not a dating app or single piece of technology involved. She hadn't checked emails or her phone all morning. She was becoming a Katianna she didn't recognise. Now, she looked forward to a Saturday night of music and dancing and hoped her now throbbing ankle would not spoil her evening.

She showered, tied one of her cotton shawls around her, like a beach wrap, and padded barefoot into the kitchen. She flicked on the kettle before stepping out onto the patio. A shimmering sun, a low-hanging fireball on the orange and pink-streaked horizon, forced her to shade her eyes from its glow. She pictured the early morning sky in London; heavy with slate clouds and a grey mist, she shook off the tiniest shiver.

She listened for Nino's now familiar braying. The church bells pealed, and the screech of a motorbike shook the silence. A welcome kind of chaos, different to the revving traffic of Camden; the screech of taxis, rumble of buses, whizz of weaving motorbikes on delivery deadlines. The air was cleaner, fresher; no carbon-monoxide pollution threatening to clog her lungs as she got older.

She breathed deeply and focused on the here and now; the salty sea air, the warmth of the sun on her skin and the empowering feeling the mountains gave her. She untwined the tight scrunchie. Setting her hair free, she ran her fingers through the soft ends, relishing the sensation across her bare shoulders and down her back. She felt free. Her *yiayia's* house was going to unlock more than a commercial deal for her; a flutter stirred within her, and a tingle of magic seemed to whisper as it travelled down her spine and up her neck; poetry spun on a golden thread of hope, a path of new beginnings.

She sipped her rich-roasted coffee and bit into one of the custard-filled pastries Sofia had insisted she bring back with her.

'My first homemade *galatoboureko*,' she said, smiling to herself. And then she licked her lips, savouring the surprise burst of orange zest which laced the cream like a ray of sunshine at a window. 'So that's your secret ingredient,' she whispered.

She squinted against the sun, flicking absentmindedly through the magazine she'd bought at Heathrow. She rarely had time to read anything other than end-of-month reports and the Sunday papers at home. She felt a little guilty doing nothing business related. But she trusted all was going well; her team had worked with her for over twelve years between them and had plenty of experience.

An hour later, walking along the quiet road towards her *yiayia's* house, women hunched over their needlework and embroidery bid her *kalimera* and she nodded good morning, just as Savva had taught her so as not to be delayed with their chatter. Careful on the uneven cobbles, she turned a bend and recognised Polis' red beat-up truck parked with its tail-wing open. Of course, he was working today.

'*Kalimera*, Katianna,' he said when she entered. He was gently hammering at the old cement around the bedroom floor slabs. Careful not to break them Polis worked diligently and with precision, lifting out one of the slabs and propping it against the wall with a dozen others already rescued.

'Good morning. Thank you for being so careful,' Katianna said. She wanted the solid blocks worked back into the renovation.

Katianna surveyed him... he would certainly be a catch for someone; hard-working, polite, well-organised, thoughtful, musical... fit and lean. His rolled-up T-shirt sleeves revealed bronzed muscles; his veins pumped as he worked.

'Almost done,' he said.

'I can see,' she said, fighting the urge to stop staring and failing.

'All on target apart from the area around the well, this is obviously on hold. Waiting on the report.'

'You're doing a marvelous job,' said Katianna, pulling her gaze up to his face.

'The kitchen walls have been skimmed and plastered and the tiles will go on next. I'm hoping enough of the original tiles have been saved to incorporate into a design above the old stove once it's delivered.'

'That's great.'

'We'll start the tiling on Monday and work around the area where the old basin and stove you've ordered are to go,' he said, pointing to the area already marked out with chalk. 'The electrics have been run on a first fix and the new fuse box is in ready for the final fix and connection to the fuse board. It's going surprisingly well.'

'I'm pleased,' said Katianna, but inside she wasn't feeling so happy. She was falling in love with the old place and battling a tug of war. Her ankle throbbed as if it too was being pulled back, not willing to move forward.

'Me too. You never know what these old houses will reveal when you're renovating but this is a sturdy house. It's certainly stood the test of time… I bet it has some stories to tell.'

Katianna hesitated, too afraid to speak in case her voice cracked. She swallowed. 'You don't know how happy that makes me, Polis. I'm glad you're enjoying the job. It makes an enormous difference when one enjoys the hours they spend at work. It's more fulfilling, more than just a pay packet,' said Katianna.

'These are the jobs I look forward to the most. All these new builds with columns here and marble floors there… too much money for sense… and there's no soul in those new builds… but this… this speaks to me.'

Katianna listened to him talking about his work; there was more to him than his building knowledge. An abundance of empathy and vision and an endearing boldness in his creativity came from the heart. She also liked his modern twist on things and was confident in his abilities, trusted his judgement.

'And what about the well?' she asked.

'There's a water supply there. I'm waiting on the reports as to whether it's potable. The villagers are already discussing the impact it will have on them… their land, their farming, their livelihoods. They pray to keep the house in the hands of a local, someone who cares about the village and its survival,' he said, wiping the sweat from his brow.

'I don't want to upset anyone, but I may have a buyer already,' said Katianna, biting down on her lip, her eyebrows raised in uncertainty.

'That's quick.'

'One of the three agents I contacted before coming out here emailed to say they have a serious buyer.'

'You won't have any problems selling this. There're so many companies fattening up their Airbnb portfolio with properties just like this one. But that surely… that can't be your only option.'

'That would be the best. No chain. No messing around,' she said, but inside she felt disheartened.

'Looks like you'll be shot of the place before you know it. And your *yiayia's* house, and the well, will be gone forever.' Polis' words rang in her ears and pounded in her heart. *Gone forever.* Was he being deliberately provocative?

A *hello* interrupted them.

Katianna was relieved to see Savva strolling towards them, two take-out cups in each hand. He proffered one to each of them.

'For me?' asked Polis.

'Guessed you'd both be here,' said Savva, proffering a handful of sugar sachets from his back pocket.

'Thanks, no sugar for me. Need to watch my spreading middle,' he laughed, pulling up his T-shirt and patting his stomach.

Katianna thought it looked far too much like an ironing board to be spreading anywhere and wondered how old he was. Polis caught her eye; she felt her face reddening brighter than the blush of a ripened pomegranate. *How embarrassing.*

'How's it all going? When I didn't find you bent over your laptop at home, I knew I didn't have to look far to find you.'

'Actually, I was up before sunrise cooking with Sofia.'

'Cooking? You really are taking the Cypriot wife comment seriously.'

Savva ducked as Katianna swiped him round the back of the head playfully. 'I'd watch your mouth,' she said, punching him on the arm.

'Ouch. You'd better not mess with her, Polis, or she'll beat you up.'

Polis smiled and Katianna noticed the crinkling at the corners of his eyes. He took a swig of his coffee before placing it on the stone hearth. 'It won't come to that,' he said, giving Katianna a side-long glance before getting back to work.

'If there's nothing more here, I'll be off,' said Savva. 'Are you still okay for tonight?'

'Sure. See you all at nine,' said Polis.

'You can hop on the back of my bike if you're coming back to mine now,' said Savva to Katianna.

'I'll walk back, thanks. Take in the scenery. Flex the ankle for some dancing,' she said, placing her hat back on at a jaunty tilt. 'And I want to breathe in the fresh air.'

Chapter 14

Katianna walked back at a leisurely pace; she quickly discovered walking any faster too strenuous in the mid-morning sun, and too much for her ankle. She settled into her unhurried steps and took in the view; the lush slope of the mountain meticulously marking out the vineyards with row upon row of vines on one side and the open blue sky above.

Butterflies danced round her hair as she passed a frothing buddleia plant, cascading down the wall of a weathered, stone house. The derelict house's broken windows and missing shutters were giving her a lopsided smile. Faded blue drapery hung behind the cracked and dusty panes.

A fat cat, sprawled next to an ornate collection of terracotta pots and tall pithoi, lay still as two kittens suckled greedily. Katianna watched as she protectively pulled a third low-meowing kitten towards her nipple. The kitten seemed to struggle but then settled between the others, happy now. An abundance of mixed herbs cast a cool shadow across the old, cracked paving of the front garden, their scent rising as the morning warmed; she recognised the smells: rosemary, coriander, oregano, flat-leaf parsley.

Next door a double-storey house with a modern red tiled roof stood tall and proud; huge pots painted a magenta pink flanked either side of an arched doorway and a tall iron gate kept unwanted visitors out. The contrast between the two properties exaggerated the contrast between old and newly updated, traditional, and modern.

She arrived home to find Savva sitting on the patio with a towel round his waist and tousled, wet hair.

'Enjoyed your walk?'

'I did,' she said, realising the pain in her ankle had faded. 'Who owns the property with the red-tiled roof?'

'A Russian billionaire. He made an offer to three different families to get his hands on that land. Luckily, he wasn't able to raze the original buildings. But he still managed to restore them in a way which stands out.'

'I'm guessing the owners of the tumble-down house next to it wouldn't sell.'

'No. And they've since died but their will stated it couldn't be sold outside of the family for the next 200 years.'

'So, what's going to happen to it?'

'Nothing. The siblings all live in the US.'

'That saddens me,' said Katianna.

'One of the neighbours potted the flowerpots so at least it looks decent.'

'I saw the flowers. So pretty.'

'At least you're giving your *yiayia's* house some love.'

'Yes,' she said, and she felt her heart flutter.

'You're quite a sentimental old thing aren't you, dear cousin. When did that happen? You never used to be,' said Savva.

'Less of the old please. I've got some emails to catch up on, then I plan to do some shopping for a new dress. And if there's still time after that, I'm going to take a little siesta... tonight we three are going to dance,' she said with a cheeky grin.

'Three?'

'Sofia's coming.'

'Nice cosy foursome, then,' said Savva.

'Foursome?'

'There's Polis, of course,' said Savva, enjoying his little jab.

***

The taxi dropped them a few minutes' walk from the restaurant in Old Limassol just after nine. Savva insisted he wanted Katianna to experience some of the ancient city's marvels including the medieval castle whose walls shone like gold in the lights along the way. Katianna took in its splendour and made a mental note to visit the museum housed within its walls. She navigated the cobbled streets in her high heels, conscious that any slight uneven pavings might push her not-quite-fully-healed ankle out of joint again.

They continued past the castle, Savva leading the way, until Savva pointed out the restaurant tucked at the end of a narrow side street off the main square. As they walked down the street, the noise and merry making of the bars and restaurants behind them receded.

The taverna initially seemed more subdued than the cafes, bars, and eateries they passed along the way even though the restaurant was already near full. They crossed the dance floor, the waiter showing them to their table. The upbeat melody of the live band started up and the atmosphere instantly became one of effervescing merriment.

'You made it. Good to see you,' said Polis as he shook Savva's hand warmly a few minutes later. He gave Sofia a customary kiss on each cheek. He leaned in to do the same with Katianna; her lace shawl fell from around her shoulders, and she felt his warm breath against her neck sending the faintest thrill through her. She hastily pulled the scarf to cover her new strappy dress, suddenly conscious of her bare arms, revealing too much cleavage.

'How's your ankle?' he asked Katianna.

'Definitely up for some dancing,' she said, too boldly and she felt herself colour in front of him. He looked different not stooped over a wheelbarrow and out of his work overalls; his hair darker, his stance assured, a singsong beat to his movements and his voice.

'I'll be back soon,' he said and disappeared to join the band.

She took a seat at the table, her back to one of the five-foot walls. The lanterns set at every three feet or so on the arched balustrade threw soft, amber arcs onto the old bricks. She looked up; positioned directly across the dance floor and the small area set out for the band Katianna realised she would be facing Polis all evening. She wouldn't ordinarily have worried about such a thing, but she felt unusually exposed as he nodded in her direction; the colour rose in her cheeks and she picked up the napkin, shaped into a sailboat, and shaking the fold apart, played with it, passing it back and forth between her hands which felt clammy.

The waiter poured out white wine. Katianna, fighting her nerves, eagerly made a toast and tipping back her glass, drained it in one.

'If you're thirsty there's water,' said her cousin.

'Thirsty? I want to shake out my inhibitions and dance the night away as if I'm the only one on the dance floor dancing my dreams.'

'This is going to be good,' said Savva, teasingly. 'And if you stumble you can pretend it's part of the dance.'

'Ha, ha,' said Katianna.

'I'll drink to that,' said Sofia, raising her glass.

'And to dancing as if no one's watching,' said Katianna.

'I don't think you'll get away with that. Your dress is just incredible,' said Sofia.

'Thank you. It's as daring as I could get without revealing everything,' laughed Katianna, swigging the bubbly amber, and enjoying the numbing feeling it cocooned her in. Katianna bubbled inside too. Was it the heat, the carefree feeling enveloping her, or something fizzing elsewhere?

She stretched her arms above her head and swayed them to the music. A trellis of old pipes and wire weaved an arbour above them; a woody vine clung with clusters of semi-hidden purple and green grapes, the shiny leaves an array of green. The sweet smell mingled with the aroma of baked onions, fresh fish and barbequed meat and the fresh scent of oregano, coriander, and fresh parsley. Katianna's stomach rumbled.

Deep aubergine-coloured tablecloths and the same white napkins creased into sail boats sat comfortably alongside tarnished cutlery creating a worn but inviting look to the table settings. On each of the square tables tall wine glasses and short tumblers for water fought for space with the menu cards and a porcelain vase holding a single rose. A mish mash of solid wood-stained chairs—which Katianna recognised as *Phini* chairs—packed the sides of the tables. Overall, the impression was one of a taverna frozen in time.

They enjoyed their meal, choosing to share the meze. The array of small taster dishes was served at an unhurried pace; cracked black olives drizzled in olive oil and garlic shaves, beetroot slices, boiled beans swimming in olive oil, potato salad, homemade *houmous*, *taramosalata* and *tzatziki* dips. They ordered extra pitta and olives. They squeezed fresh lemon over the sea bass; its crispy skin sprinkled with freshly chopped parsley and savoured the charred slices of charcoal grilled *halloumi*.

'This is heaven.' She smiled through her mouthful. 'Cyprus and *halloumi*,' she said, running her tongue over her lips.

Katianna drank her second glass of wine and relaxed. She even gave her widest smile to Polis as he played the first notes of a new song, standing at the other side of the restaurant, a few feet from her. He adjusted the mic and dedicated the song to the beautiful woman of the village house; Sofia nudged Katianna in the side. Katianna got over her embarrassment and then the thrill of his dedication hit her, and she thrummed along to the beat of the music; her fingers tapping the side of her chair. The music was beautiful and not as overpowering as she imagined a live band in such a small space to be.

The dance floor, alive with dancing patrons, young, old, children holding hands and twirling round and round, seemed to beckon Katianna. She tugged Sofia and Savva by the hands and nudged into the space in front of their table.

'Come on, Savva. We haven't danced together in years,' said Katianna, but Savva pulled back and sat firmly on his seat.

'I'm happy admiring the two of you from my seat,' he winked. 'Just watch that ankle of yours.'

Katianna raised her hands to her sides and clicked her fingers. She mirrored Sofia's movements from left to right and back again repeating the basic step of the most common Greek Cypriot dance, the *tsifteteli.*

The familiar song flooded Katianna with memories of long ago; family celebrations, her *yiayia's* courtyard garden overflowing with family and dancing. She clicked in time to the music just like her

77

yiayia and mother used to. A nostalgia brimming with happiness filled her.

When the music stopped both women clapped in appreciation of the others' dancing and Savva teased, 'Have you been practising?'

He stabbed a piece of honey melon with his fork; a platter of juicy red watermelon wedges, peeled prickly pears, sweet purple figs, apricots, and quartered peaches had been brought to the table.

'We just found our rhythm,' said Katianna.

'You attracted a lot of attention, especially after Polis' little dedication to you,' he said.

'What a sweetie,' said Sofia, fanning herself with her napkin. Little patches of sweat trickled down the side of her face.

'It's been a long time since I've danced like that,' said Katianna.

'I miss dancing,' said Sofia.

'I don't get the chance anymore and certainly not Greek dancing like this,' said Katianna, in a nostalgic whisper.

'I used to at weddings but they're so expensive now. More couples choose to escape…,' said Sofia.

'And have those dreamy-beach or mountain-top weddings on a tiny unknown Greek island in the middle of the Aegean, with white-washed houses and pretty little churches overlooking the blue sea,' said Katianna dreamily.

Savva nudged his head in the direction of Polis who was approaching their table.

'You're a beautiful dancer Katianna and you too Sofia,' Polis said.

'It's all down to the music. Your bouzouki playing is wonderful,' said Sofia.

'It is,' agreed Katianna with an enthusiasm she realised usually only made an appearance at work. *Must be the wine.*

'Thank you. It belonged to my great-grandfather on my mother's side. I found it in the bottom of a dowry chest when my parents decided to finally sell the old house. It needed some restoration, and cost a fair bit, but it was worth it.'

'It's just wonderful,' repeated Sofia.

'Join us for a drink?' asked Savva, waving to the waiter for another chair.

'Thank you. Let me finish my set. Another half an hour or so.'

Sofia and Katianna danced some more and joined in the *kalamatiano,* traditionally danced by the bride and her female friends and relatives by holding hands and taking steps back and forth to the left and right, moving clockwise in a circle. The women shimmied and twirled to a belly-dancing song and joined in the Zorba's dance; its energetic pace left them out of breath.

By the time Polis sat next to Katianna she could feel the make-up running down her face in a sea of perspiration. Sofia fanned Katianna's face with a menu card, but it seemed not to make the slightest bit of difference sitting within the walled area.

'I'm going to step out onto the street for a few minutes. It's so enclosed in here I'm going to faint,' said Katianna.

'I'll come with you,' said Polis.

Katianna waved a linen napkin around her face to cool herself. She sat next to Polis on an old wooden bench a few yards from the restaurant; a scattering of cigarette butts littered the ground and two skinny cats fought over a chicken bone while a stray dog barked in the distance over the partying and singing floating up from the other restaurants and bars they had passed earlier.

The moon, hanging like a silver coin above them, created a magical surreal atmosphere. Polis sat so close to her she could feel the hair on his arm tickling her elbow. She liked the way it felt soft and gentle yet so manly, strong. A heat rose in her and she suddenly felt a shift in her.

'There's something quite inexplicably magical about Cyprus. I'd forgotten the feeling until now.'

'Business colleagues tell me London has no soul; full of people driven by money and power.'

'Unlike Cyprus?'

'Sadly, not unlike the modern Cyprus; we've had our fair share of greed.'

'You mean the banking crisis?'

'That was only part of the problem. Hardship is what plagued the whole country for a long time. Cypriots grabbed as much as they could from the banks, withdrawing their savings before the banks could get to it but before long there was no cash. The cash machines were empty. People were desperate, became bankrupt overnight, losing as much as ten percent of their money.'

'But the economy is recovered. It seems so normal here. I mean look at how busy all the restaurants are, people out enjoying themselves,' said Katianna.

'The Cypriots are tough people, resilient...' His voice tailed off and she picked up a sadness in him. He had suffered, she was sure of it. 'Feelings still run high,' he continued. 'They have huge self-efficacy, have doubled down and tried even harder to survive but most have a long way to go.'

'And you?' she asked boldly.

'I've kept going. Adapted the business. Took on smaller projects. But my biggest regret is not finishing the renovations to my aunt's house, my mother's last living sibling, before she died.'

'I'm sorry you have suffered. Life is cruel.' Suddenly Katianna understood why he approached her *yiayia's* renovation with was such an ardent passion.

She looked into his jet-black eyes, and he looked back at her intently, his eyes sparkling, teary-eyed. He coughed and said, 'Tell me where you learnt to dance like you do.'

'My mother loved dancing. She would dance in the kitchen while cooking, making the beds, even while mowing the lawn. She danced at every opportunity singing or humming her favourite songs as they blasted out from the Greek radio station she used to listen to.' It was her turn to will the tears back.

'And you?'

'Not much opportunity recently. Not until now. Cyprus has got under my skin,' she said, looking away.

'Is Cyprus the only thing that's got under your skin?' he asked. He moved in for a kiss, his lips brushed hers for a second. She felt the world shift under her.

But before she had a chance to respond, to take in what was unfolding between them, Savva and Sofia appeared.

'Time to go,' said Savva. 'It's way past our bedtime.'

'Sorry, we got chatting,' said Katianna, running her fingers over her tingling lips.

'Of course,' said Polis, having pulled away. 'I have to be up early too.'

'*Kalinichta,* Polis,' said Sofia. 'And thank you for such a fun night.'

'Goodnight and thank you. The ladies certainly enjoyed themselves,' said Savva, shaking Polis' hand warmly.

'Yes, thank you, Polis,' said Katianna and Polis held her gaze a fraction longer than necessary, and that crazy, leaping swoon filled her.

'The thanks are all mine,' said Polis and he bid them goodnight.

***

At home, washing her face with cold water, Katianna shook off a shiver. Polis had kissed her. A tiny kiss, but a kiss all the same and she had wanted to feel his lips on hers, liked how they felt. But then what? She had no time or room for complications in her life. The sooner the village house was ready the sooner it would be sold, gone. She did not have the time or the inclination to be holding onto a past she had barely considered until these last few days. Her return flight was booked for three days' time. How ridiculous... what had got into her?

An overwhelming feeling of helplessness filled her, and her mind raced like a plane on a runway. But despite her thoughts, she lay in bed, the shutters partly closed over the open window, the night's heat fighting, despite her protestations, with the heat burning within her.

Chapter 15

The journey didn't take long despite the traffic and everyone, it seemed, having the same idea. However, the newer, modern mountain road, now tarmacked meant that at least traffic could easily and safely pass in both directions simultaneously despite the twisty bends and steep incline.

Katianna remembered how scary the drive had been as a child and how she had often shielded her eyes from the view over the mountain's edge. Vehicles had to pull precariously over to the edge of the cliffs, but now solid barriers offered reassuring protection from the sheer drop into the deep valley below.

The twenty-five-kilometre drive to *Platres*, a mid-point up the southern face of the Troodos Mountains, proved uneventful. Katianna crossed one leg over the other trying to ease the numbness which had settled in her thigh. Savva concentrated on the road ahead. Snuggled in the back, between two ice boxes, Sofia tucked her elbows into her sides to get comfortable. All three wound open their windows, giving up on the inefficient air con.

'Fresh mountain air,' said Savva, breathing in deeply.

'A relief from the annoying hum of your air-con,' said Katianna.

'The higher mountain altitude is certainly cooler,' said Sofia, leaning forward between both.

Savva's car continued the steep, winding climb to their destination. Their convoy made its way to an area called *Mesa Potamos*, literally translated as Inner River; an area traditionally frequented by generations of Greek Cypriots to celebrate the Assumption of the Virgin Mary, or *Tis Panayias*, as locals referred to this religious holiday where many Greek Cypriots booked their annual leave too, leaving the villages and cities for the cooler temperatures and open space of the coast.

The sheer craggy mountain sides rose to the left and then right as the car meandered along the alpine route, the sharp drop over the side too frightening for Katianna to look at. Huge tree roots protruded from the thin dry earth like veins searching for blood, struggling against the increasing heat.

'Those pines are so regal, tall, strong,' said Katianna, pointing to their branches, emerald green and splendid black against the sky's blue canvas. 'Reaching up,' she said, stretching and pushing her hands against the roof of the car.

'They're black pines, some older than five hundred years. They're the diamond of

Troodos' natural heritage.'

Katianna looked back and swept a wave of her long hair behind her neck and across her left shoulder, holding it there to stop it blowing in her face. She gave Sofia a smile.

Sofia's soft auburn curls blew around her face as the pine air, fragrant and sweet, whirled inside the car and she blew away an errant hair caught between her lips.

'That clean smell of pine. Reminds me of years ago, with Mum and Dad,' said Katianna, turning back to face the front and closing her eyes.

'That smell brings out those memories for me too, growing up, road trips…,' said Savva. 'Shorts and scuffed knees, splashing around in the stream, playing hide and seek amongst the pines. Such happy days.'

'To be that age again,' said Katianna.

'You're as young as you allow yourself to be,' said Sofia.

'That's good philosophy. Philosophy for a real life… for today's living.' Katianna let out an undignified whoop of joy. The women looked at each other and laughed.

A funky modern Greek pop tune blared from the radio. Savva blasted the volume a notch, breaking into song, 'When you find me... I will be just what you're looking for...'

Sofia joined in, '...like stardust nights... we will soar to new heights...'

'Listen to you both. A duet,' said Katianna, sneaking a sideways smile at Savva.

Savva kept his eyes fixed on the road, but Katianna wondered whether he was hiding his true feelings. *And what about Sofia? Did she harness any feelings for him?*

The sign for *Platres*, partly hidden by low cone-weighted branches, showed another five kilometres. The two cars ahead of them indicated left at the last minute. Savva slammed on the brakes and took a sharp turn, following them along a bumpy dirt track enclosed by overgrown vegetation.

'You're joking,' said Katianna, coughing against the dust billowing around her as the car trundled over a pothole and shook her back and forth. She wound up the window to stop the dust from filling her lungs and huffed, fanning herself with a folded newspaper she tugged out from down the side of her seat.

With skillful navigation, Savva avoided the rest of the uneven ground, zigzagging along the path until it eventually led to a level clearing in the woods.

'Thank God for that,' said Katianna, swinging the car door open. She shook her arms by her sides and kicked out her legs to ease the numbing.

'That wasn't exactly a joyful ride,' said Sofia.

'It never is, but it's always worth it. You'll see,' said Savva, winking.

'At least it's not too hot up here,' said Sofia.

'Not yet, but it'll soon warm up,' said Savva, changing from his soft leather loafers into his trainers.

Parked up, everyone helped to carry the cars' contents to the picnic spot one of the family members said would not be overcrowded. Sofia carried one of the cool boxes and Savva took two large tote bags; one filled with soft drinks and the other with two huge watermelons and three honey dew melons. The men unloaded and carried the barbeques and the skewers, bags of charcoal and firelighters, foldaway tables, and camping chairs.

A boy, no older than seven tucked a folded blanket under his arm, hoisting it back every time it threatened to fall and two girls, possibly even younger, wrestled with a plastic bag of salad vegetables between them: the plastic handles cutting into their palms. Katianna took the bag from them, and they skipped off ahead singing a rhyme.

Navigating the hilly trail was a challenge; thorny undergrowth and tangled underbrush made it difficult to avoid the bumpy, uneven ground. Katianna shuffled *through* detritus, seeking the brilliant white shaft of light as it appeared momentarily between the canopy of dense pines, to guide her. Branches snapped and crackled above, and the ground felt soft in places where pine needles created a springy carpet.

Katianna, relieved she had grabbed a jacket, slipped it on, shivering against the coolness of being in the shade of the tall pines. She guided an old lady, the grandmother of the family in the car in front of them in the convoy, dropping behind the others to walk at the old woman's pace. The old dear chatted and intermittently stopped to catch her breath, a shallow rasping coming from deep within her chest, but she persevered and with the aid of her walking stick kept a constant pace all the way to the picnic spot.

'I told them to leave me at home,' said the old woman, 'but they wouldn't hear of it.'

'And rightly so,' said Sofia. 'There is no distinction between ages and generations, here. You know that. How could we have left you at home on one of the biggest religious days on our calendar?'

'You're right of course. It's how it should be,' the old lady chuckled.

A tiny trickling stream tinkled over rocky buttresses and a bed of pebbles; the location took Katianna by surprise. The beauty of the destination was certainly worth the uncomfortable walk. For a moment she imagined she had passed through a secret doorway; the early morning sun tipped over the tops of the trees sending a shaft of golden light into the clearing, the forest's multitude of greens brighter than ever. Two grey-black warblers, with jet black heads and black streaked underparts, hopped across one of the rocky slopes between the low bushes. The invasion of their solitude sent them flying, deeper into the forest. A light brown lizard with thin white stripes shot across the rocky, forested area and disappeared between two boulders another smaller one, camouflaged against the rock, moved, and ran behind its companion.

'They're harmless, right?' Katianna pulled a face. Sofia laughed her hearty laugh and focused on the group of women unfolding the blankets and picnic rugs. The men kicked away larger stones and smoothed out the dry earth with their hands, careful to avoid the prick of pine needles and the women laid out the blankets in a mishmash of rainbow stripes, blue stars, and the Cyprus flag.

Katianna ushered the old lady towards a pop-up camp chair and helped lower her into it. Taking Katianna's hand, she gave it a squeeze. 'Thank you for helping me, God bless you child. I won't move from here for the rest of the day,' she smiled.

Katianna noticed the woman's hazel eyes and wispy strands of silver hair coming loose from under her head scarf and wondered what stories she had to tell, of love and war, home and country, sisters, and brothers. Something in her expression reminded Katianna of her *yiayia*; she fought the sting of tears as her eyes filled.

'I miss my family here, my roots,' Katianna whispered to herself, examining her feelings cautiously.

Katianna quickly joined the hive of activity and devoted herself with intensity to the task; she erected picnic tables and unfolded chairs for the adults and older generation amongst them to sit on and laid out cushions and pillows around the edge of the jumble of floor coverings for the teenagers and children.

The men got busy too; positioning their equipment for cooking the meat a few feet away to avoid smoking everyone out. They emptied chunks of charcoal into the metal barbeques from huge paper sacks, and made their 15th August toasts to each other, clinking their cooled bottles of beer, their laughter punctuating the air with loving warmth and notes of easy comradery.

Katianna wondered whether the roles naturally divided between the men and women would ever change. Even in modern-day Cyprus it seemed the traditional roles existed from generations before, and it surprised her to see she found this a comfort. 'Some things don't change,' she said, nodding towards the men and women working separately yet in harmony.

'No, they don't,' said Sofia. 'The good traditions remain and anyway, I wouldn't want to stand over a smoking barbeque or clear the rough ground with my hands, would you?'

'I guess not,' said Katianna, shivering against the bite in the air. 'I'm glad I listened to Savva and grabbed a shawl.' She shook off a shiver, tugging the soft cashmere wrap over her jacket.

The chink of glass echoed above the merriment and Katianna smiled. She was reintroduced to neighbours from the village, long-distance aunts, and cousins she hadn't seen since she was eight or nine, now with husbands and families of their own.

One of the teenagers, prompted by his mother, put on some music, and increased the volume; it pumped out across the space from the little speaker perched on a wide gnarly trunk behind him, fallen amongst a mountain of dead branches and wildflowers.

Sofia passed Katianna a tumbler of red wine and they made a toast to each other with their plastic cups.

'Wine o'clock already,' said Katianna.

'What a wonderful day this is already turning out to be,' said Sofia.

'And wait until you're eating, said the old lady to Katianna, slurping the sweet pink nectar of her rosewater cordial through a paper straw. 'You'll think you've entered another realm.'

Close to two hours later, one of the men announced the first skewers of meat would be ready in fifteen minutes. The women all took to work; chopping vegetables into big plastic bowls, fresh flat-leaf parsley to garnish the meat, cutting *makaronia tou fournou* ready for serving and opening Tupperware filled with *kioftethes* and *koubebia;* the homemade meatballs and stuffed vine leaves testament to the effort put into preparing the picnic days in advance. Freshly made *houmous* and *tahini,* dips made from sesame seed paste and garlic, lemon and olive oil shone in the sunlight.

A little girl tucked packets of pitta under each arm. She jumped across the boulders to where the men cooked, her long plaits swinging against her back, and passed the floury artisan bread to be warmed and crisped over the hot charcoals.

London felt distant and though Katianna was happy to be booked on the flight home, a touch of sadness tugged at her. She wasn't ready to leave. The genuine, warm closeness so different to her isolated existence back home hugged her like her *yiayia's* cosy hand-crocheted blanket, taking her back to those long days on the beach, warming her long after the sun dipped behind the horizon.

She shook herself out of her downheartedness. She picked up a huge catering pack of serviettes and handed them out with paper plates and plastic cutlery, delighted to be a part of this wonderful group of women who made her feel so welcome. Their patience had proved fruitful; not only had Katianna's understanding of Greek improved but her conversation had improved too.

'*Ade, oli… to kreas einai etimo,*' Savva announced.

Everyone cheered as the first sizzling chunks of lamb and pork were forked from the skewers into the waiting plastic containers; the smell of meat marinated in oregano tickled Katianna's nose and her stomach rumbled.

'You look relaxed today,' said Sofia. 'Like one of the locals.'

'I am. To be connecting with my roots and a language I thought I'd forgotten feels good,' she laughed.

'Cheers, and welcome Katianna. May Cyprus' hospitality and its people persuade you to keep your *yiayia's* house and enjoy it for a long time to come,' Savva toasted, and everyone joined in.

Katianna hesitated, Savva's words unexpected. 'It's good to be here,' she said, surprised also at the joy the thought of keeping the house brought her. Secretly she enjoyed everyone's reference to her as *the woman who was rebuilding the village house and found a magical water source for the whole village.*

'You're our superhero. Sweeping in to save our village from more looming mansion-sized properties being erected, not only on the outskirts of the village, but on inner plots holding the secrets of old village homes,' an aunt said, a distant family member.

'The water supply will be a God send. It will help us tremendously,' said another.

One of the younger children theatrically bowed and his mother reprimanded him with a playful slap on the backs of his legs. He giggled and run off, his mother warning him to be careful of the thorny bushes.

'God works in mysterious ways. We must trust Him. Now, eat more,' said another woman, proffering the last few *kioftethes* rolling around in the bottom of the deep lipped bowl.

'Thank you, no. I've eaten enough food for a week,' said Katianna. 'It was all delicious.'

'Many hands make light work of cooking,' said Savva's mum.

'It's how we always enjoy such a feast when we're together,' said one of the neighbours.

'I think it's lovely. The family, the celebrating together like this,' said Katianna.

The conversation turned to the new high rise planned for the seafront and another set of Twin Towers nearer Old Limassol. Katianna shivered at the obtuse name given to the development given 9:11.

She discarded her empty plate and cutlery into a bin liner hanging from a tree branch and made her excuses. She escaped the animated conversations growing in pitch and seriousness and headed uphill in the direction of the stream's source; the tinkling running water taking her back to carefree childhood days when she visited as a young girl. She let herself be led by the sights and sounds, birds tweeting, the rustle of leaves, the whistle of the warm breeze, all the while a gentle pull tugging at her heartstrings.

With no path but Katianna stepped tentatively in and out of low vegetation, boulders, and craggy rocks, glad for the borrowed pair of trainers from Sofia. She ascended a set of wide steep steps, logs set into the ground. The voices faded giving way to nature's soft rustle and her faintly echoing steps on the woody ground.

The sun dappled through the overhead canopy of tall pines warming her head. A mountain face swept steeply upwards, affording a breathtaking spot to sit.

Perched on a boulder, not caring it was damp from the splash of the stream; Katianna stretched her legs towards the water and ran her fingers over the wide rock. She pressed her hand on its cool surface, drawing strength from its solidity. She closed her weary eyes, her early morning rise, and the excitement of the celebrations, catching up with her.

She didn't know how long she sat there, tuning into the heartbeat of the forest when a twig snapped, startling her.

'I'm sorry. Did I frighten you?'

'Polis?' she asked, twisting round to face him.

A two-note hooting interrupted her, making her jump again. Then another, like an echo.

'That's a duet of sorts... you don't often hear them anymore,' Polis said, walking closer. 'Owls. Cyprus Scops Owls to be exact. They thrive in these high altitudes.'

'I can't see them,' said Katianna, shading her eyes from the yellow midday light.

'The higher pitch is the female, responding to the call of the male.'

'The repetition is like a musical symphony,' said Katianna, composing herself. 'What are you doing here?'

'Same as you I'm guessing... escaping the noisy celebrations for a while, seeking the calming call of nature, of the stream.'

Sustained hoots, two notes in a rigid sequence: quiet note, short silence, loud note, long silence, continued.

'Not so quiet.'

'No,' he said. 'But quieter than London?'

'Have you been to London?'

'I've had no wish to go until now,' he said, holding her gaze.

'I didn't know you'd be here today,' she said, the idea of him being in London colouring her cheeks.

'Half of Cyprus is in these mountains today,' he laughed and as if laughing too, the cicadas began their crescendo of high-pitched buzzing.

She stared at his slightly crooked teeth, remembering the first time she noticed them. Prickles ran up her spine and spread into her chest; warm tingles, lots of them, tap-tap-tapping, dancing in tune to the cicadas' tymbal vibrations as they sang across the afternoon.

The sound fell away and a long silence stretched between Katianna and Polis until she eventually asked, 'How come you wandered up here?'

'I don't know. Something was pulling me this way,' he said.

She was sure he noticed her flushed cheeks.

'It's a beautiful spot. I'm surprised more people haven't found their—'

'Don't move,' he said.

Chapter 16

'What?'

'Stay still.'

'Oh my God, what is it?' cried Katianna, her hand flew to her chest, her body rigid, a cold sweat enveloping her.

Polis pulled slowly at a semi-concealed branch by his feet, his gaze holding hers the whole time. He stretched the bough towards her and stabbed the forked end into the ground. Katianna looked down. The stick pinned the trailing body of the coin snake to the earth. Polis grabbed the snake with his hand, his jumper wound around it, and threw the creature towards the stream where it quickly disappeared into the dusty undergrowth. Katianna screamed, a delayed reaction, and she burst into tears.

'I've got you,' he said, rushing to her. She didn't stop him as he folded her close, his body hard against hers, massaging her shoulders. He pulled back, cupped her face, and kissed her. Then, he kissed her again. A soft, lingering kiss. She breathed him in, squinting up at him into the sun, eventually closing her eyes. She pressed herself against him, lost in the smoothness of his full lips and the bristle of his three-day beard. His smell. His taste.

She wanted time to stop still.

Simultaneously, the cries of the cicadas stopped. A stitched mélange of peace, made up of the trickling stream, their own beating hearts, and that of the forest, fell upon them. They eventually pulled apart; she opened her eyes and smiled. They remained silent, a few stretched-out moments, one after the other, as if both afraid of spoiling the magic, losing the connection, between them.

'Looks like you were meant to have that kiss after all,' she said eventually, leaning in to kiss him again, her eyes searching his.

'I thought I'd frightened you off after the other night,' he said.

'You did?' said Katianna, surprised at her flirting.

'You haven't been to the house for two days.'

'I've been busy.'

'So have I,' he said, 'thinking about you.' He kissed her cheekbone and forehead, found her lips again.

Katianna felt the heat of their mutual desperation and tried to fight the sensations rising within her.

'Polis, there can be nothing between us. I'm going back to London, I've got responsibilities.' But even as she uttered the words, she feared her heart would not be the same again. She had stepped out as one person and now stepped back as another. The feeling unnerved her. She pushed her desire back into the wings. She didn't have time for this. Katianna was ambitious. Katianna was razor sharp. A heart on fire had no place in her life.

'Don't say that. Not yet. Not without giving it a chance.'

'This holiday romance, infatuation–'

'I'm not a teenage boy. I know what I feel,' he said with fire in his eyes.

'What you feel and what can happen are two different things. Please Polis, what chance do we have?'

'We have every chance we make. Every chance we take,' he said, holding her hands in his, turning them over and stroking her palms. And then, as if grappling for some sort of further explanation, assessment, he said, 'Did you know that mulberry trees are commonly dioecious?' Katianna gave him a quizzical look. 'They are male or female, and the female-bearing trees require the pollen of the male, non-bearing trees to set fruit. One male and one female, supporting each other.'

'Mulberry trees…' she said, trying to slow her breathing, to take in what he was implying, what was happening.

'I'm not explaining this very well. It's not by accident that we've met,' he said finally. 'I need you and I think you need me.'

Katianna, taken aback by his forwardness, said, mocking him, 'Now you're going to tell me the moon and stars have aligned to bring us here.' But as she said the words a sparkle of fireflies seemed to dance inside her, lighting her up from the inside. Her pulse quickened.

She took in a deep breath in an effort to calm herself. This was impossible. A silly fantasy. Heightened with silly romantic holiday notions. The sun was getting to her. That was it. Exhaustion. She was out of her routine.

'I don't know what it is. But I know you feel what I feel. Don't push it away before it has time to grow.'

'And when it grows so big, we cannot do anything but crumble under its weight, its expectations… what then?' she asked, searching his eyes.

'We'll be strong enough in unity to bear it all and throw happiness and joy at it.'

'I didn't realise you were such a romantic. An optimist.'

'I wasn't until I met you. At least not like this.'

They stood looking into each other's eyes until the spell was broken.

'I'll see you at the house soon,' she said to Polis and turned her attention to Sofia and Savva calling her name.

'I'm over here,' she called, and then louder, 'Here!' She uncurled her hands from Polis' grip, the sensation, that of the gentle pressure of his fingers around hers, still there. She ran her fingers through her hair.

'You've been gone an awfully long time,' said Savva. We thought you'd got lost.'

'The scream. Are you okay? Polis?' Sofia asked.

'I probably am lost, but not in the way you think,' she whispered. 'Polis found me. Apparently, this is his favourite spot. And it is the favourite hideaway for snakes too.'

'I bet it is,' winked Sofia who sank into the mossy ground.

'I wouldn't sit down,' said Katianna. 'I'm serious. A huge snake.'

'Not that huge. A coin snake, not poisonous,' said Polis, straightening, his face serious.

'Polis, you're Katianna's hero,' said Sofia, clasping her hands in glee, like a child in a sweet shop.

'We're going to be heading back to Limassol soon,' said Savva.

'What a day,' said Katianna.

'And how's your day been, Polis?' asked Savva. 'I'm surprised I haven't seen more people I know.'

'More families opt for trendy sea-side fish restaurants or air-conditioned five-star hotel eateries,' said Sofia.

'True. But you can't beat the mountain air and the smell of those black pines,' said Polis.

'And the love in the air,' Sofia giggled into Katianna's ear.

Katianna straightened, brushing the back of her skirt, she twirled a lock of hair in her usual way across the back of her neck and over one side over her shoulder; the ends felt dry, and she made a mental note to make a hair appointment as soon as she got home. A stab of regret came at her; she was going to miss all this, miss Polis.

'Thank you for rescuing my London-city cousin,' said Savva.

'My pleasure. Glad I was there.'

'We'd better get going,' said Katianna. 'Thanks again for saving me,' she said to Polis and with a thrill of alarm, desire filled her again.

They all turned to leave. Katianna stopped, glancing back. Polis turned too and they smiled.

Chapter 17

The drive back seemed interminable for Katianna, the glare of the sun unrelenting, blinding, as it bounced off the windscreen. By the time they arrived home, and unloaded the car, the church bells rang out for the evening service. The ding-dong reminded her of the acoustic reach of the church bells in London. She didn't hear them often but when she did it was as if they came from another world, pushing the traffic-stifled streets of Camden out of the way. But here, the celebratory hum of families still enjoying the day's gatherings echoed across the cobbled streets.

'At this precise moment I'm missing London… and the English weather,' said Katianna, shading her eyes against the dipping sun. *Under the Setting Sun*, she thought… the romantic connotations associated with the business name didn't quite fit in as well here when she was fighting a headache.

'You'll soon be back there complaining about the cold,' said Savva.

'You're right. I don't mean to sound ungrateful. It's been a glorious day. Thank you.'

Savva turned to Sofia, who unceremoniously stretched her arms in the air.

'Won't you stay for a drink?' invited Savva.

'I'm exhausted,' said Sofia, letting out an elaborately noisy yawn. 'But thank you. I'll see you soon.' She kissed them both on each cheek and waved goodbye.

'See you soon,' called Katianna, blowing her another kiss, and then yawning, Sofia's yawn contagious.

***

Showered and changed into fresh clothes, Katianna and Savva sat in the back garden under a darkening canopy of fading light, the sky turning a deep blue. Savva drank a cold beer straight from the bottle and Katianna was enjoying a cup of tea in one of Savva's art mugs. She massaged her temples, small circular motions.

'What's with you and Polis?'

'There's no me and Polis,' said Katianna, turning towards the sudden buzz of the cicadas from the highest branches of the pomegranate, orange, and lemon trees behind Savva's walled garden. Conscious too much emotion spilled from her, she concentrated on the shrill, relentless buzz which tormented her and beyond to the vine-filled slopes and the ghost of an abandoned minaret.

'So, we didn't catch you kissing earlier?'

'He kissed me and… it was one kiss. It's hardly Klimt's kiss,' said Katianna, raising her mug with the image of the lovers embracing in a cloak of shimmering gold. Her cheeks blazed hot; her head thrummed.

'And you liked it. Why deny it? He's a good man.'

'I hardly know him.'

'You can get to know him. Isn't that how relationships start? You do run a dating agency.'

'What's that got to do with anything?'

'Why the guard rails? I'm just saying you know how it works.'

'In theory, maybe, but it never works out for me.'

'Never is a long time… believe me, I know.'

Katianna pondered his words; her heart raced, and her reluctant smile grew of its own accord. She ran her fingers up and down her arm, chasing the tingle. She knew he was right but not ready to admit anything, not out loud anyway. Instead, she said, 'What does that mean? What are you not telling me?'

'Nothing's going to happen any time soon, if ever. But I still hope, still want to love someone.'

'Or do you still love someone?'

'Love, the idea of loving someone is painful for me.'

'Why?'

'Because the past, however much you try to escape it, will always catch up with you.'

'How can you be positive with me but not as generous with yourself?'

'Because the risk far outweighs my possible joy.'

'You need to change your mindset,' said Katianna.

A rattle at the back gate ended their conversation. Katianna let out a sigh of frustration.

'I changed my mind,' Sofia said, and the gate swung shut behind her with a gentle click.

She wore a cotton dress, the matching sash pulled tightly around her tiny waist. The swirling black and white pattern suited her and the extra height her open-toed wedges gave her was flattering.

'You look lovely,' said Katianna, feeling guilty about her conversation with Savva.

'Less dusty that's for sure, thank you.'

'Your timing's perfect. You've saved me from my dear cousin's interrogation.

Perhaps he'll turn his attentions to you,' said Katianna, noting again how Savva's posture changed in Sofia's presence.

He pushed himself upright in his seat expanding his chest and pulling in his stomach. Katianna smiled knowingly.

'Of course… come in. Good to see you again.' Savva stumbled over his words. Sofia smiled, her hazel eyes reflecting the final amber-gold rays of the setting sun.

'It's only been a couple of hours,' said Katianna playfully, part of her enjoying how he squirmed.

'I feel better after a shower. You forget how grimy you get in the mountains,' Sofia said.

'But what a day? I loved every second of it,' said Katianna.

Savva smirked. 'Every second?'

'Apart from the snake,' she giggled, knowing that if it hadn't been for the snake she and Polis might not have kissed and she laughed a little harder, nerves getting the better of her. Perhaps she did enjoy the kiss; more than she admitted. And Savva was right about Polis being a good man; she could almost touch the intense goodness which radiated from him. He certainly hadn't given her any reason not to trust him both in matters of the building work and the heart.

'What happened with Polis is a good thing, right?'

'Not you as well, Sofia. Yes, maybe. Now change the subject please,' said Katianna.

Sofia dropped two overstuffed paper bags onto the table. 'I've brought treats.'

'We're all maxed out on food,' said Katianna.

'This'll change your mind.' Sofia took out two tubs; she pulled back the lids to reveal pistachio and *anari*-cream ice creams.

'I'm in heaven,' said Savva and quickly dived into the kitchen, returning with three bowls and spoons.

Sofia gave Katianna a twinkly wink.

'So, how did you know it was my favourite?' Savva asked Sofia.

'I just knew. This is from a batch I made last week with Petros. We sweetened the whey cheese with my aunt's mountain honey, cream, and freshly ground cinnamon. My customers can't get enough.'

Katianna dipped her finger into the pot of already melting ice cream. 'I can see why it's a popular flavour,' she said. She closed her eyes and licked her fingertip. 'Delicious.'

'What are you waiting for? If you don't scoop up, I'm taking the whole tub,' Savva laughed.

They tucked in and talked animatedly about their day. The setting sun casting faint shadows before finally sinking behind the mountain ridges and within half an hour the glowing sky, tinged red and gold, transpired into a deep navy cloak scattered with flickering stars.

'The perfect end to a wonderful day,' said Katianna, looking up at the black, star-studded canopy and in that moment *Under the Setting Sun* felt totally right.

'Sure is,' Savva said. Katianna sensed her dreamy comment was not wasted on him. He licked his lips slowly and Katianna guessed it was in appreciation of more than the creamy dessert.

'You're easy to please,' teased Sofia.

'I am and I'll take you out one night next week to say thanks,' said Savva.

'There's no need,' said Sofia.

'Of course, there is,' said Katianna, enjoying her mischievous interjection.

'Only if you want to,' said Savva, backtracking, awkward again.

Katianna and Sofia dabbed at the melted dregs in the tub and licked the stickiness off their fingers. Sofia. That's who Katianna had reminded him of... a memory stole into his thoughts of Sofia picking at flakes of pastry and sugar grains as a child. He always found it a bit disgusting and had often teased her, calling her a *gourounaki,* a piggy, which sent her into a rage and a bout of play fighting with him. But she ended every meal with little sweeping dabs of the plate just in case she left anything behind. Savva smiled at the recollection.

'I'd like that,' said Sofia, the slightest quiver in her voice baring her nerves.

'Don't have too much fun without me. Save some of the entertainment for my return.'

'Soon, I hope,' said Sofia.

Katianna checked her vibrating phone. 'I'll know more after Polis' update. He's just messaged. I'm meeting a prospective buyer tomorrow morning, so who knows? It may be soon. But I'm thinking October.'

'That's only a couple of months away,' said Sofia.

'Watch out for crooks. Is the buyer through an agent?' Savva asked, revealing his protective side.

'Yes, we're meeting at the house. I feel nervous. Not sure why.'

'Good luck cousin. Just don't be persuaded by the first person who comes along.'

'And Sofia if you can, I'd still like to go ahead with the party I mentioned before. I want to celebrate my *yiayia's* house and her life, and to thank everyone for making me feel so welcome.'

'I'll make the time. Sorry I hesitated when you first asked.'

'I was a bit pushy, I suppose.'

'Not at all,' said Sofia and Katianna noticed the tiny, powdered freckles across Sofia's face shone like stars.

'And you're welcome to stay with me again, you know that.' Savva reached across and gave Katianna's shoulder a squeeze and a pat.

'Or you can stay at mine. It's not full of mod-cons like Savva's place but you're more than welcome.'

'Thank you. Both of you. You've made these last few days so enjoyable. In fact, I'm not sure I want to go back. I didn't realise how much I'd missed this place, the people, the slower pace... life has a way of unfolding differently.'

'People work to live, not the other way round, even with the struggling economy,' said Sofia.

'I can't explain it,' Katianna said.

'People have and will always hold onto their *kefi*. Their spirit of joy, passion, has seen us through a lot and I'm sure a lot more too. But you're right, there's something special here,' said Sofia. 'You hear all the tourists trying to put their finger on it.'

'Your hearts beat to a different rhythm,' said Katianna.

'It's the mountain air and the magical sunsets,' said Sofia.

'You don't have to leave, cousin. You can do everything on your phone and laptop. We're not exactly out in the back of beyond.' said Savva, practised patience playing out in his tone.

'Easier said than done. I've a lot to sort out with the business and need to get back to the office. Unlike you I do live to work. Without my work I'd have nothing. Everything I do and think, and plan is done with my business at the heart of it.' Katianna took a deep breath, surprised at her sudden outburst but the strength of her emotion genuine. It was time to fly back to London.

'We all need a passion. And we'll be waiting for you when you do come back, won't we?' Sofia looked at Savva and he nodded, avoiding eye contact with her. Katianna noticed the heightening colour on his cheeks and again wondered was it more than a flush of sunburn.

'Sure, we will,' he said, excusing himself.

Katianna waited for him to be out of earshot but lowered her voice just in case. 'I think Savva likes you. There's mischief in his eyes and a kind of crazy.' *She's a tempest of stardust and scars, ruling the moonlight and touting the sunrise,* thought Katianna, the words of a poem filling her thoughts.

'I like him too,' admitted Sofia with a sparkle. 'But I think you're wrong. He finds me too independent. And there's this, it reminds him too much…' she said, running her fingers over her scars.

'What do you mean?'

'Our family's rift… the years of guilt and blame and trying to forget when for the longest time all I wanted was to move on.'

'I'm sorry but I don't know what you're talking about. How's Savva involved?'

'We were messing around as kids, in one of the open fields. Building a fire to roast chestnuts. Savva threw paraffin onto it to speed it up… the dry cones and twigs caught suddenly, flared, spat wildly. Apparently, I was lucky to be alive. He smothered me in his jacket, dampened the flames.'

'I didn't know.'

'I was in hospital for ten days… had two excruciatingly painful skin grafts over the next eighteen months.' She visibly shivered, as if suppressing the dark memories stirring in the depths of her memory.

'How old were you?'

'Nine. It was the day after my birthday.'

'My mum never mentioned it,' said Katianna, an overwhelming sadness coming over her. It was too late to ask her mother anything now and she couldn't quite believe that both her parents' memorials were approaching.

'Too many of the villagers blamed him, unfairly, of course. There was a lot of shouting, arguing. It was horrible. It divided the village. Our families fell out, and even now if you look closely, there's only forced politeness, nothing more.'

'That's a terrible thing to have to live with as a child. For both of you. And to live with after all these years but Savva must have paid the price for what he did.'

'It's been lonely. No one mentions it. I hide my scars most of the time, conscious not of the way they look but of how they make others feel,' she took in a long breath and exhaled slowly. 'It must've been lonely for him too, but I don't blame him. I could have stopped him, but I liked the thrill of being around him, the danger. I even encouraged him.'

'I'm so sorry you've had to go through that. To still be living through it.'

'It's my life's trajectory, I can't change it.'

'Sofia, change your path and your life will change. We are fusions of mind, body, and spirit. Mould these, manipulate your core beliefs and your heart's desires and you can be on a different path altogether.'

'That's what this café's all about. A different focus.'

'We're not too different you and I,' said Katianna, taking Sofia's hand and giving it a gentle squeeze.

'Perhaps,' she said, shaking her head. 'Not sure where that all came from but thank you. You're easy to talk to. You're more like your *yiayia* than you imagine.'

'I feel her close to me here.'

'And she always will be.'

'You and Savva... there's no argument between you now?'

'Argument?' Savva's voice cut across their subdued voices.

'Yes, in the office,' said Katianna, pulling her hand from Sofia's. 'My team doesn't always get on. You know what it's like when you're together day in day out, tempers rise when there's too much work and too little time, deadlines, tight schedules, tech issues.' Katianna looked at Sofia, took a slug of her drink. Sofia nodded her thanks, but Katianna was concerned and wanted to delve deeper, know more. More about how something so long ago was still impacting on Sofia's life, on Savva's too. Had they even spoken about it together since?

'All the more reason to stay here and let them get on with it,' said Savva, popping open a beer. 'Anyone joining me for another?' He wiped his sweaty brow with the back of his hand and slumped into his seat, more relaxed.

They listened to music the rest of the night, talked about the banking crisis, the growing economy, finally after all the months of hardship, and how they still dreamed of a solution to the island's division forty-two years after Turkey's invasion.

The humidity, despite the hour, stifled Katianna and, suddenly exhausted, she longed for the coolness of London, her huge sofa, and the calming space of her deluxe flat.

Chapter 18

Katianna pushed open the gate recognising how nervous she felt about seeing Polis again.

After the trip to the mountains, he had sent her a message to say he would happily rescue her from a snake anytime, but she had not replied unsure of what to say.

Polis, wheeling a precariously over-filled barrow across the little garden, stopped before looking up, seeming to sense her presence. His eyes brightened instantly, and Katianna blushed, the awkwardness of seeing him again evident in her hesitation.

She turned her full attention on the immaculately dressed woman introduced as Ms. Anichka Lebedev by the equally polished estate agent. Katianna kept her attention; the woman's limp handshake a contrast to her self-assured Russian-accented voice.

'It's exactly what I want. Size. Position. Potential to modernise,' she said, fluttering her fake eyelashes furiously as if batting at a fly. Katianna watched her lips moving, fascinated with her pout. 'I would like to make an offer. A serious one.' Katianna waited, crossed her arms, unsure whether to cry or whoop with joy. '200,000 euros. I can complete with no delays. I assure you my funds are in place.'

Katianna hesitated, the words modernise and no delays ringing in her ears. She became aware of her palms sweating. 'That's more than the agent estimated... I don't think the refurbishment will be finished any time soon. I'm waiting for confirmation from my builders.'

The woman batted her lashes again. 'This does not affect me. My plans are for this old house to join the next century... marbled courtyard, modern open-plan dining.'

Katianna stumbled back as if the woman had pushed her. She touched her throat, caught off guard by a nauseating catch, gasped for air. This wasn't what she expected. This wasn't something she had anticipated feeling so strongly about. Could she let her *yiayia's* house become a state-of-the-art mausoleum?

Memories pulled her back; rocking in the iron swing in the courtyard, her *yiayia's* freshly squeezed lemon juice, washing her sandy-crusted feet with the hose, wrapped in a huge scratchy beach towel. Her personal narrative dragged her back to a time she was happy, a carefree and joyous childhood full of love and innocence, family, and security. She found it surprisingly arousing, the vibrancy and warmth. She wanted to cling to it, to all of it.

Perhaps selling the house wasn't the right decision. Perhaps holding onto her heritage was better and with a touch of sadness she realised she wouldn't see the house finished, someone else would be making the bed, brewing coffee, sitting in the shade of the olive tree.

'I will let you know as soon as I can,' said Katianna, conscious of the things she once loved, still loved, being torn away.

'I don't have time to waste. Let the agent know by this afternoon. Thank you for your time,' she said, waving at a waft of dust.

Katianna watched the woman's retreating back, the agent shuffling after her like a trained monkey. She exhaled only once the hum of the waiting car's engine had faded. She hadn't even realised she was holding her breath.

'Can you believe the cheek?'

'Bad news?' asked Polis.

'Did you hear what that woman offered me for the house?' Katianna ran her fingers through her tangled hair, the gritty grains of construction already settling.

'Katianna, you told the agent you wanted a quick sale. Now you're stalling. You need to decide what you really want.'

His words hung in the air like the echo of a tolling funeral bell.

Katianna walked towards him and at the same time, she in English and he in Greek, said, 'about yesterday.'

'What does that mean?' she asked, a kinetic energy running through her.

'It means we kissed. A proper kiss. And yet you're ignoring the kiss, ignoring me and now, I sense, you're ignoring your intuition.'

'Polis, I'm not ignoring anything. I'm being realistic,' she said, trying to convince herself that what she was saying was right, was the truth, though perhaps not an unvarnished one. She could not look at him, yet she knew, felt even, the truth of what he said.

Polis sighed, refrained from pushing her. 'If you don't want me to continue with the refurbishment, tell me now. I don't want to waste any more time on something which I've so lovingly restored,' he gulped, 'if it's going to be destroyed the minute the house is sold. And, as a businesswoman, I'm sure you don't want to be wasting your money either.'

'I'm sorry. If I'd known…'

'How were you to know what?'

'This… how I'd feel,' she said, nervous prickles of electricity coursing through her, across her scalp, down her arms.

'Our roots are called roots because they have a pull on us. They pull at our heartstrings, muddle our feelings. But they also ground us. Give us somewhere to call home. To feel at home.'

'But home for me is in London. I'm getting confused. I need to remain realistic,' she said, chaos surging through her veins, her palms sweating, and she felt him evaluating her.

'You're not confused. You know exactly what you want. You feel it here,' he said, placing his palm over his heart. 'It's in your blood. Your whole demeanour changes when you speak of your *yiayia*, your childhood memories.'

As he spoke, Katianna experienced a resurgence of emotion, a curiosity for what she was feeling. He was right, of course. She could no longer deny her feelings, however confusing.

Polis took a step closer and taking both her hands in his gently kissed each one in turn.

Electricity ran through her; immeasurable, powerful. She couldn't fight her sudden overwhelming desire, her logic desperately trying to work out a realistic strategy.

'How's ignoring your gut instinct realistic?' he asked.

'I'm not sure what's happening,' she said, fighting to demist her brain.

'I do. You were already falling in love with Cyprus and then I kissed you... again.'

'I know but...'

'There's no but, Katianna. There's only when... when will you be ready to face a new future and,' he paused, a smile playing on his lips, 'when will I see you again?'

'I don't do romance... I don't do boy meets girl and happy ever after. That's the job of my business. I can't stay here indefinitely, there's so much to think about.'

'Don't think about it all. Think about the kiss for now,' he said.

Katianna became aware of her own heartbeat.

She swallowed.

'The kiss was... a surprise,' she said, unblinking.

'And?'

'And it was lovely,' she said.

It was lovely. Relief flooded her. *It was lovely.*

Polis' face lit up.

'Good. As for everything else you don't have to think about it all at once or on your own. I'm here. I can help you. Savva's here. He can help you. You've a whole family here from what I've seen, all willing you on with the refurbishment. Your *yiayia* was loved by so many.'

Katianna crossed her arms over her front like a child being told off. Her lower lip dropped; she was sulking and was annoyed with herself for being so transparent. 'There's still a lot to do,' she said.

'One thing at a time.' He took a step closer, prised her arms from her chest, held onto her hands. 'Look at me. I'm not going anywhere. Unless you tell me to.'

'I can't do it all.'

'You don't have to. Let me do that for the both of us.' Katianna, wide-eyed, stood in silence, her heart beating faster, faster than a woodpecker's beak against a tree trunk. 'I'm serious. I want to see you again. I want to get to know you. Maybe even make a life with you.'

'Make a life with me? How? We live two thousand miles from each other. My life's in London. Your life's here.'

'That's just geography,' he said, gently massaging her palms with his fingers.

'It's a lot of geography.'

'But you're not denying there's something between us… a spark?' he asked, almost pleading.

'Maybe,' she conceded, her voice a whisper.

'Maybe, is good.'

'So, what now?'

'Let me fill you in on the building progress and then let's have a coffee at Sofia's. Talk properly.'

'By properly you mean?'

'Head strategy first because that's what makes you tick and then heart strategy. Deal?'

Katianna nodded; the relief in Polis' face evident when the tiniest smirk played across his lips.

Chapter 19

Alex, the porter of Katianna's apartment block, dropped Katianna's luggage just inside the flat's front door and bid her a good morning. He handed the bundle of mail to her, secured with a red rubber band. The door shut with a soft click behind him.

Kicking off her shoes, abandoning them where they fell, she drifted down the narrow passage and pushed open her bedroom door throwing her jacket towards the bed. The garment slipped off the silky duvet. It landed on the thick pile carpet where Katianna left it; she needed coffee.

She wandered towards the open plan kitchen-lounge-diner. The vase of flowers on the work top had long since wilted and died; their water gave off a rancid, sewery smell and she gagged as she tipped it down the sink.

Within minutes the coffee maker gurgled and bubbled. She breathed in the rich aroma of her favourite coffee, Fortnum & Mason's Jamaica Blue Mountain. No fresh milk. Thankfully, she always kept an emergency supply of powdered milk.

She carefully set her mug onto one of the strategically positioned coasters on the glass coffee table, mirroring the coffee-table book stack. Her soles ached; too quickly accustomed to padding around in flip flops her feet were sore after being pushed into closed-fronted, high heels for over eight hours. With both legs tucked beneath her, she massaged her feet and propped with a couple of cushions on the enormous cream couch, then checked the mail. Two neat piles emerged; read now and read tomorrow.

Her mobile buzzed. She hesitated for a few seconds. It rang off. Within moments a Facebook message came through... Savva checking her safe arrival back in London and to say she had forgotten her lipstick, flip flops, and sunhat.

She smiled and little shiver, a tingling sensation like fizzing sherbet, filled her, at the thought of a little bit of her still in sunny Cyprus, close to the house and Polis. Her heart fluttered as Polis' goodbye kiss tingled as real as if he were standing in front of her. She thought back to their last meeting at her *yiayia's* house; the early morning sun drenching the clay roof tiles and two desert-blue butterflies flapping gently around their heads.

'You'll be back in October?' he had asked.

'To finalise the house sale, yes.'

'Maybe to see me too?'

She took a sip of coffee, their kiss, long and gentle, stealing into her thoughts, sliding under her skin. She looked around... she had longed for the comfort of home; everything shiny and clean. But now it felt sterile, cold, she was rattling around in the huge open space.

The village's dusty air had at first been tiresome; wiping furniture and work surfaces multiple times a day irritating, an inconvenience, but over time she came to enjoy the regular circular motion of cleaning; it had become therapeutic, calming. It became a routine. She liked routine.

Her phone vibrated again, and she answered, 'Hello.'

'Welcome home,' Angie said. 'I don't mean to bombard you but what time will you be coming into the office today?'

'I'll be with you by two,' Katianna said, and the work adrenaline kicked in, forcing her back into work mode, but the fire in her had shifted. *Had Cyprus done this?* She shook off a shiver, determined to jump straight back in.

'You've got two meetings scheduled... conference call re the new TV show I talked to you about at three and then John at four.'

'John? What does he want?'

'Something about the figures for the last quarter. You know him and figures… it's one love affair after another, his face lights up...'

'Right, see you soon,' Katianna said.

'And I want to see some photos,' trilled

She checked the time on her phone; an hour and forty minutes ample time to arrive promptly.

Katianna, showered and dressed, felt a spark of the usual adrenaline rush present when psyching herself for work. She arrived at Broadgate at a quarter to two. The weak summer sun had enticed dozens of people outside; every bench, seating area, and patch of weathered grass, accommodated chatting office workers enjoying a break from their desks and computer screens.

The air smelt different in London.

Within seconds the lift pinged her arrival to the 12th floor. A quick swipe of her entry card and she walked across the open-plan concourse to her office bidding her team good afternoon. Everyone welcomed her back, nodding and smiling.

In her office, the usual titillation of being at the helm did not fill her. Something felt off. Maybe she was jet-lagged.

The London skyline, had other ideas, and seemed to welcome her back with open arms. She leaned back in the leather swivel chair, adjusting to its contours again. Katianna toed off her red heels, kicked them under the glass-topped desk. How did she ever wear these all day? She pulled herself closer to the table, wriggling the cramp out of her toes. She took out the ridiculously tacky Cyprus mug–a farewell gift from Savva–and placed it on her desk alongside the framed wedding photograph of her *yiayia* and *bapou* she had swiped at the last minute.

She consciously tore herself far from Cyprus.

Angie had kept everything immaculate. A neat pile of opened mail on her desk was tagged red, amber, and green. Bull dog clips held open copies of magazines and newspapers headlining advertorials and feature stories on the agency.

'What's different about you? Have you changed your hair?' Angie asked as she breezed in with Katianna's coffee.

'No. And now's not the time. I have a lot to do but thanks for leaving everything so orderly for me.'

'I'm just outside if you need anything else.'

'Thanks, Angie,' said Katianna but a tinge of guilt made her pause.

'Nice mug,' Angie said, lifting it from Katianna's desk. 'I'll put it in the kitchen for you.'

Katianna pushed the mail to one side, smiling at Angie's retreating back, her humming light and bouncy. The write ups, in two of the most prominent Sunday newspaper magazines, caught her eye. Both shone a light on the ethics and social responsibility rules embedded within her dating agency and how these made it the firm choice for the majority of 25 to 55s. This was, according to a study carried out by Your Date, Your Life UK, why she continuously featured in the top ten agencies in the UK.

She scowled at her bio picture, faded highlights, her face pale, a spot on her chin. She had struggled to cover the eruption with her usual concealer, but the photo shoot had been confirmed and she had not been able to sidestep it.

She made a mental note to ask Angie to remove the image from the media kit on the press release website page so it could not be used again. She read the questions and answers, lifted from the media kit, and smiled. Katianna came across knowledgeable and professional in her responses, natural.

The newspaper advertorials highlighted the simplicity of the membership levels and how anyone, whatever their budget, could enroll. She cringed at the headlines *Perfect Partner* and *More Than The Dating Game* but the overall coverage pleased her.

She stacked the papers, scribbled a note to Angie asking her to frame the articles and find some wall space for them behind the reception desk.

The unopened letters were brown envelopes; marked private and confidential. She picked up a pen, a gift from one of her successful couples, and pushed it down the side of the first envelope, tearing it open. What? She opened the next... the same... she threw down the pen and ripped open each envelope... the same repeated letter. *What was going on?*

She buzzed Angie.

'Can you call John and tell him I want to see him within the next half an hour… here. Don't take no for an answer. And can you re-schedule the TV appointment to next week. I can't think straight. And bring me another coffee, extra strong, black. It's going to be a long first day back.'

She stared at the torn envelopes discarded on her desk. Her dad had raised her to never tear open an envelope. Absolute savagery, he would repeat. And yes, that's exactly what it was. She fought back a welling urge to scream and thumped her fist on the desk.

Finally calmer, Angie entered and placed the coffee on Katianna's desk. 'Just how you like it,' she said. 'And John's on his way.' Angie appeared nervous, as she pressed her hand to her chest, a flush spread across her neck and face.

'Is everything okay?' asked Angie.

'It would have been good to get the heads up from you before all this came at me at once,' said Katianna, looking her straight in the eye.

'What's happened?' asked Angie.

'All this,' she said, pointing at the piles of paper, 'unpaid bills and final demands.'

'Right,' said Angie, the colour across her cheeks heightening further.

'What is it? Do you know something?' asked Katianna.

'Not really. John assured me it was all just a misunderstanding. Nothing to worry about.'

'I know you and John have a past but where the business is concerned, your loyalty has to lie with me.'

'It does. I promise. I'd have said something if I'd realised it was serious.'

'And what do you know?'

'Nothing. I heard John promising the bank transfer would be made and that the missed payment was simply an oversight.'

'How long ago was this?'

'A few weeks ago,' said Angie, mumbling into her frilly neckline.

'How many weeks exactly?'

'Eleven, twelve…'

'And you didn't think to mention it?'

'I'm sorry. I've had other things…'

'Other things don't cut it, Angie,' said Katianna, dismissing her with a wave.

Chapter 20

Forty minutes later, a gentle knocking on the door interrupted Katianna's reading. John strolled in, wearing jeans, a shirt, and a lightweight bomber jacket. His light brown hair was gelled back and his smile wide, but his demeanour seemed less confident than usual.

'John.'

'How was Cyprus?' he asked, leaning in to give her a kiss on the cheek.

'Cyprus was surprisingly good. I needed the break… the refurb is coming along.'

'Good to hear. At least you didn't have to fork out for an expensive hotel.'

'Talking of costs. I've come back to a pile of bills and final payment demands, added interest, court threats. What's going on?'

John visibly stiffened in the seat across from Katianna. 'I wanted to speak to you about that face-to-face,' he said, sweat building across his forehead.

'Go on. I'm listening,' she said and rested her elbows on the desk, her chin on her clasped hands. She held his gaze. She felt the imbalance of their competing egos.

'I agreed and planned to cover those charges in a single payment at the end of the first three-year period. But there were several overspends back in 2016 and 2017 which have caught up with us. And the hike in annual rent and ground maintenance charges for here are crippling. We're in negative equity, cash flow is irregular.'

'So, the company doesn't have the money to pay? Is that what you're telling me?'

'On paper it does. On paper you're strong.'

'And what about the loan for the court fees? I thought they'd been cleared?'

'I extended the loan.'

'When? Why?'

'You're asset heavy which means cash and other sources of income are tied up in buildings...'

'But putting us into more debt hasn't worked.'

'Look your overheads are high... this suite of offices and you've been overspending on luxuries... like first class flights. You didn't have the funds to pay the monthly premiums. I had no choice but to extend it.'

'Are you implying I've been mismanaging the company's money? What do I pay you for?'

'That's not what I'm saying. It's just that...'

'How did this happen? How do we sort this?' She snatched the letters, shook them in his face, then threw them back on the desk. 'Why didn't you just tell me sooner?'

Angie popped her head round the door. 'There's a caller who won't take no for an answer.'

'Who is it?'

'The builder from Cyprus.'

'I'll call him back.'

'I've tried fobbing him off twice.'

'Go grab a coffee or something, John. I'll be five minutes.'

Katianna ran her fingers through her hair and paced behind her desk. Polis had tracked down her business number. She gave him full marks for tenacity.

She coughed a couple of times, cleared her throat.

'Polis, hello.'

'You're a difficult woman to get hold of,' he said, his voice smooth as buttermilk.

'Sorry. It's been a mad first day and I'm in the middle of a meeting.

Can I call you tonight?'

'Yes, but promise me one thing.'

'What's that?'

'That you will smile all day after you put the phone down.'

Surprised at the romance of his reply, she ended the call already smiling, picked up a leather-bound pad embossed with the company name and her Cartier pen and walked to the conference room.

Chapter 21

Katianna winced as she massaged her temples. The conversation with John had been heated and uncomfortable, a chaotic onslaught. She insisted on listening into his telephone conversation with the office responsible for ground rent and service charge collections. The seriousness of her situation sunk in; without a hefty cash injection she could run into further debt and risk losing the business.

She shook off a shiver; the proposed sale of her *yiayia's* house and the TV company's pitch to feature the agency in a fly-on-the-wall series went some way to soothing the sting. She never imagined being the focus of such a TV programme, but she was not in a position to be choosy.

Letting go of the house would mean severing inseparable ties looping back generations and now felt like her homeland more than ever. Accepting the deal on the show would impact her privacy and that of her team. Asking her solicitor to look over the final proposal and paperwork would also cost a lot. She mulled over her predicament. Could she ask the TV producers to absorb these costs?

Her usual dose of migraine tablets, downed with a glass of water, did nothing to ease the flashing across her eyes or the cutting pain across her brow. The evening's light bounced off the office windows; she gave the city scape none of her usual attention.

Despite, knowing she had to rake back on unnecessary expenses, she hailed a black cab home, unable to shake off the stuffiness pressing down on her.

* * *

At home, Katianna unpacked a ready-made lasagne and pierced the film lid. She set the microwave for eleven minutes and turned on her multi-room speaker system. Amy Winehouse filled the apartment with her deep, expressive contralto vocals. The notes sat comfortably with Katianna's sadness.

In her bedroom, she stripped off and stepped under the hot spray of her en-suite shower. She began to relax, the water instantly washing away the tightness across her shoulders and upper back, like lapping waves against the shore. She closed her eyes and allowed the pulsating body jets of water to ease her stress and she felt the knots loosen up and disappear with the gush of water as it gurgled down the plughole.

She unscrewed a bottle of Rioja and filled a tall wine glass. She emptied the overcooked pasta dish onto a plate and perching on the chrome stool, ate at the granite-topped kitchen island. The meal tasted like card. She pushed it aside after two mouthfuls. She longed for the rich flavours sampled in Cyprus.

The wine warmed her, but she grabbed the remote and upped the heating another three degrees; London's "summer" nipped at her after the blissful temperatures of Cyprus. She shouldn't be drinking, but after the day she'd had, she was counting on it to knock her out. She needed a good sleep, was desperate for it, and forced her mind not to think about the meeting scheduled with her team the following day. It was already gone ten, just after midnight in Cyprus.

Her phone rang. "Polis Builder Cyprus" flashed on the screen. He was keen, too keen but then she knew she was being unfair; her headache talking.

She hesitated. What was she doing? Thinking? This whole thing, whatever it was, wasn't going to work. How could it? It was all moving too fast...

'You're calling late. I've had a rough day. My head's pounding.'
'I'm sorry to hear that. You work too hard.'
'I have a lot to sort out...'
'Businesses always need our attention. Other than that, how are you? Are you glad to be back in London?'
'It's always good to be home but I'm missing Cyprus' easy pace.'
'So, London is home?'
'It has been nearly all my life.'
Silence. Katianna took the phone from her ear and checked the line. 'Polis?'
'Sorry, yes. But they also say home is where your heart is.'
'Now that's a cliché I haven't heard in a long time,' she giggled, her nerves filtering through her effort to be calm, finding their way through her exhaustion, the wine beginning to work its soothing magic on the overactive, overthinking mess of what she was facing. Her bubbling feelings fought their way to the surface.
'I'm missing you,' said Polis. Katianna took in a sharp intake of breath as she let the words sit just above her ribcage, warming her heart, surprised at how comfortable they felt there.
'That's nice to know.'
'Are you missing me?'
She bit her lip. She'd been too busy all day to think about him but now, hearing his voice,
imagining the flop of wavy hair over his left eye, something deep inside yearned to be with him.
'Yes,' she said, her voice a squeak, unable to deny her feelings.

Chapter 22

From behind the glass partition of her office Katianna watched everyone arrive one after the other. She read through the letter from the TV company and felt the tiniest butterfly flutter. Never do anything important on an empty stomach, came her dad's words and Katianna tucked into a halloumi and tomato wrap from the local deli.

At exactly nine o'clock she walked into the central office area and announced, 'I'm bringing today's meeting forward to eleven o'clock. I want everyone there. No excuses, so if anyone has any other scheduled meetings or calls, re-jig them.'

At eleven Katianna walked into the boardroom to find everyone either seated or jockeying for a spot around the oval glass-topped table. The caffeinated chatter stopped and a prickle of uncertainty, panic, replaced it. The dull ticking of the giant white-faced chrome wall clock seemed to take on an ominous persona, counting down the seconds to something hostile. She felt its ticking; snuffing out each breath she took and then, to push the ill feeling aside, pushed her shoulders back and held her head high. Business as usual, she reminded herself.

She took the few strides towards the empty seats at the far end of the room, at the head of the conference table; one for Katianna, the other for Angie, who took the Minutes.

'Good morning,' Katianna said, 'and thank you to those of you who've rescheduled diary appointments to be here. This is important. Though I hate to be the bearer of bad news this isn't going to be the happiest of meetings, but I hope we can remain positive.'

Someone sneaked in a few seconds later and loitered behind the coat stand. Katianna made a mental note, careful not to reveal she had noticed his late arrival; she had to remain whip-smart from now on. She had let things slip. Let the success of the company blinker her typical astuteness, even allowed her personal relationships with her employees to cloud her judgement. *Not anymore, she vowed silently.*

Katianna looked at each of the faces; brows furrowed, wide eyes, expectant expressions. A pang of regret hit her point blank in the chest. 'Without going into too much detail, we are facing financial pressures which require cutbacks.' She paused for effect. Everyone focused on her.

She continued, 'I've asked Angie to draw a simple spreadsheet. On this spreadsheet will be…' she turned round and pressed the clicker; an image of the spreadsheet appeared on the interactive white board. 'The overheads for each department and a column pertaining to each of your own cost areas. I want you to go through your expenses for the past three years and send me a follow-up email by 8pm this evening listing five areas, at least, where you can cut costs by a third to a half, right now.'

'This is a joke, right?' blurted Warren.

'Do I look like I'm joking Warren?'

'No… but how have you allowed this to happen?' Katianna gave him one of her diva stares and he backed down. It didn't help that she felt guilty. She had taken her eye off the ball; the staff knew it and she knew it, but she was not going to admit it.

'What about our jobs? Are they safe?' asked Jenny, pregnant with twins.

'There are no job cuts planned. That's the last thing I want but this is serious.' Jenny's shoulders visibly relaxed and then tensed again. She cradled her tummy, her gesture instinctive, protective.

Katianna continued, 'We're a formidable team. I want us all to work on turning things around which I'm certain we will. The cost-cutting exercise is a starting point. Our priority lies in reducing overheads. Any questions?' she paused for three seconds, counting them in her head. 'Let's meet again on Monday at 2pm.' She placed the clicker on the table and nodded at Angie.

'If any of you wish to talk to Katianna privately, I have cleared her diary this afternoon,' said Angie.

'That's all,' Katianna said. 'You can get back to your desks now. And thank you for your support and attention.' She stood up, smoothed out her pencil skirt, and ended the meeting.

Everyone filed out of the conference room; hushed whispers and tuts cut through the tight atmosphere.

When the last of her employees pulled the door closed behind them, Katianna flopped back into her seat and, lowering her head into her hands, fought back the tears.

'It'll be okay,' said Angie.

'We have to make some serious cutbacks, Angie. This isn't just going to disappear,' she said, looking up.

'And the whole team is rooting for you. Even Warren. He'll come up with the most innovative ideas. His brain's a strategy board. It's like playing chess with him. He's always two moves ahead.'

'I hope so. I don't want the last ten years to get swallowed up by a pile of unpaid debts.'

Angie sank further into her seat, unfamiliar with how to behave around Katianna's despair. 'I'll get you some coffee though it might have to be one of the first things to go.' Angie looked at Katianna. 'Sorry, I can't believe I said that out loud.'

Katianna smiled weakly. At £25 per 125ml, her favourite Jamaica Blue Mountain from Fortnum & Mason was an extravagance. She did the maths… £50 a month… £1250 a year. Damn it.

'I'll get on it immediately. I can't be home late.'

'Oh?'

'Mum's dementia's getting worse. I have to be home by six to relieve her carer. He's lovely but won't stay a second later than I'm paying the agency for. Extra hours are charged at double time.'

'Why didn't you tell me sooner?'

'I was worried. Processing it all. And I didn't want my loyalty to you or the company to come under scrutiny.'

Katianna nodded and ran a reassuring hand over Angie's arm.

'You're one of my most loyal employees. And you're a good friend. I'm sorry about your mum.'

Half an hour later, Katianna hovered over Angie's shoulder; Katianna's eyes travelled down the screen.

1. *customised paper cups, napkins, etc.*

2. *private catering for meetings*

3. *staff taxi account*

4. *Premium two-friend package, Royal Opera House (3 x per year @£2,100 each, £6,300 per year)*

5. *Ascot (£13,500 with food, beverage, and transport)*

Katianna sighed and carried on reading:

6. *ladies' weekend at Champneys, Henlow (£230 per night = £1,380 without treatments)*

7. *private Club Box at Chelsea F.C. (£4,200 for 14 guests)*

Angie pulled up a spreadsheet headed sundries: stationary, telecom and utilities, equipment, fixtures and fittings, insurance, professional services, and catering.

Katianna walked away. She recognised Angie's immediate response as a sign of worry; Angie knew how much that side of the business meant to Katianna. The branding, the corporate events.

Katianna took in everyone's demeanour. None of the usual late afternoon banter or joking around; each had their heads down; no doubt working on those figures. She knew how some of the six-strong sales team would struggle with the cutbacks.

But without the four company cars, she reasoned, there would be no parking hire charges, insurance, servicing, valeting bills, road tax... unnecessary expenses and luxuries. She knew there was argument to keep these expenses and hoped her team would see it too.

At her desk, Katianna mulled over the figures from John. How could he have allowed this to happen? As a professional accountant he worked with the big fish. Perhaps that was the problem; her dating agency was mere plankton compared to the steely sharks he dealt with daily in his vast sea of corporate numbers.

Her mobile vibrated. Polis; two attachments. She opened them; a photograph of her leaning against the olive tree at her *yiayia's* house, and another one dancing at the taverna.

Unaware he'd taken the photos, she marvelled at how relaxed she was; her wide smile, her hair gleaming in the light, her eyes sparkling. She almost didn't recognise the carefree woman looking back at her. She certainly didn't feel effervescent today or since she'd returned.

'What's it all for?' she muttered, throwing the phone onto the desk. 'Who am I doing all this for?' She ran her fingers through her hair, 'I'm tired. Tired of running the show alone.'

An email pinged from Angie and Katianna looked up. She caught sight of Angie still in the office, tidying her desk, and a stab of guilt came at her; nearly seven o'clock.

A few minutes later she waved goodnight to Katianna and turned out the lights; the others had long gone. Katianna resisted the urge to open Angie's email. She would read it at home, prepare for her meeting with John tomorrow. And open a bottle of wine and watch a movie.

Chapter 23

Katianna put the key into her front door and pushed it open. She stepped in; the lights instantly illuminated the passageway. She left her shoes by the coat stand and padded to the kitchen. Recessed lights flickered on leaving a trail of twinkling, guiding stars. She reached for a bottle of already-opened Merlot and poured a generous measure into a wine glass, twirled the stem of the glass between her fingers. Looking out across Camden she surveyed the moored river boats and canal boats, the lights of the bars and restaurants strung across the buildings and a hazy moon suspended in a darkening sky. Not the clear indigo expanse of Cyprus, or its beautiful mountains, but a beautiful view all the same.

She took two long sips, but the wine tasted bitter, caught in the back of her throat reflecting her foul mood.

Office workers and market traders weaved in and out of the slower paced tourists along the canal's path and disappeared under the bridge.

She wondered how many were going home to a cheerful home and how many just existed, moving their energies from one place to another but never actually fulfilling their dreams. Pedalling hard on the wheel of life; did they have a destination, a happy ending, a chance to change the way things were or did they savour their lonely existence? Was she destined to find achievement only in business or did she have a chance of finding success with love too?

The intercom buzzed. She grabbed her purse rooting for a tip for the pizza delivery; ordered on her way home in the taxi.

As she placed the pizza onto the kitchen island, Polis called, and they exchanged warm pleasantries.

'And news of the well?' she asked, and her voice emitted a sultry and sexy sound surprising her.

'There's been a delay.'

'How long? Why?'

'There are rules and regulations, they go back to 1955 governing the conservation, development and use of water resources as well as coordinating the distribution of water supplies within an area. It's all necessary yet so unnecessary but unfortunately the water wheel moves slowly here,' he said, as if reading from an information leaflet.

'So, the water supply may have to be shared? That's a huge responsibility.'

'It is. This may impact on the sale, but don't worry. I will keep you updated.'

'What else have you been up to?' she asked, less enthusiastically. *Another delay.*

'I saw Sofia earlier and she sends her love. Savva passed me in the street, but he didn't stop to talk.'

'That's not like him. I hope he's okay. I must get in touch.'

'I'm sure he's just preoccupied with work. I heard there are many changes in the government offices where he's based, my nephew works there too. Bureaucracy… it leaves no man untouched.'

'I will message him after our call.'

'And what else will you do after our call?'

'I don't know… watch a movie, sleep.'

'I too will sleep soon, but I will sleep with my window open and staring at the stars I will think of you under the same sky as me.'

Katianna, sidetracked by his words, fought to form a reply, eventually saying, 'Under the same sky, Polis.'

After the call, she pondered whether she was any happier than the lady pushing the pram along the walkway every evening, her hunched shoulders and matted black mop of hair tied in a ponytail. Or the entrepreneur who sold screen-printed T-shirts made from organic hemp and linen in the market, or the Bulgarian woman she had said hello to a couple of times, who cleaned the apartment block's common parts early morning, invisible to the multi-million traders, and then went home to feed her children breakfast before walking them to school.

In bed, having checked in on Savva, she succumbed to going through Angie's email, she drank the last of the wine and succumbed to the maudlin arms of Netflix and The Beach starring Leonardo Di Caprio.

Her thoughts took her deeper than they had in a long time, it was the wine, maybe it was the mess at work, maybe it was Polis. She thought about what it meant to be thinking about him. To allow him into her thoughts.

She stared at the huge mirror standing at the foot of her bed. A piece of Cyprus, reclaimed, uprooted, sitting in her London abode. She wondered whether this was the piece of Cyprus she yearned; the traditional, the simple, the tarnished yet beautiful. She sat up in bed and looked at her reflection. For an instant, she imagined Polis' looking back at her but shook off the tingling sensation. Instead, she made a note to ask Alex to organise someone to hang it for her.

Happiness was a state of mind. Was that what she was looking for but lacked? Her long working days, drive, and single-mindedness to make the company the best it could be had cost her. Was it worth her happiness? Was it worth sleeping alone every night?

Whatever it was she fell asleep wondering whether paradise was just another word for happiness and whether it wasn't a physical, geographical place but something inside yourself, intangible yet so powerful it could make you soar physically.

Chapter 24

'Let's compare what we've got,' said Katianna, scanning the team's printouts with John the following morning.

'Refreshments for you,' said Angie, bringing in a large pot of coffee. Katianna noticed the absence of warmed pastries which would usually accompany their refreshments. Inwardly, she smiled. Angie was already saving her money.

'The biggest is this,' said John.

'How's this a viable option?' Katianna was pointing to the red circle around the rent for the offices and the words "move elsewhere."

'I know this is hard. And I'm sorry. I really am. But surely you can see the obvious benefits of relocating. Don't write it off,' said John, dabbing at the beads of sweat on his forehead.

'Go on,' said Katianna.

'I've done the research. Square meterage might be less, but you can still operate the business successfully and have the amenities you need. The rent comes in at six thousand less per annum.'

Katianna watched Angie make for the door and how she avoided John's gaze. Katianna automatically mouthed "thank you" to her and wondered whether they had fallen out.

After almost two hours and endless cups of coffee Katianna pushed her chair back from the conference table and stretched. With every saving ticked off she breathed a bit easier until John mentioned redundancies. 'The savings we can make over a year are incredible but how do I choose three people to let go? This is going to be hard. I know them and their families. This is rubbish, John and I blame you. You took your eye off the ball.'

'It hasn't got to that,' said John, shifting in his seat, reaching for his vibrating phone. 'With the possible savings in place we can run for another year, maybe eighteen months.'

Katianna struggled to find a calm response. 'We have to do everything we can to save the company. Figures on paper won't do that. Action will,' said Katianna.

'There's no other way,' said John, glancing at his mobile, his hand shaking. 'Cuts have to be made.'

Katianna felt a ticking time bomb inside her. 'We're like a family. Family makes sacrifices for each other. We have to make this work.' She held John's gaze for a few seconds and dismissed him. Something didn't feel right. What else was he hiding? And had Angie known more than she admitted?

Each time Katianna surveyed her team through the glass wall, she sensed the atmosphere in the office; an undercurrent of anxiety, the unusual silence spoke volumes and snaked its way around her until she felt strangled. Everyone seemed subdued, no Friday office banter and the relaxed atmosphere of the week's end quashed. She felt awful for them, responsible for this mess.

'I'm going to miss this,' she sighed, pointing to the cityscape stretched against the summer sky along the top of the clouds in the distance. The vista unfolded as far as the eye could see. The sun struggling to peek, just visible. For an instant, it made her think about Angie and suspected John may have persuaded her to be quiet.

Chapter 25

The next morning John showed her the updated cash-flow forecast for the next twelve months. 'I'll present our case to the bank on Monday morning,' said John.

'Before all of that, tell me this: did Angie know we were in trouble?'

'She overheard a conversation.'

'So, she knew,' Katianna huffed unable to contain her feelings.

'Not really. I fobbed her off. Assured her it was nothing. Don't come down on her.'

'Come down on her? This might come down on all of us.'

'This is my fault. I'll fix it, Katianna.'

'You're damn right about that,' Katianna said, looking him straight in the eye. 'Are we likely to get the loan?'

'I hope so. It'll give you enough to keep the business afloat.'

'And everyone in a job?'

'No, not everyone. It can buy us some extra time. We've got a solid and workable plan in place. The business will be okay, but jobs may have to be cut, hours reduced.'

'The team has been incredibly supportive. How am I going to explain three of them might be out of a job within the year?'

'Well, I'm sure they'll see it coming.' His petulant whine grated on Katianna's nerves and in that moment, she wanted him to be gone.

'How? I didn't. You didn't. And if it was your job on the line? How would you feel? I pay you a huge retainer to keep an eye on the finances, not just to do the accounts.' John's demeanour changed, he nodded, sheepishly acknowledging the implied meaning of her words. 'And there won't be a next time,' she said, opening the boardroom door. 'This is not a situation I want to find myself in again. I've worked too hard to lose it all and our relationship with our management company is now tarnished. I mean it, John. I'm watching you.'

Her pulse quickened. A sudden heat almost took her breath away. This was not going to be easy but with every box ticked and every area cross-checked and checked again, she tried to convince herself it had to turn out alright. She still had the sale of her *yiayia's* house. Or was this the end of her dream?

There's always a new dream, don't you forget that. Her mother's words came at her and she shook off a little shiver. She missed her mum so much. She wished she had spent more time with her. Katianna's business had always taken priority over everything. It was her way of coping. Of proving that what she did she did well and failing was not an option; never had been and never would be. But she had not been the generous, kind daughter she should have been. She knew that. The admittance stung her. Her mum had not only said wise words but had lived by them too. She had been lucky in love and life... right up until the end.

Katianna, fighting her tears, watched John retreat. His steps echoed in her ears, a metronome of failure. He crossed the office, avoiding eye contact with those looking up from their desks, his briefcase and laptop bag swinging by his side; his hesitant strides breaking the silence.

Half an hour later, Angie shifted in her seat, crossing, and uncrossing her legs, as she sat opposite Katianna.

'Despite this one indiscretion relating to John I just wanted to say thank you, to acknowledge what an excellent job you did not just with the task at hand but with holding the fort. I haven't thanked you properly for that.'

'Thank you. I appreciate you saying that. I won't ever let you down again.'

'I know that which is why I wanted to talk to you about a new responsibility.' Angie's
eyes widened in disbelief.

'I'm proposing a re-shuffle.'

'Oh?'

'John will take more of an administrative finance role – the company's accounts and taxes–but with regards to the day-to-day financial outgoings and overheads, I'd like you to oversee the budget and allocate funding alongside me.' Katianna had also calculated the savings she would make on John's retainer fees.

'Why me? Surely Warren or…'

'Because you're the only one who suggested cuts which impacted not only on you, and your role, but on me directly and therefore indirectly on the business. You're the only one who exceeded my expectations. You looked at the situation holistically and logically; transport, entertainment, catering, the coffee…' Angie blushed, but sat beaming all the same.

'Thank you. But there's something I need to say. I should've mentioned this before, but I've been so emotional about everything…'

'What is it?'

'Mum's dementia is progressively worsening, and it all feels too big. I don't know if I can take on a new role. I'm really grateful to you but you might like to reconsider your offer.'

'I'm so sorry. That must be tough watching her go through something like that. What can I do to help?' Katianna asked, walking to the other side of the desk, giving Angie's shoulder a squeeze.

'Nothing… there's not much I can do other than give her as much patience, love, and care as I can.'

'The new role is still there, it's yours. Any increased hours can be done from home when you need to be with her,' said Katianna, thinking on her feet, unswayed by Angie's honesty. 'Family must come first. I wish I'd been around for my mum more. Those last few days, after Dad passed, she became so frail. Her face pinched from refusing to eat, her bones sticking out through her favourite jumper. The guilt I still carry is crushing.'

'Guilt solves nothing,' said Angie.

'I guess not,' said Katianna, remembering where she was. 'Let me ask HR to draft a new job description and contract next week and we can take it from there. Sound fair?'

'I also want you to know I wanted to be straight with you, about John, but the timing never worked. With Cyprus, now this.'

***

Katianna spent the rest of the afternoon making calls to suppliers. It was an exhausting task but one she felt she needed to do herself. This needed her touch and as the face of the business it was only right and fair, she communicated personally with those she had been doing business with, in some cases, for almost half a decade or more.

Some were shocked to hear Katianna concluding her contract with them; others took it in their stride with graciousness, while others shared her concerns and revealed their own extreme cost-cutting exercises to keep their enterprises afloat. She appreciated their kind words and their understanding, though they made her task more difficult, emotional.

Emails drafted, she pressed send, relieved the end of the day neared and she had tackled the most difficult part of the cost-cutting exercise. She prayed for a lifeline during John's meeting on Monday morning.

She swiveled round in her chair; her stockinged feet tucked snuggly under her bottom. The London skyline floated in the haze, bleeding light pink to orange, filling the floor-to-ceiling windowpanes like a huge painted canvas. St Paul's iconic green dome, framed by Wren's City church spires and The London Eye's big-wheel silhouette, dominated the horizon. The view wouldn't be the same from the fourth floor, but she recognised a sensible decision and when to follow through.

Angie had already made an appointment for her to view the available suite. Thankfully, their current contract did not expire until April; the filming, if it went ahead for the TV series, would take place in the current offices. The view was certainly one the film crew and directors of the programme could take advantage of.

She turned off her laptop and tidied her desk; tidy desk, tidy mind her psychology teacher used to say. The tidy desk was the easy bit but the tidy mind... she needed to work on that and hoped the weekend would rejuvenate her. She suddenly missed the carefree, uncomplicated time she had in Cyprus; slow, unhurried, peaceful. Her thoughts drifted to Polis and the village house.

Chapter 26

Katianna paced the pavement in front of the bank, stopping every few steps to sip her takeaway coffee. Where was John? This wasn't like him. He was a stickler for punctuality.

She looked up at the tall buildings, old and new, side by side. Limassol's charming historic centre filled her thoughts; where colonial buildings and traditional workshops also sat in harmony with modern cafes and bars, encircling the town's landmark medieval castle. But there was a difference. The air was different. The sounds were different. And it was that difference she missed already. The fresh sights and sounds had soothed her, given her a sense of freedom, unshackled her from the constant demands, the stress.

A black cab pulled up across the street. John jumped out. He dodged the morning rush of city traffic and was hooted at a number of times, his suit jacket flying like a sail in the wind behind him.

'Cutting it fine,' said Katianna, pushing her cup into the overfilled dustbin. 'You okay? You didn't answer any of my calls.'

'Let's get this over with.'

'John, if you're not up to this, let me go in without you,' she said, grimacing at his bed-head and general crumpledness. 'This isn't something we need to get over. It's something we need to achieve, to win in our favour. We need this loan.'

'Sorry. That came out wrong,' he said, avoiding her eye.

'Let's go in and secure the best terms, but before we go in...' She rested her handbag and laptop bag between her feet and pulled at John's tie, tightening the knot. 'That's better,' she winked.

***

'Well, that's an interesting proposal and I appreciate the efforts you're putting in to actively reduce your overheads, however...'

The relationship manager's words rang in Katianna's ears, relationship manager indeed. What was wrong with the title bank manager? Everything about the man's demeanour had irritated her. She pushed back into the taxi's seat. 'He was an absolute pompous arsehole... bloody hell... what do we do now? We haven't got the luxury of going back to him in three months' time. We needed that cash injection now.'

'There's always those sexy investment angels,' said John, undoing his tie and unbuttoning the neck of his shirt.

Katianna gave him one of her looks; trying to be funny was not even remotely entertaining right now. She knew their debt signaled a red flag, but John had persuaded her that the meeting would be just protocol, ticking boxes.

The energy and positivity of earlier fell away. 'You look how I feel,' she said.

'It's unbearable in here,' said John, his voice strangled. He wound down the window.

'So much for fresh air,' she said, her throat tightening against the mugginess. She looked over at John, his face a shade redder than her lipstick. 'Are you angry?'

'I don't feel right.'

'You need your coffee fix,' she joked and then, 'You don't look so well.'

'I'm not f-e-e-e-l-i-n-g... g-r-e-e-a-t...' he slurred his words; his head slumped to one side.

'John, no... no...' Katianna banged on the partition screen, her eyes wide in panic, 'We need to get to a hospital... now!'

The force of the taxi driver's acceleration sent her slamming sideways against the door. She winced and rubbed her elbow.

'Right, you are,' he said without the slightest inflection, as if used to emergency-hospital diversions. The driver's eyes flicked back and forth between his rearview mirror and the road as John blinked furiously, one arm hanging limp across his lap.

'John, can you hear me? John,' begged Katianna.

Within a few minutes the taxi pulled up outside A& E the Royal Free in Hampstead.

'Thanks so much,' said Katianna, thrusting a twenty-pound note through the opening in the front window. 'Keep the change.'

Before the driver had a chance to say goodbye Katianna turned her attention to a nearby porter and called for help. He rushed towards John with a wheelchair.

Inside, with John still slurring his words, and unable to respond to some of the receptionist's questions, he was surrounded by nurses within minutes. The worry of what had happened, and the tediousness of registering John's details at reception, deflated Katianna's mood further.

Katianna sat on one of the scuffed plastic chairs lined up in rows like at a bus shelter. On the seat opposite someone had scratched the words *house of horrors* and she shook off the ill-feeling smothering her like a winter fog. The clock on the wall behind the reception desk tick-tocked; the minutes passing like a slow-mo movie scene, the wheels of the NHS moved slowly.

She stepped outside and got three bars on her phone. She punched out a message to Angie to say she had been inevitably detained and would be in as soon as possible

Forty minutes later, Katianna followed the duty nurse dressed in blue scrubs and croc-clad feet along a maze of freshly painted corridors. She had a stethoscope hanging around her neck, the bright red tubing clashing with the flash of orange in her hair. A loose thread on one of her trouser leg hems threatened to unravel, leaving one trouser leg longer than the other. Katianna was tempted to offer to sew it for her.

A little tug threw her back to the village and sitting on her *yiayia's* lap while she showed her some basic embroidery stitches on a piece of linen stretched across a wooden hoop. She hadn't done any sewing in a long time and wondered where her *yiayia's* sewing box was. She had not come across it at the house.

Katianna shook away the thought and peeked behind the bay's flimsy curtain. John lay attached to various tubes and IV equipment. 'What's happening?' she asked, taking in the sterile space around the wheeled bed.

'Mild stroke, a TIA I think they said. I need another MRI and Ultrasound scan to find the possible underlying cause.'

'I'm so sorry.'

'I'm still here, aren't I?' he smiled weakly. 'Though, I'm guessing if I'd gone it would have saved one more job.'

'Stop that. How long are they keeping you in?' Katianna stared at the yellow stain on the thin blanket folded over his legs.

'He needs to be kept under observation, at least the next twelve hours,' said a heavy-set duty nurse, who appeared behind Katianna. 'Thankfully, his speech is improving; this is positive news, yes?' Passing two pills to John, she continued in her Polish accent. 'Take these. It's Aspirin.' She poured water from a plastic jug into a blue beaker. John's hand shook as he tipped the cup and swallowed.

'You go. I'll phone Vicky, my sister, to come in and sit with me,' said John, his breathing heavy with the exhaustion of getting his words out.

'Are you sure? I don't like to leave you like this,' said Katianna, twisting her gold band back and forth on her ring finger. The ring was her mother's wedding band, given to Katianna just before she passed, saying she hoped it brought her as much love as it had to her with Katianna's father.

'She'll be here in no time. She's on leave this week.'

Katianna waited another hour until John got his sister's message that she was ten minutes away; she'd had to cross London from Waterloo.

The hospital seemed to burst into a flurry of activity; a wailing man was pushed along in a wheelchair with the letters A & E painted across the back. Two porters helped him into a bed opposite, his cries getting louder. A crying baby obliterated the soothing words of its mother, as she rocked the child in her arms. Further along the corridor the screech of squeaky gurney wheels, preceded the arrival of another patient and an oxygen tank crashed against the flooring. All the while, the constant clack-clack of a keyboard and the main doors along the corridor whooshing open and shut added a kind of bass to the cacophony of sounds like an orchestra. And then Vicky swept in.

She burst out crying as soon as she saw her brother in the hospital bed. Katianna took in the sight; the raised, metal side railings, the pillows propping him awkwardly. No wonder Vicky was upset.

Katianna looked away, not wanting to invade their privacy. Her heart leapt and her thoughts, surprisingly, went to Polis. She had to admit she missed him and suddenly wanted to hear his voice. Exhausted she felt smudged and dirty. She wanted to feel someone close, someone near and she realised it was a yearning for Polis, but she still had to have the meeting with her team.

She just made it back to the office for the two o'clock meeting and after briefly recapping on the cuts identified which would make the most impact on reducing their overheads, she congratulated the team and assured them of keeping them updated through Angie. Everyone seemed less emotional in their reactions than during the first meeting and that was a huge relief for Katianna.

Jenny, restless and teary-eyed at the end of the meeting, announced her husband had been offered a promotion and that she may not be returning after her maternity leave. This softened the guilt Katianna was carrying at the possibility of having to make her redundant. She uncharacteristically hugged Jenny who was trying to control her emotions.

At the end of the day, Warren, the high-flyer, knocked on the glass door of Katianna's office and handed in his notice. Katianna, though shocked and a little sad, marvelled at how the power of the universe was working in her favour; she had to trust that whatever unfolded would give her, and the business, the best possible outcome.

Chapter 27

In the back of the taxi to Broadgate, the traffic seemed heavier than usual, and the squealing of brakes and snarling motorbikes and weaving couriers made her headache; maybe Polis's assessment of London was right after all. She closed her eyes against the whoosh of traffic and tried to shut out the noise; she gave up after a few moments. She messaged Polis instead: "Hello. Just to say I'm thinking of you."

At the office, she greeted everyone with a smile until her jaw ached and relieved to be behind her closed office door exhaled a long sigh. Angie walked in with a coffee in Katianna's Cyprus mug.

Katianna was instantly reminded of Polis and checked her phone. No message. A little pop of deflation hit her, as if her skin pulled inwards.

'So, the meeting didn't go as you'd hoped?' Angie deposited the mug in front of Katianna, careful to position it on the ceramic coaster embossed with the company logo.

'How did you...?' Katianna asked, taking a sip and though the mug looked out of place in the office she liked it; it gave her a cosy, reassuring feeling.

'I know you, Katianna, and I know when your smile is heartfelt and when it isn't. You were struggling out there.'

'No, it wasn't what John and I had hoped and John's in hospital... he's had a stroke... straight after the meeting.'

'Oh, my God. No. He's so young.'

'And stressed.'

'Is he going to be alright?'

'I hope so. His sister's with him.'

'And the business?'

'I need to work on my plan B,' Katianna said, leaning back in her chair and crossing her legs. She stifled a yawn, so much for her relaxing weekend.

'You've always got a plan B.'

'Will you get the TV company on the phone and schedule another meeting? I want to clarify a few points, finalise the details for filming with them. And John's health is confidential for now.'

'Of course, I won't mention it to a soul. Anything else?'

'Yes.' Angie, already having taken a few steps towards the door, turned around. 'How's your mum? How are you? You look beat.'

Angie's eyes clouded, she flopped into the seat opposite and burst into tears.

'Hey, what's happened? Can I do anything?'

'No, no, thank you. She's not so good and it's been a horrendous weekend. Sorry, you've got enough going on without me and now John too.' Angie sniffled, fighting more tears. 'She left the house on Saturday afternoon and ended up in Shepherd's Bush. The police called to say they'd found her walking up and down the station platform calling for Joanna, her sister. My aunt's been dead for nine years.'

'Poor thing, she must've been terrified.'

'Thank goodness she had her little address book in her handbag. The police found me listed under 'B.''

'B?'

'Best daughter.'

'She's got that right,' smiled Katianna. 'So, what happens now? Can her dementia be treated? Slowed down?'

'I've an appointment with her GP tomorrow afternoon so will have to leave here by two the latest if that's okay with you. But she's so loving and kind and doesn't want to trouble anyone. She even invited the police round for tea.'

'You take the day off, paid of course, and do what you need to do with your mum. Life is too precious,' said Katianna and wiped a rolling tear from her cheek.

'Thank you. That means a lot to me. I can work from home in the morning.'

'If you so wish, but I'm not expecting you to,' said Katianna. 'You've given me hours of your time beyond the call of duty over the years and it's my turn to do the same for you.'

Angie's face crumpled. 'Sorry, I'm fine, I'm fine,' she mumbled. Katianna passed her a tissue. Angie blew her nose and dried her tears. 'Now, back to work,' she said, squeezing Katianna's hand.

'Okay. If you can get that email out to everyone to postpone this afternoon's meeting and hold all calls for the next couple of hours that would be great. I don't want to be disturbed.' She hesitated, and then added, 'And Angie, take a proper lunch break today. Go and get some fresh air.'

Katianna waited for Angie to leave and stretched out her legs. She took a sip of her coffee and stared out across London. Ground-rent-gate and now John-gate. This was not going to get the better of her. This was merely a puddle she needed to get through; a deep, muddy one… but she had her wellington boots ready.

She scanned the TV company's proposal again, focusing on the details of the contract, the filming schedule, the payout. She would need to be clever about this. If they were offering remuneration, then this could be used as a starting point for negotiation. She needed to think what her carrot would be and then it came to her; an observational documentary taking in the lives of those behind the scenes as well as the dating clients.

That evening she called John but got no answer. She cursed for not getting Vicky's details. Her phone buzzed a few minutes later. An unknown number, but she accepted the call anyway.

'Katianna, it's me, John,' he said, as if they had telepathically communicated across the miles.

'How are you? I've been trying to reach you.'

'I know. Sorry. I'm waiting for the consultant to see me, but it looks like a blocked artery in my neck.'

'It sounds serious. Can they do anything about it?'

'Blood thinners for the moment and if the consultant and doctor agree I may need a small operation.'

'Surgery? John, you are going to be okay, aren't you?'

'Yes, yes, of course. The procedure will reduce the risk of recurring strokes and I won't have to be pill-popping for the rest of my life. But I'm going to need some time off for physio and the like.'

'Do you want me to do anything?'

'I've had two missed calls from the bank so do you mind following up? I couldn't risk calling back with my phone's battery so low. I'm calling you from the ward's mobile phone at the hospital.'

'Sure yeah, of course,' she said with a lightness in her voice that she didn't feel. 'Sleep well and call me in the morning. I'll swing by and see you.'

'Yeah, you too. And thank you, Katianna. You've been great.'

'Hey, we've worked together a long time...it's what friends do.'

Chapter 28

Katianna tucked her crisp white shirt into the top of her skirt and straightened her collar. This was it. The meeting with the TV company had been cancelled and re-booked twice; this meeting needed to go well. She was either going to make it or break it. It was surely written in the stars that when you want something this badly the universe contrives to bring it to you. She'd read that somewhere and while the logical side of her thought it mumbo-jumbo, her spiritual side, which seemed to be revealing itself more, believed it as strongly as she once believed in fairy tales as a child with red-ribboned pig tails and patent navy Mary Janes.

Angie laid out the boardroom with blotters and pencils, glasses, and bottles of still and sparkling water. Katianna had to live up to her reputation and she had to prove her agency would fit the director and editing crew's vision for the fly-on-the-wall series. If successful, the small print clause promised to extend the contract and rewards would incrementally increase with each series. She had done the maths and the remuneration outweighed anything forecasted by the business even if it continued to increase at the rate of the last eight months.

At three o'clock Angie buzzed to say she had shown five people into the conference room. Katianna, put her mobile on silent, grabbed her *Cartier* pen and leather-bound pad. She dragged her four-inch stilettos towards her with clenched toes, slipped them on and walked towards the conference room, pushing the butterflies in her stomach downwards, while mustering renewed confidence.

Charles introduced himself; she had spoken to him on the phone before. Everyone quickly said hello in turn and she made a familiar connection in her head to recall each name; a little trick she'd learnt at a team-building course which had stuck with her.

She took her seat after asking them to sit with a wide show of her hand and in her head, she repeated, 'birth mark, melanin, that's Melanie, my best friend at school, that's Tina, my battered denim Levi's jacket, that's Levi, strong in Hebrew and he sure had muscles, that's Ethan.

'So, Angie's assured me you're not ready for coffee just now, shall we get started? I'm excited about this. So, thanks so much for being here. I'm just going to click the link with John, my accountant, who can't be here today but it's important he's privy to our discussions.' Katianna pressed connect, ensuring the volume was on and John simultaneously turned off his video connection; being propped up in hospital was not the most professional of looks. John introduced himself, his voice clear but Katianna recognised a forced chirpiness in it, and she hoped this wasn't going to be too much of a strain for him.

She swiftly continued, 'Observational docs are familiar to me but only from the comfort of my couch. This is totally new for me, and the company, but I'm ready to embrace the challenge and hope it'll be hugely successful for us all.'

'Thanks Katianna,' said Charles. 'As I've said before, this series has done tremendously well in the US. You'll be the first to air a version outside of the states. We've spent months researching the market and have updated the way the series will be presented, filmed, and edited to meet UK protocol. We wouldn't be here if we had doubts about its potential success.'

Melanie chimed in, adding, 'I've checked current filming regulations and attended meetings with lawyers to ensure privacy laws are upheld during filming, what information can be shared with the media and what can't be unless we have the express written permission of anyone taking part in the show.'

Clearly the legal lady.

The meeting continued and they agreed on and clarified all the details of the series regarding filming, editing, production, wardrobe and make-up, props, lighting and a hundred and one other aspects Katianna hadn't been aware of.

An hour into the meeting, Angie knocked on the door and, propping it open with her foot, nudged her way into the room wheeling a silver trolley. She unobtrusively placed cups, two large silver coffee pots and a white teapot on the sideboard as well as an oval platter of pastries, side plates, napkins, and extra bottles of water.

'Okay, I'm sure you could all do with a break,' said Katianna, 'and if anyone needs to freshen up the toilets are at the end of the office suite, turn left out of here, all the way to the end and you'll find them on the right.'

Katianna switched off the video link and ceased the moment to slip back to her desk. She dialed John's number and after a brief conversation delved in with her proposal. She was glad to hear his thoughts mirrored her own; despite his recent lapse with the accounts and his health scare, she still trusted his judgement, his wider business experience. She was also aware of how his slow recovery was impacting on his mental wellbeing and so including him in negotiations was important to her.

Back in the conference room she sidled up to Charles who was pouring milk into his coffee.

'So, we're going to be working together,' he said.

'We will be if we can get that remuneration up. I've mulled over your latest proposal and I'm looking at another 15%,' said Katianna. 'Given everything you've seen here today, and know about the firm, it's a fair request.'

'Our offer is a generous one…'

'It is… but it doesn't go far enough. The disruption to the office, to the way we operate, our clients… it all needs to be recompensed fairly.'

'I can't sign off on that,' said Charles.

'Charles, you, and I are both head of our game. We're powerful decision-makers. It's obvious to me you can make the decision. So why not close the deal, here and now?'

By the time half past five came around the atmosphere had moved from one of formality to all-time old friends. Katianna's note pad and proposal papers were scribbled on, highlighted, and filled with notes, representing the possible exciting future of her dating agency and the world of TV. But the deal still hung in the balance.

Charles gathered his papers, and suddenly stopped. Katianna, conscious they were the last in the conference room, looked up from her position at the head of the table. She levelled her gaze with his.

'Well?' she asked.

He leaned across the table. 'Your proposal's a deal,' he said. 'You've got your extra 15%.' He extended his hand in a handshake.

Chapter 29

Over the next two weeks Katianna and Angie scheduled meetings with eighteen of their newest clients and proposed they take part in the show. Melanie drafted sample contracts and the tentative dates for filming were scheduled and shared by Ethan.

At six o'clock Katianna ran out the door and took a taxi to UCH in Euston; John had been transferred to the specialist stroke unit. She mulled over their brief conversation mid-morning; he'd had a carotid endarterectomy; a procedure which removed the spread of plaque blocking the artery in his neck which had caused the first and second minor strokes. The operation carried out under local anesthetic allowed monitoring of his vital signs throughout the procedure. It appeared successful though he still had some paralysis along his arm and in his leg.

Part of her still worried about visiting him. She pondered on her own parents' final days in hospital almost two years before. Both had died within ten days of each other; her dad of a double heart attack, the second one killing him in hospital three days after the first and her mum of a broken heart. Everyone expressed their heartfelt thoughts about how kindred spirits, soul mates, can never be apart, and their beliefs, eventually, had comforted Katianna knowing that although her parents were no longer here, there was a chance they could still be together on some other plane. That belief was the only thing which kept her from falling apart.

Sitting in bed, John chatted slowly but happily to one of the nursing staff. She bent over laughing and Katianna knew instantly that he was okay; a shiver of relief shook her.

'Looks like you've got a visitor, so I'll leave you alone. Just press the call button if you need anything.'

'John. How are you?' Katianna moved the chair nearer and hooked her feet between the crank and the bed frame, trying not to stare at the bandage around his neck and the series of tubes and wires, noticing the snake trail which disappeared under the thin blanket.

'Surprisingly well. I've been nicknamed the bionic man. I'll be back in the office before you know it.'

'There's no hurry,' laughed Katianna. She knew the attention from the female staff had undoubtedly increased his positivity and attitude to his recovery. But she also recognised how long it would take for him to be fully mobile again.

'Fill me in. First the bank and then TC Productions' he said, struggling to push further up the bed.

'This can all wait, you know.'

'I'm not a total cabbage,' he said and then in a softer voice, 'I'm feeling a bit useless being molly-coddled here so a bit of normality would help.'

'The bank didn't go so well. They're asking for collateral and guarantees... that's all going to take some time I imagine.'

'Guarantees are standard procedure, not unreasonable.'

'But the TV deal is on, and they took the bite. We got the extra 15%!'

'That's fantastic news,' he said.

'You're on the mend, the deal is done. Looks like we'll both have something to celebrate,' she smiled. She leaned into her bag and had a rummage. 'The grapes are for show, the sausage roll is so that you don't say I never do anything for you,' she said, handing him the still warm savoury.

John took a bite of the sausage roll and struggled to lick the errant puff pastry flakes off his lips. He looked embarrassed; the flakes eventually fell onto the front of his T-shirt. 'You've been so good to me after everything...' he said, his voice breaking.

Katianna pulled a grape off the stalk and popped it in her mouth. 'That's because I'm a good person,' she said, dispelling the awkwardness of the moment, and then, pulling a face said, 'Not as sweet as the grapes in Cyprus.'

She put the carton on the bedside cabinet, her mind filling with the sweet taste of the grapes Polis had picked straight off the vine. They had tasted as sweet as honey and, with the sun warming her face, had taken her time plucking them one by one, relishing each little berry. She shivered recalling the sensation of Polis' lips on hers, the sweetness of the inside of his mouth as they kissed. She pulled at the silk scarf around her neck, a heat filling her.

John laughed, pulling her back to the present, and then he winced. 'Gotta watch those stitches,' he said, touching the bandaged incision in the soft folds of his neck. 'Still thinking about Cyprus, are you?'

'There's been too much going on here but yes. I didn't think I would. Life seemed… less complicated there.'

'Life anywhere but here would be less complicated,' he said.

'Have you had many visitors other than the swooning female staff?'

'Vicky. She's planning on coming every day despite being up to her eyes looking for her next project.'

'What does she do?'

'Investment… she works for independent big shots, more money than they know what to do with, all a bit hush-hush, but she likes it, and she must be doing well. She's always dining in the best places and on holiday somewhere further than a three hour hop on the plane. Her Instagram account is full of post after post.'

'Lucky woman, but I bet she must work hard for a lifestyle like that.'

'She does.'

'Do you think she might be able to help us with finance?'

'Let's focus on that TV deal for now. It's just the news I hoped for. But I could put some feelers out there,' said John, hesitating and then he succumbed to Katianna's pleading eyes. 'Leave it with me, she'll be in soon. I'll feel her out.'

'Not talking about me again, are you?'

Vicky appeared at the foot of the bed.

'Hello,' she said, addressing Katianna while casting a scowly, but playful, look in John's direction.

'Hello, we didn't get a chance to meet properly yesterday,' said Katianna, extending a handshake.

'Vicky. Unfortunately, John's sister,' she said, shaking Katianna's hand with vigour.

'John says you're in investment. We should talk.'

'Sure, anytime,' she said but Katianna sensed a hint of hesitation, an uncertainty in Vicky's tone and demeanour, but her smile seemed genuine.

'Anyway, I'll say goodbye. I'll leave you two to catch up. Hope you sleep well John and I'll keep you in the loop if anything else confirms with TC Productions.'

'Make sure you do,' he said. He wriggled, settling back into the pillows his sister busied plumping. She certainly had an air of matronly command, yet Katianna sensed a sweet kindness towards her brother.

Katianna left not sure what to make of Vicky. Vicky visited John every day so she must be warm hearted under that fierce business exterior John mentioned.

Chapter 30

By the beginning of September, the day-to-day routine of running the business began to find its flow again and, though a little slower than Katianna had hoped, she recognised how small steps in the right direction supported the business's best chance of recovery.

Since her trip to Cyprus something in her had shifted, like sand particles, new thoughts and feelings filled the tiniest crevices she had forgotten even existed and, sensations she had long forgotten, rose to the surface. She became less urgent in everything she did, demanded perfection less of herself and recognised a deeper association with those around her. She came alive; noticed more, felt more, yearned connection beyond instruction and correction. She pushed worries about the business to the back of her mind; it would work out in the end, she kept hearing her mother's words: *There's no point in worrying about something that might not even happen.*

As time went on, her new-found optimism was mirrored by John's steady recovery. He phased his return to work, splitting his time between home and the office, and he threw himself back in as energetically, almost maniacally, he enthused and offered his support to Angie, and towards himself demonstrated an abandon tipping on recklessness, which Katianna put down to fear of not living to the full. It was evident to Katianna John's rehabilitation and physio appointments sapped his time and energy, yet his outlook was one not previously associated with the calculating focus of John-the-accountant but rather John-the-man-who-wasn't-going-to-be-held-back.

'I got scared,' he declared down the phone. 'And now I'm all out to do everything I can to feel alive. What's the point of playing with fire if it doesn't burn a little?'

'John, stop,' Katianna said.

'I thought you'd be all for my new go-get attitude.'

'It's just reminded me of someone I met in Cyprus. Her and flames don't get along…'

'I didn't mean to offend. It's just a figure of speech, you know.'

'No, it's fine,' she said. 'And it's good you're finding the energy to be so… passionate.'

'Anyway, I've had discussions with the authorities and agreed a realistic payment plan for the overdue ground rent and service charges.'

'That's such a relief to see us breathing again. Hopefully, we'll continue to thrive despite the cutbacks,' said Katianna.

'You're still able to continue offering the same professionalism and standard of care to your clients.'

'And how's your physio going?'

'The physio… let's just say it's not my favourite pastime right now,' he said. 'So, fill me in.'

'We're all set with TC Productions too; sixteen signed contracts, one couple have dropped out, and our contract is with the solicitor. The team's on board; agreed to be involved in the "behind the scenes" filming and day-to-day footage. It's really excited them and taken the focus away from cost-cutting.'

Katianna ended her call with John when Angie rushed in.

'Sorry to burst in,' she said, taking hurried steps into the room. The door swung open behind her, the force quaking the books piled on the wall shelf. 'It's my mum. She's been in some sort of altercation near her house. The police are with her at the local off license.'

'Has she been drinking?' asked Katianna, trying to keep the alarm out of her voice.

'I hope not. They didn't say. I'm sorry but I have to go.'

'Let me know if I can…' But Angie had already bolted out the door, her long cardigan a flash of scarlet fluttering like a matador's cape to a bull.

Suddenly feeling deflated and alone, Katianna walked to the door, pushed it shut. She lowered the blind, before sitting at her desk; the window covering diffusing the low-setting sun's glare on her lap top screen. She reluctantly finished updating new entries in the five-star membership bracket; she insisted on doing these herself and her mood improved by the time she finished.

With everything that had gone on recently she wanted to show her empathetic side; show some concern towards her team, show not only ruthlessness in the boardroom but compassion outside of it. Polis had shown her there was more to live for than work and though she had her doubts as to where their relationship would go, she was thankful for him in her life though their contact was sporadic and became less and less as the weeks wore on, distance and work keeping her from him.

***

The day's melancholy continued into the night and Katianna realised how much she missed her evening conversations with Polis which had dwindled; she had spent more time sorting the business. What did she miss the most? Was it his company or the routine she'd fallen into with him?

She supposed his warm-hearted conversations made her feel less alone mentally and physically; his voice filled the empty space not only in her heart but in her apartment which felt too big, a void she could no longer sustain like she used to. She had been disappearing, hiding, when all along she wanted to be found. And then an unwelcome thought about her life invaded her thoughts; wondered whether she was designed to be alone; she had no parents, no siblings. Her empire filled the biggest part of her life and now she struggled to stand tall beside it. Once a sure-footed woman she now found herself floundering, doubting her ability to emerge victorious, her hormones raging and she recognised that she wanted desperately for someone to care for her, wanted Polis' love and attention, craved it.

She stared at her mobile phone, willing it to ring. She thought about her parents and what had been important to them, love first. Their love had set an insurmountable bar; one she could not dare to imagine for herself, the kind of love she had never known, not as a mature woman, and in recent months realised not as her younger self either. Their words rang in her ears; she had approached much of her adult life running in the opposite direction of love. Running the agency created a screen which camouflaged her crushed dreams. Quite suddenly she felt crushed.

In giving her all to the business she had pushed away love, pushed everyone away from her; even friends over the years had dwindled. There were only so many times backing out of an invitation or a day out could be tolerated. Her clients became the most important people in her life, but eventually moved on without a backwards glance.

In seeking self-actualisation, she had isolated those who would have otherwise contributed to making her life a better one, more fulfilling in ways she couldn't touch or see but only feel, love, understanding, patience, compassion.

She decided to take a walk, get out of the apartment. She wanted to be outside, in the fresh air, around people, and Camden Lock offered both. She changed out of her two-piece trouser suit and snuggled into a fleecy-lined pair of jogging bottoms and matching grey hoodie, pushed her feet into her black trainers. She stuffed her keys and mobile phone into her pocket and slammed the door behind her.

Cooler than anticipated, she shivered against the drop in temperature and pulled her hoodie around her neck to stop the biting chill. Another few weeks and the clocks would be going back marking the end of summer in her mind, the start of Autumn already changing the colour of her days, present in the fading light and the yellowing leaves.

She walked along the canal, following her usual path, noticing the golden and rust hues of the trees still clutching onto their leaves. Conker-fights with her dad and warm bonfire nights occupied her thoughts; childhood images flashed before her, filling her with a strange feeling of floating in midair; a lost helium balloon with no direction, dancing on the wind. She had never felt like that. What was wrong with her?

'I've lost myself,' she whispered to herself, and nausea surged, aware of the tenuousness of all life.

Chapter 31

Katianna fumbled for the glass of water on her bedside table. Her tongue stuck to the roof of her mouth like sandpaper against old wood, her throat as dry as a snake's sluffed skin. She took two long slurps, last night on her mind. Her safe, successful world was teetering on a cliff edge; was the universe trying to tell her something? What was once a source of joy, no longer nourished her.

She checked her phone, nothing from Polis. And why should there be? The last few days she had pushed her feelings aside and put all her time and energy back into the business. She was feeling more energised yet there was a niggling worry sitting just under her skin.

She took a power walk before work, but it did not help ease her apprehension. She suddenly wanted to be away from London, longed for Cyprus's pink blooms, blue alkanet and creamy delicate flowers of Queen Anne's Lace, the mountainsides filled with nimble goats and curly-haired sheep and the salty sea air. She longed too for the simplicity life in the village afforded, the city she had loved all this time now too big, too much for her. She still longed for Polis' warm embrace but fought her feelings, she was not a teenager. She needed to stay on track, focused on what mattered and right now that was the survival of her business. Without it, who would she be?

***

Katianna surveyed her empire, trying to shake off her previous melancholy. Across the sky a plane marked its path with a white contrail and a checkerboard of grey-black glass rooftops dotted the skyline. Normally the view would fill her with pride and a feeling of accomplishment but today she felt empty, disappointed. It was very different from the Cypriot landscape which had greeted her from the village.

She picked up the framed photograph of her taken the day she moved into the offices eight years ago. One of the removal men had snapped it, insisting she have a memento of the day. Self-conscious she had smiled too wide, baring all her teeth.

She replaced it on her desk; it served as a reminder of how much of herself she had invested over the years into making the business a success. She certainly wasn't ready to let it go just yet but also toyed with what else she would do if she did. Increasingly, her *yiayia's* house edged into her thoughts and so did Polis. With her parents gone, the prospect of selling the house was unravelling the already-fraying thread connecting her to Cyprus.

Angie walked in with Katianna's morning coffee; Katianna had quickly become accustomed to the bitter roasted coffee from the local supermarket and drinking out of the Cyprus mug took her focus off the taste. She still pulled a face.

'Missing your Jamaica Blue Mountain?' asked Angie but she seemed distracted, her magenta blouse jarred with her usual style of dress and her mood; it was showy; shouty, sure.

'I still treat myself to a sneaky cup in Fortnum and Mason when I'm in that part of town and I'm still drinking it at home, at least while my supply lasts.'

'Anyway, here's the files you asked for and last month's expenditure,' she said, little intonation in her voice.

'Thanks Angie. That's great. You've really settled into the new role. You're an absolute Godsend.' Katianna, acutely perceptive, tried to inject some light energy into the room.

'Thanks. If there's anything else…'

'How's your mum now?'

Angie hesitated, 'Confused. Deteriorating faster than the doctor warned. It's so hard watching her disappear. Some days she calls out for me when I'm standing in front of her. She doesn't recognise me...'

'I'm so sorry, Angie.'

'I just need to be there for her. It puts things into perspective. It's the people around us who make life worth living, who we should devote time to, not spreadsheets and algorithms which will continue long after we're all gone.'

'If there's anything you need. Please let me know.'

Angie thanked her, then turned and said, 'I hope you don't mind me saying but Polis hasn't called in a while. Is everything alright?'

'The refurbishment is almost finished. In fact, I'm looking to fly out again, maybe next week.'

'I meant between you. I thought I detected a spark there.'

'There're sparks and there're sparks,' said Katianna, shifting in her seat.

'They won't catch light if we don't feed them,' said Angie and she disappeared in a puff of pink chiffon and black Lycra.

Katianna let her words sink in. She should take a step back from the office and see how things worked without her here. Angie was loyal and hard-working and proving herself more than capable, in fact better than Katianna anticipated, but she wondered how long Angie could continue at this level of commitment before burning out.

Katianna had noticed the change in her. Angie, now less talkative and more withdrawn, took lunch at her desk rather than going out like she used to, and she hadn't suddenly forgotten to wear concealer, her dark circles a clear sign of sleepless nights, broken sleep, and worry. She made a note to broach the subject with her again.

The other options were still available; flexible working hours, working more hours from home to fit in around her mum's care. Katianna wanted to support her; prove she was more than the work-driven boss whose key focus was single-mindedly the business's success.

Angie's words hung in the air. Katianna instinctively picked up her mobile and called Polis. He answered on the third ring just as she almost lost her nerve, he didn't want to talk to her.

'Katianna, what a lovely surprise,' he answered. Instantly her doubts dissipated, leaving an excited thrum in her belly.

'Hello,' she said.

'How are you?'

'I'm very well, thank you. I'm thinking about coming over next week to settle with you and put the house back on the market.'

'So, you're still selling?'

'That was the plan all along…'

'Plans can change, no?'

'I'm sorry I haven't been the person you wanted me to be.' Katianna fumbled with her words, surprised at her own outburst.

'That's not what matters here, Katianna. It's about whether you're being the person you want to be.' His words, direct and full of emotion, cut through her; it wasn't what she expected to hear. He was right. It wasn't about what other people wanted her to be it was about the person she chose to be. She had lost herself along the way, her soul was tired, her mind confused. She knew what she had to do, had to face it, take a chance.

The moment she got off the phone and before she could change her mind, she logged onto British Airways and booked a flight out to Cyprus. The First Class offers popped up, but she resisted and confirmed her Premium Economy seat for the following week.

Chapter 32

'Polis, what are you doing here?

'Here let me help you with that.'

'Where's Savva?' she said, quickly embarrassed by the hostility in her voice.

'We both agreed it would be better for me to meet you,' said Polis. His face, despite his three-day growth, flushed pink and Katianna's heart skipped a beat. She'd forgotten his good looks and as he took the suitcase from her, she couldn't pull her gaze from his muscles, firm and taut, under the fabric of his shirt. 'Aren't you glad to see me?'

'Of course, yes. Sorry, yes, I am,' she said, aware of an internal weakening, aware he was evaluating her. His smile hugged her, hugged her ribcage and she tried desperately to keep her voice even. 'That's kind of you, thank you.'

She leaned in to give him a kiss on the cheek and they both went the same way; her kiss brushed the side of his mouth. She jumped back as if a lightning bolt had gone through her; the musky smell of his aftershave and slightly sweaty scent sending her pulse pounding like rain on a tin roof. Katianna suddenly felt vulnerable as she fought against the prickle of electricity running up her spine. Talking on the phone had become infrequent and cordial and seeing Polis again in person she felt shy, unsure of how to explain the feelings exploding within her.

In contrast, Polis seemed happy around her and, on the drive, back to the village he chatted animatedly, filling her in on the renovations which he proudly described as a project of love and respect to her *yiayia* and all the family before her.

As Katianna listened to him a rush of love for her roots pulled on her heartstrings; this place had something over her. Outside the house she gasped at the beauty of the cascading bougainvillea; its fragrant blooms filling the front wall of the house like a rose-pink waterfall. It instantly called her home and despite being exhausted, she smiled at the sight before her, picture postcard pretty.

Polis ran ahead of her and pushed open the gate. The courtyard had been totally transformed; the olive tree pruned back and tidied, the old pots planted with herbs. A rusty metal table and two chairs under a makeshift awning rekindled a long-forgotten memory. The old lace curtains still hung at the bedroom window.

'This is just beautiful,' she gasped.

'Wait 'til you see the rest,' said Polis and unable to contain his excitement pulled her towards the kitchen.

The previously dark space now flooded with light pouring in from the new skylight. In the sitting room the old fireplace was lovingly restored, and Polis had left one wall unplastered exposing the original brickwork.

He had even hung her *yiayia's tsestos* and *tatsia,* flat wicker basket and fine sieve, above it. 'I found these and thought you'd like to keep them,' he said. 'The basket's a little ragged and the sieve bent out of shape on one side but they're heir looms all the same.'

She recalled Savva and a group of his friends dancing with the *tatsia;* a dance of skill and non-stop movement which involved holding the instrument and twirling it around on four fingers. She had tried to copy her cousin a few times but failed every time she raised it above her head, the *tatsia* flying from her fingers' hold and nearly decapitating her laughing audience in the process.

In the bedroom her *yiayia's* old furniture stood proudly against the roughly rendered walls and the soft-white painted expanse of the ceiling.

'You found the blanket!' Katianna enthused. 'And the silk-worm cocoon frames.'

'It was in the wardrobe, just like you said it would be,' said Polis. 'And the frames I picked up in the village market for you.' His kind gesture filled her with genuine warmth for him.

The shutters, stained natural, trussed the bedroom's re-glazed windows. Lastly, the tiny bathroom with its original lamp, and her *yiayia's* old mirror above the sink, looked like something from the pages of a country house interiors magazine.

Katianna skipped from one room to the other taking in the sheer magnitude of the work completed and the sympathetic way it had been crafted. Her heart filled with warmth, cast only through heartfelt appreciation and love. She wanted to hug Polis and even kiss him but she daren't. She had to remain fair to him, not lead him on and after last time she knew how easily emotions escalated and it wouldn't be fair, wouldn't be fair on either of them.

Chapter 33

'What are you afraid of?' asked Sofia.

'I don't want to get into that complicated situation again.'

'From where I'm standing the only person making it complicated is you. You don't know how much he mooched around after you left and I knew when you stopped talking; he was like a cat whose saucer of milk had been stolen.'

'I didn't realise it was quite that bad. I just thought he'd get over me.'

'Get over you? How?'

'Meet someone else. Someone here.'

'When you've fallen in love with someone it's not that easy. You must know that' said Sofia, tipping back her wine glass. She swiftly refilled it, emptying the bottle.

'In love?'

'Yes, in love. He really fell for you. Has fallen for you.'

'Did he say that?'

'He didn't have to… it's there in his expression, the way he used to talk about you.'

'I suppose talking on the phone it isn't quite so easy to fully appreciate someone else's emotions. It was easy to put distance between us,' said Katianna, crossing her arms defensively. Had she realised just how strong Polis' feelings were? Maybe she wanted to deny them, deny he had feelings for her. Maybe even deny she had feelings for him. *She had feelings for him.*

'But you're here now. He's here now. Don't you think you should at least talk?'

'You're right, but how do I even start to explain everything… the relationship that's left me scarred, forced me to put up barriers, barriers still there?'

'You don't have to explain it all… take it one step at a time,' said Sofia and then, 'Pretend you've just met and you're going on a date. You should know all about that…' The wine had begun to loosen her boozy, inebriated tongue, she spoke more loudly, slurring slightly so her words came out with an American-Cypriot twang.

Katianna brooded on their conversation. Then in a burst of silliness she took a selfie with Sofia, both pouting, wine glasses filled, the nectar leaping over the rims as they shook with laughter and sent the image to Savva. She also messaged to say she would be staying the night at Sofia's and not to wait up for her.

She was grateful to him for putting her up again and hated to be a burden. If she had bed linen, she could have stayed at her *yiayia's* house now that it had water and electricity but something in her didn't want to chance staying there; she already hated putting it back on the market and the most recent snotty-nosed agent had scoffed at the original features saying new owners would likely modernise it.

The agent's words had stabbed Katianna in the chest, and she had instantly retaliated by saying she needed to think through her decision to sell. *How dare she after all the effort sourcing original materials and Polis' hard work.* The anger Katianna felt, like a ringing alarm bell, screamed at her not to sell the house. She wanted to protect the house and preserve the efforts made by Polis, yet she needed to sell. Surely the right person would materialise.

She knew her decision had to be based on sound business-making and not yo-yoing emotions. The cash injection would ensure the business stayed in the black. She had worked far too hard to lose it all now. The business had ultimately saved her from herself and a time when she quite easily could have spiraled into depression and happily stayed there popping tablets, disappearing into her own darkly morphed world of make-believe. She owed it to herself to make it successful again.

Sofia and Katianna talked past midnight, chatting under the arbour of tangled woody vine stems and scattered bunches of wine-red grapes. Sofia stumbled into the flowerbed stretching to pick the fruit and kicking an array of tiny terracotta pots they skated across the pathway.

Katianna tried to grab her and lost her footing on the uneven slabs. She crashed into Sofia, and they landed with a thud. They held onto each other stunned for a few seconds and then burst out laughing at their clumsiness.

The following morning, nursing hangovers, they sipped black coffee in the shade of the striped umbrella in Sofia's little garden; Katianna forcing herself to drink it. She surveyed the carnage of discarded bottles, now empty, they had drunk their way through; two bottles of red wine and half a bottle of *Commandaria;* a sweet, oaky, and richly fruity wine Sofia used for flavouring some of her more adventurous desserts.

'Thank goodness it's Sunday,' moaned Sofia.

'Stop the bells, stop the bells.' Katianna cupped her ears with fisted hands against the clang of the church bellringing. She closed her eyes against the rising sun despite wearing her sunglasses.

'No one can stop the bells,' said Sofia.

'Too loud,' Katianna replied and scrunched her face in retaliation.

'Sounds like you're having fun,' said Savva as he peeked over the wall.

'Good morning to you too,' said Katianna.

'Last night yes… this morning… not so good,' said Sofia, opening the once bright, blue-painted gate whose paint now flaked off in shaves.

'I've brought you breakfast,' he said and with a showy gesture opened bags and wrappers and laid out a morning feast of pastries, bread rolls and *tiropittes* for the girls.

Katianna and Sofia groaned.

'Not the reaction I'd had hoped for,' he laughed looking from one to the other in mock confusion as he took a bite out of a cheese pie.

Chapter 34

The end of September came round quickly. Katianna had checked her online banking which confirmed the advance from the filming company; she transferred all of it to pay most of her debts. She also gave the management company three months' notice to vacate her present suite of offices and downsize to the space on the lower floor.

In letting go and moving forward Katianna found a resemblance of happiness. With it, she had found a renewed lease of energy and she threw herself into her business and the filming.

The morning filming began Katianna fought an irrational fear everything was going to go wrong. The house is Cyprus had not yet sold and her world felt increasingly discombobulated. A dream the night before about her *yiayia* Anna's patchwork quilt sewn inside out plagued her.

'It's going to be so good,' cooed Angie, who looked stunning in a new two-piece trousers suit and fresh highlights running through her hair. 'I can't wait to be on camera.'

'We'll interview you at your desk. Angie, you can walk into the office, stand here,' Ethan said, indicating to an X marked on the floor. 'You don't have to tidy anything away unless it's confidential. The camera will focus on you and your computer screen. We'll cut into the bookshelf and then across to the view across London,' said Ethan, as Tina added the last touches of blusher across Katianna's cheekbones and Ethan's team nodded their understanding.

The area surrounding Katianna's desk, and beyond, looked like a movie set; tripods, light stands, trailing leads and cables, microphones, recording equipment, sound equipment, cameras, more lights, a ladder. And people. There were people everywhere. The rest of the staff already knew their day's productivity was questionable.

Filming took three hours until twelve o'clock and after another touch of eye shadow and lipstick Katianna breathed a sigh of relief when at four o'clock, and after three changes of clothes, Ethan announced they were done with her.

'We should have enough for an hour's film after editing,' he announced. Everyone clapped. Angie looked extremely proud. It had been a grueling day with the lights and concentrating on answering all the questions posed. Dehydrated, despite having drank two bottles of water, Katianna followed Angie into the kitchen stepping between and over lengths of cable and extension leads and around tripod legs.

'Tea?' asked one of the sound crew already pouring boiling water into a mug.

'Yes please. I'm dying for a cuppa. White two sugars,' said Angie.

Katianna shook her head, reaching into the fridge for a bottle of water.

'You did well out there. You've got a great voice. It's news reporter clear.'

'Thanks. I was nervous,' said Angie.

'You did great,' he said. 'I'm Jamie.'

'I'm Angie,' she said.

'I know,' he laughed shyly and then handing her a tea said, 'So you're in charge?'

'Katianna here is the owner and the boss. I just look like I'm in charge. And you?'

'Mainly sound, but I've trained in recording too and the basics of filming. I did a college course and then a Level 4 Apprenticeship, 4 years.'

'It's paid off. You look like you enjoy what you do.'

'Definitely. Travel around the country. I've done filming abroad too.'

'Thanks for the tea,' Angie said, accepting the mug.

'What do you do for fun round here?'

'Not much to be honest. Some of the gang gets together after work but I normally have to get back for my mum.'

'You live at home?'

'No. She's got dementia and so I like to pop in on her. Check everything's okay, you know.'

'My mum's the same. She's James this and James that.'

'It's not Mum, it's me. I like to see she's okay.'

'Sorry, I wasn't criticising. Must be hard.'

'Yeah, sometimes.'

'How about I take you for lunch tomorrow? No strings.'

Katianna pretended to be checking her mobile but noticed how Angie's face reddened, suspecting it was not with anxiety but excitement. She knew since Angie's divorce three years before, at age twenty-nine, she'd not had much time for dating and now with her mum's dementia worsening it was not a priority.

His consideration of her situation touched Katianna; lunch seemed perfect, and she hoped Angie would accept.

'I'd like that,' she said, taking a sip of the hot drink but her sudden flush didn't go unnoticed.

With each day's filming an excitement buzzed around the office suite, which was undeniably contagious; everyone seemed happy and above all else the crew involved in the recording, although clearly exhausted, ended each day on a productive high. The staff, overall, thrived on the thrill of being on television and though they were not allowed to forecast their involvement publicly they at least had each other to show off to.

Within a day or two everyone had found their rhythm and a routine which worked for the TV crew and Katianna's team; when to be quiet, when to have a break.

The rest of the filming went better than expected with no hiccups or problems. The acoustics were good, the sound was great, and everyone took their parts in the filming seriously.

By the end of the two-week shoot the office team and the production crew knew everything from each other's favourite take-out meal to their worst ever embarrassing moment. The banter was cordial, and at times too loud and, Katianna, in those moments found herself closing her office door and plugging in her ear buds, but the job got done and, surprisingly, on time.

Katianna, during the daily sessions, waved her phone around capturing the organised chaos for the company's social media posts which she had express permission to use during and after the airing of the programme.

'So, you've found a new lunch buddy,' said Katianna one afternoon. 'I'm glad for you.'

Katianna observed their tall, slender frames mirroring each other as they walked out of the office hand-in-hand or sat huddled by Angie's desk chatting over a cuppa.

'And how's it going with Jamie?' asked Katianna a few days later.

'He's pretty shy but I took things into my own hands and invited him to dinner last night.'

'And?'

'Apart from being wrapped like an Eskimo?' said Angie. 'The care worker agreed to sit with mum until eight o'clock. Our meal was delicious; pie and mash in one of the local pubs and a pint each. Jamie was surprised with my knowledge of brewing.'

Katianna raised an eyebrow. 'I didn't expect that to be a topic of conversation.'

'Dad used to home brew and so I often spent my weekends hidden in the shed with him syphoning and breathing in the fermented brew. I'm sure I used to get drunk on the fumes some days,' she joked.

'Are you seeing him again? You look close,' Katianna said wistfully.

'Well, put it this way. We kissed.'

'I've got a feeling this year will be extra special for you. I'm so happy for you,' said Katianna and as she said it, she wanted it to be true for herself too. And she thought of Polis.

***

It was the end of the last night of filming and Katianna had thrown a party to thank everyone for their patience and support and made a toast to their mutual success. The cheers reverberated around the office suite.

It seemed as though the interviews about modern love and meeting the right one had infused the air with some sort of lover's potion, and everyone appeared high on love and life. It created an incredible shift in the atmosphere and Katianna marvelled at how even the usually grumpy IT technician whistled as he dealt with a frozen computer screen.

Everyone reluctantly began to drift off at around half past six when the cleaners came in, chatting in Serbian and Polish between them. They smiled through the drudgery of clearing the party mess; plates, glasses, empty packets of peanuts and crisps and platters still full of sandwiches and filled wraps. Katianna watched as one of her team nodded and gestured towards the pile of unused plates, saying they could help themselves to the food.

Most of the recording equipment had been packed and loaded onto the waiting vans at the back of the building. The last of the trolleys disappeared into the lifts, just beyond the glass wall of the office suite and Katianna swung round one of the swivel chairs and flopped into it, her slim legs sprawled out in front of her like Bambi's.

Someone lowered the music, and she pressed her hands over her ears still thrumming from the beat.

'I'm off,' said Angie. 'Better get home to Mum.'

'Thanks again for all your help. You've been incredibly generous with your time and energy. Have a good evening.'

'You too,' trilled Angie and buttoning her coat, double wound her scarf before knotting it.

Outside London's skyline twinkled with glittering orange and yellow lights shining out from buildings old and new, creating a magical scape of illuminations against the winter sky, heavy with cloud. Katianna pushed her glass of champagne to the side and closed her laptop. She felt done in and she had to admit nervous about seeing Polis again.

She wondered how she would feel seeing him after all this time.

She pushed down the bubbles of anxiety and looked back at the blackness... tiny flecks of snow filled the sky, and her heart skipped a beat at the thought of a white Christmas, the space in her heart filling up too.

Chapter 35

With the work on the house Katianna had to face selling it and she realised too Polis had no reason to return to the village unless she gave him one. She missed his now long-ago sweet messages and berated herself for avoiding them, not giving anything back. She had persuaded herself it was the best decision, but it had been the worst. She knew it. She felt it.

Sofia's words swirled round and round in her head like a snow-globe flurry; she deliberated as to whether the flakes would eventually settle and reveal a clear image. Sofia, though younger, possessed a wise intelligence, a deeper, spiritual understanding of people and emotions and all the stuff Katianna avoided; ran from. Being in Cyprus, she increasingly found it difficult to forget Polis and subconsciously willed their paths to cross again. It bothered her that by now he may have found another to pour his affections and she longed for his attention.

One morning, Katianna found herself on a bus which took her out of the village. Alighting twenty minutes later, she stumbled across a tiny beach set in an alcove; secluded from the road and to her delight it appeared undiscovered by the hundreds of tourists still vacationing on the island.

She slipped off her canvas shoes, and felt the soft, golden sand sink beneath her feet and settle between her toes. It was warmer than she expected it to be despite it being early October and she liked the way the sun still shone, as if to say, you're not going to get rid of me just yet.

Looking out across the ocean for a few minutes, Katianna watched the white-crested waves as they crashed and hurled against the beach, changing the colour of the beach from golden to a deep rust, each new break bringing with it a mess of tangled seaweed.

Polis crept into her mind, and it was as if she could hear his name being carried on the crests of the waves as they came closer and closer up the narrow beach towards her.

Picking up her shoes she continued to meander, glad to be cloaked from the rest of the world by the bay. Her phone vibrated in her shoulder bag. She ignored it not wanting her moment of quiet to be broken. It vibrated again. She looked at the screen. It was Polis. Her heart raced and pounded like the sea, the waves breaking white against the shiny black rocks at the far end of the cove. *She panicked, should she pick up?*

'Hello,' she said, trying to steady the tremor in her voice.

'Hello, Katianna. How are you?'

'Good thanks. I'm just out for a walk on the beach.'

'I've got some news.'

'Go on.'

'There's a buyer for the house.'

'That's amazing. It's too good to be true. Who are they? Is the offer genuine?'

'They've instructed a prominent solicitor in Limassol. I'm sure they'll be in touch via the agent.'

'Everyone knows what's going on before I do,' she said.

'That's Cyprus for you,' he said. 'The sale means you'll get the money to help your business, no?' Katianna flattened her palm to her chest trying to calm her thumping heart. 'Katianna, are you there?'

'Yes, sorry. It's just a huge shock, a surprise,' she said and shivered against the slither of warmth from the sun on her back. 'Thank you. My guardian angel is looking over me right now.'

'As am I,' said Polis, his voice suddenly thick with emotion.

'I know. And thank you. You've been so kind to me and I'm grateful, truly.'

'I don't want your thanks, Katianna. I want your presence in my life.'

Katianna's heart raced. His directness shocked her and seemed to contradict his otherwise gentle and easy-going nature. Was this how love burst into flames and engulfed you? Is this how love was meant to be? But before she had a chance to say anything Polis ended the call.

Katianna spent the next hour in a confused melee of thoughts. She wondered who the buyer might be and whether turning up in the middle of Polis' revelation was a coincidence or something more, unsure how she felt about either situation. She dwelled on Polis and whether his love might be the love to sustain and keep her happy.

Vicky had found two possible investors, but Katianna would have to relinquish 20% of the business in return. It was an attractive offer but after fighting to keep the business perhaps it was too risky letting someone take such a big bite. Selling to her would provide the investment she needed for the business, and more, but something niggled at her insides, and she couldn't quite admit it to herself. A question hung over her; did she want to save the business over losing her *yiayia's* house? And was this about control, her *yiayia's* house or was it really about Polis? Was she willing to lose the first thread of love in her life in too long to even think about?

Her phone vibrated and this time she accepted the call without hesitation.

'Don't say anything. I will be at *E Petaloutha*. Meet me there at nine o'clock. If you don't come, then I will accept there is no chance for us to make a life together.'

She dropped down onto the sand — what was there to talk about?— Polis had made his feelings clear, and her heart had already spoken, if only a mere whisper, to her and her alone. *He was giving them a second chance. Giving her another chance. At love, at happiness.*

She got up, her feet sinking into the silky sandy grains and, after pushing into her shoes, made her way back up the sharp incline to the rough path that led to the main road, noticing a fleet of bikes propped up against one of the boulders. Laughter floated up from another narrower cove she only noticed from her vantage point now and she was glad she had not bumped into anyone, enjoying the cloak of anonymity the deserted beach had afforded.

She needed to speak to Sofia. Her heart fluttered and she almost walked straight into the path of a motorcyclist. She stepped back, the whoosh as it passed at full speed knocking her back and onto her bottom. She put out her hands to stop herself from bumping her head too, scraping her palms on the rough ground. She coughed as the rising dust off the road caught in the back of her throat. She waved her hand in front of her face to waft it away. Choked, her eyes filled. Defeated she dropped to the ground, tears streaming. She didn't know what to do. She didn't feel strong enough to face this crossroad in her life, she didn't want to be hurt and humiliated again. She wanted to be the strong, successful entrepreneur everyone knew, everyone relied on, and everyone went to for support. *If she crumbled now, would Polis hold her up? Did she even want to be held?*

She wiped the falling tears with the back of her hand and shook her head to pull herself together. The bus trundled along, and Katianna hardly noticed the landscape which she would usually have marvelled at with a deep joy.

***

'What's happened?' Katianna crumbled into Sofia's open arms, fresh tears falling all over again. Eventually, her sobbing abated, and Sofia guided her friend to the garden and the swinging two-seater and with her feet firmly on the ground she anchored the gently rocking seat so Katianna could sit down.

Katianna talked and talked; the words tumbled, leaving her breathless, yet she carried on desperately letting out wave after wave of pent-up emotions. It was as if the words had been stored in her for too long and they fell like toys from a toy chest, one after the other, noisy, and messy, making no sense, then making the best sense ever, sounding impossible and then sounding totally possible and utterly real.

She had no idea how long she talked for, or how long she sat cushioned in Sofia's embrace. When she finally stopped her voice was hoarse. The sun had dipped behind the mountain slope striped, green with a verdant carpet of vines; planted in neat rows across one section of the mountainside; the vineyard represented years of order and tradition and hours of painstaking labour going back to ancient times. Some things didn't change in Cyprus.

'It sounds like you know exactly what you need to do and what you want to do but you have to push doubt and fear and obstacles and excuses to the side. This is your chance to express the happiness that is within, to release all the love inside of you and share it with someone who is equally willing to do the same,' said Sofia and she gently dabbed antiseptic cream into Katianna's sore palms.

'But what if it all goes wrong?'

'Then it goes wrong... but have you considered what if it all goes right?'

'I don't know...'

Sofia looked straight into Katianna's eyes and said, 'If it goes right, a moment...'

'...can last forever,' said Katianna finishing her friend's sentence.

Chapter 36

It was close to sunset, that moment when the sky bleeds pink and orange and purple, when Katianna finally left Sofia's and took the walk back to Savva's. She kicked off her shoes and gave them a shake before stepping into the house. Savva wasn't in and his note on the kitchen worktop said, "Out with some work friends. Don't wait up. ☺"

She was quietly relieved he wasn't home and taking a quick look through his music collection was surprised to find a Jay Sean album she used to listen to. She slipped the CD into the player and turned up the volume. The mellow tones bounced off the walls mingling with the warm glow of the final beams of sunlight as they drenched the white walls with golden arcs. Under the Setting Sun, she whispered.

Time edged towards eight o'clock. Her stomach knotted into a tight ball of frustration, and she reluctantly took a shower which went some way to easing the tightness across her shoulders.

She slipped into a three-quarter length sleeved dress with a scooped neckline, its frilled hemline skimmed her ankles. It was perfect for this time of year, and she smiled at Sofia's generosity; a farewell gift received earlier in the week. Sofia's words chimed in her ears: what if it all goes right?

The dress fitted perfectly, hugging her in the right places and hanging loose where she needed to hide a bump or two. She had put on weight since her arrival; everything the Cypriots did seemed to evolve around food and eating but she liked the way it brought people together; sharing food, sharing stories, sharing life. Her existence in London was so far removed from this, those she knew lacking the genuine warmth and hospitality of the Cyprus people.

She dabbed moisturiser over her face and rubbed it in gently with her fingers. The music made her tingle and she relaxed. Perhaps meeting Polis was a good idea. She couldn't just jilt him, not after all the work he had put into the house, his love and attention, and not after making so obvious his ongoing adoration for her. She had to admit that, for a time, he had filled that space behind her heart with heat, with passion, with a desire to keep living and to keep breathing. Was she heading for heartbreak? Was this a chance she should walk away from or towards?

She thickened and lengthened her eyelashes with layers of mascara and added her signature red lipstick. She pouted at her reflection in the mirror. She sprayed herself with the last of her travel size perfume and grabbing her handbag was on her way by a quarter to the hour.

The village was dark, the streets lit by intermittent pools of light from the streetlamps, the sky a dark mass of low puffy clouds. A cat and her kitten, meowing for attention, chased Katianna and her clicking heels. She tried shooing them, but they kept coming back until eventually realising she had no scraps they reluctantly disappeared into the carcass of another derelict house on the other side of the road. The monastery came into view ahead of her, across the open village piazza, and something pushed her to veer off, and she took the narrow alley past her *yiayia's* house.

The house would be locked, and she didn't have the keys with her, but she wanted to take a look; her feet carried her effortlessly. In the darkness of night, something spoke to her and pulled at her heartstrings; the solid stone walls, the slope of the tiled roof, the slightly off-kilt windows, the freshly painted blue gate. The conversation with the agent wound its way back to her filling her with heaviness. She placed an open palm on the rough stones of the outer wall, as if feeling the house's heartbeat and then she turned and leant against it.

A breeze picked up from nowhere and she felt a tingle close to the side of her face. She turned but there was no one there. A wind chime tinkled in the wind; the tune a soothing white melody especially for her.

It was a sign. The sign she was looking for and she was plunged back to a long-forgotten memory. The chimes continued to touch her soul like someone familiar in spirit form telling her to hold on, to believe in the past, the present and the future. Could this be her *yiayia* or her mother trying to communicate with her? She welcomed the positive energy the sound seemed to bring and felt uplifted, lighter, happier.

She peeled herself off the wall and looked back towards the square; celebratory cheering and clapping echoed around her as a coachload of tourists spilled into the square and made their way to one of the eateries there. She noticed her nerves had calmed and not wanting to be late hurried to *E Petaloutha.* The song of the nightingales in the trees sent tingles of anticipation up her spine. This really was a magical place.

As soon as she took the first step into the restaurant Polis stood up from where he had been waiting at the table across from the entrance. Katianna walked over to him embarrassed under the scrutiny of his stare. She stopped a foot or so from him, the relief on his face obvious.

He stepped towards her and pulled her close and everything around her fell away. He leaned in against her and she felt his racing heartbeat bursting through the thin fabric of his shirt. His heart thrumming the same rhythm of her own.

He stepped back and surveyed her from head to foot. 'You look… just… you look stunning.' And before she had a chance to reply he kissed her.

'Glad to see me?' Confused feelings, bombarding her from every angle, crashed around her body but she welcomed them. His face broke into a smile. She smiled back. 'Red lipstick suits you,' she teased.

Mihalis appeared silently behind her and pulled out a chair for her opposite Polis. She sank without protest into the seat, grateful her legs had not buckled from the tumbling emotions. Mihalis slid the chair towards the table and vanished.

For a moment Polis and Katianna surveyed each other shyly. She hadn't been sure what he expected of her but now it was as plain as she was sat in front of him. And they were here, and they were still smiling in a surprisingly busy restaurant, noted Katianna.

'You came.'

'I wasn't sure I would,' she said, afraid the telltale throbbing in her throat would reveal her feelings.

They spoke at the same time. Stopped. Then spoke over each other. Katianna prompted Polis to continue.

'You came,' he said again, his voice full of happy notes.

Her mind roused a vision of the fluttering butterflies and tweeting birds dancing round his shoulders like in the Mary Poppins movie. A movie she recalled watching many times at Savva's house years before; with Greek subtitles she had learnt many words and still remembered them.

'*Pachia poulia…* Fat birds. *Olos o kosmos sta podia sou…* the whole world at your feet. *Mia koutalia zachari voithei...* a spoonful of sugar helps. She smiled broadly.

'I did. I wasn't sure I'd come but also knew I couldn't leave you sitting here alone.'

'Is that the only reason? To avoid me from embarrassment?'

'No, of course not. I wanted to see you.'

'That's a good start. We can talk, work this out together. But if you're here it must mean something good.'

'I care for you Polis. You're sweet and gentle and… passionate.'

'You noticed?' he teased and a flush coloured his cheeks, a flash sparkled in his eyes.

'You haven't seen his cooking skills though, have you?' joked Mihalis as he placed a carafe of white wine between them and two glasses. Katianna giggled, relieved Mihalis had chipped in, lightening the conversation.

'*Thalero*…the wine of poetry.'

Polis nodded, conveying his understanding, 'youthful and full of life.'

'You two talk. I'll serve something special for you to eat tonight. Don't waste precious time looking at the menu.' He walked off with a bounce and disappeared into the kitchen, his whistle cutting across the restaurant above the other patrons' lively chatter.

'The wine of poetry?'

'Yes. This,' Polis said, pointing to the carafe, 'is named after a famous poet, and play write, Angelos Sikelianos.'

'Everything feels poetic here, feels like a great piece of literature.'

'Does it? Look, I know you have a life in London. And I have a life here. But we can at least try to make it work. Is there enough to persuade you to try?'

'We did try, didn't we? And look what happened? It sizzled… it flopped…'

'But this will be different… it was just circumstantial before… we fell into it,' said Polis.

'And we fell out of it.'

'He also wrote the poem The Moonstruck… *If I fell in love with you, I would like to Make my dreams come true, You could fulfill all yours too, So come on, Just one look will do, I'll lose my heart to you, Like all the moonstruck do.*'

'That's beautiful,' Katianna said, and a little pocket of silence fell between them until Polis broke it.

'A toast,' he said, and he raised aloft his glass. 'To love and life and everything it may bring.'

His toast held a gentle strength in it, illuminated the space between them and Katianna was roused by the romance of it all. 'The Moonstruck,' she said and touched by his poetic recital, clinked her glass against his. Inside her gut told her to stay, to listen, to experience, to see.

Mihalis, his steps sprightly, approached their table with a dish piled high with thickly diced oven-baked aubergines with fresh tomatoes, sliced onions and fresh coriander and parsley.

Polis and Katianna shared the dish forking the soft vegetable pieces and spooning the delicious tomato sauce into their mouths. Katianna dribbled a little sauce across her lips and Polis leaned over the table and wiped it from the corner of her mouth with his thumb.

His touch against her lip sent a charge of electricity through her and she shifted in her seat trying to cover her bubbling excitement. She breathed in the meal's aromas. How could people live without ever tasting this food? Or maybe it was Polis' company which made her feel this way.

Mihalis, a towel draped over his shoulder, fussed around them. He brought a platter of fresh charcoal-cooked shrimps, garnished with wedges of fresh lemon, and a basket piled high with soft white bread. A plate of meatballs followed by a bowl of crisp salad topped with crumbled creamy feta and drizzled in olive oil fought for a little square of space on the table.

Katianna noticed how Polis relaxed more, like her, with every glass of wine and every forkful of food. He leaned across the table and held her hand, touched her face with a gentleness she had not expected from him. She stroked his hand and played with his fingers as his thumb massaged the fleshy inside of her palm. Each time she looked into his eyes it took her one step closer to the allure of the stars.

Their conversation took them to discussing everything from the house, to work and to life, and even the magic of serendipity, and by the end of the evening Polis had Katianna laughing when he added London to his weather app Katianna felt connected to him in an entirely different way; a tug at her heartstrings and she realised Polis was nestled there. A Polis-shaped future dared to twinkle at her.

'Can I walk you home?' he asked.

Chapter 37

'I'm hardly going to get lost,' said Katianna. Polis took her hand in his and they walked.

'What sort of a man would I be letting you cross the village alone at this time of night?'

'London's getting worse. Or I'm just noticing more. The attacks at Westminster Bridge, then London Bridge, those poor people at the mosque in Finsbury Park. Sorry…'

'It's not like that here but all the same I'm walking you back.'

She gazed at the clear night sky, full of wonder at the dusting of glittering stars filling it and the full moon a perfect silver disc. 'The sky's not like this in London,' she said out loud. 'It's all clouds, the stars hardly visible.'

She shivered against the cool night, suddenly wanting to be closer to him, connected to him physically. She reached for his arm and wove hers through the bend in his; their arms locked seamlessly, like puzzle pieces, at the elbows.

They continued to walk in silence for a few minutes, the square quiet, and then, by the old mulberry tree he stopped and taking both her hands turned her to face him. 'Maybe one day we can look at the sky every night and create our own star-lit canvas,' he said. He leaned in and brushed his lips gently against hers and then, with a passion that took away Katianna's breath, he kissed her deeply, melting her. Hot lashing flames devoured her as he laid a hand on the small of her back and something incredibly energising, without preamble or thought on her part, was foisted upon her.

She pulled away and ran her tongue over her lips tasting him, wanting more, her cheeks aflame with the heat of his desire for her, of hers for him.

Their steps took them in harmony, unconsciously on her part, to her *yiayia's* house. Something burst into life inside her. She wanted the night to never end. She wanted Polis to stay with her. It was as if her *yiayia* understood how Katianna felt. A high filled her, adrenaline coursing through her and she kissed Polis again.

They fell onto the bare mattress, she not caring about the unmade bed. A giggle escaped her, filling the silence; her wholehearted glee bounced off the walls. She discarded her dress, he his shirt and trousers. His hands, though big and strong flattened softly, like cotton wool, against her arms. And then they swept over her, idly tracing soothing lines down her back, his touch electric on her bare skin.

He gasped as she stroked his arms, his bare chest. He didn't rush. He didn't waiver. She wriggled out of her bra and knickers wanting to drown in the whole of him. He kissed her, his mouth lightly sweeping across her neck, her clavicle and shoulder and along her arm. He kissed the inside of her elbow and the soft folds of her thumb and forefinger. He ran his tongue down to the soft hollow of her belly button and back up to her breasts; her nipples erect as he teased each one gently.

Polis made her feel like a goddess on earth and with the light of the moon stealing into the room, she lowered herself onto him. They tossed and turned, passion taking over like a rough sea and finally spent, fell asleep spooning, as if they were always meant to be together.

The following morning, tangled in a white sheet she could not remember seeing on the bed the night before, Katianna extricated herself from Polis' arm, the sheet still wrapped around her. She turned to face him; his expression, one of peace. Rousing from sleep moments later, he opened his dark eyes and looked straight at her, his bright smile colouring his lips.

'Good morning,' he said, his whole face alight with joy.

'Good morning,' she said shyly. 'We spent the night together.'

'It looks like we did.'

They both burst out laughing.

'And you had keys,' she said, but not accusingly.

'I did. I meant to give them back to you at the restaurant.'

'So, what happens now?'

'What do you want to happen?' he asked, kissing her on the nose.

'I really don't know. All I know is that I didn't plan this. But I'm glad last night happened. Glad that we happened,' she said. He took Katianna by the hand. She shuddered as she felt his hand against hers; his touch still imprinted on her skin from their lovemaking the night before.

His expression clouded and he looked as if he wanted to cry. Katianna fought back her own tears, but they spilled over. Teardrops trailed over her cheeks and Polis licked each one up with his tongue and then kissed her; salty-tear kisses overwhelming her and touching every crevice within her, filling her with tingling joy, vibrancy. As he kissed her his hands grappled with the sheet, pulling at it urgently. She leaned into him, marveling at how her breath stirred the hair on his chest. He caressed her and she arched towards him aching for him all over again

Spent, she laid with her back to him, her bottom pushed up against his groin. He wrapped an arm around her waist and whispered to her in Greek. 'I don't ever want you to leave my side.' He gently tugged at the sheet beneath him and releasing it, tucked it around her. Within minutes she fell asleep again.

Chapter 38

Katianna woke with a start. She turned to face Polis fully dressed in his shirt unbuttoned, sitting at the end of the bed.

'Good afternoon,' he smiled.

'You're joking, right? Oh my God. I had a Zoom call booked with Angie.'

'That explains your phone buzzing continuously.'

'I don't do sleeping in the afternoon.'

'You do now. You slept like Pasithea,' he said.

'And she is?'

'Was... the wife of Hypnos, God of sleep? She personified relaxation,' Polis explained.

'In that case, yes. I slept well.'

'I'm hoping you still want me to be your Hypnos.'

'I do,' she laughed. 'But first I need to get onto Angie. And I need to let Savva know where I am... if he hasn't guessed already.'

'I'm surprised he hasn't burst in looking for you,' he said.

She pulled on her clothes. 'Four missed calls,' she said, checking her phone. 'He still just might.'

Katianna moved to the other side of the bed. Swiftly she pulled her hair into a tight ponytail to tidy herself and Face Timed Angie. Polis sat close to her, but out of shot of the phone's camera.

Their call lasted fifteen minutes. Everything was okay and there was nothing urgent to report. Katianna sensed Angie's frustration when John came up in their conversation, but let it go, knowing that his return to the office could only go as fast as his convalescence allowed. Otherwise, it seemed, Angie was taking on her new role like a new suit of perfectly polished armour.

Polis ran his finger playfully over Katianna's thigh and she playfully batted it away. Katianna finished her conversation and pressed end.

'You're insatiable,' she laughed.

'Only around you.'

'Shall we go out for something to eat?'

'I need to change first,' said Katianna.

Katianna let herself into Savva's house. Polis at her heels, his shirt still open to the waist, trying to keep his steps light, but his heavy strides reverberated around the stillness of the house.

Savva's bedroom door was closed; thank goodness he was still asleep. She tiptoed to the kitchen. Polis came up behind her. She turned round in his embrace, running her hands over the curl of his chest hair, when she heard a creak behind her. She froze in Polis' arms.

Savva's bedroom door opened.

'Good afternoon sleepy head,' he called. He approached the kitchen, still speaking. 'You must have had a good... Polis... good afternoon to you too.' He looked from Katianna to Polis who had stepped back from Katianna, trying to button his shirt.

'Looks like we've been caught out,' said Polis.

Katianna and he looked at each other grinning.

'Well, I must say this is a surprise but not totally unexpected,' said Savva.

'I take it you approve then, my dear cousin?'

'Approve? I'm delighted for you. And for you Polis,' he said, slapping Polis on the back in a show of camaraderie.

'I wondered where you might have spent the night,' said Savva.

'We ended up at the house.'

'So that's why I didn't hear you come in last night,' said Savva. 'I did try calling.'

'Sorry. I didn't see your missed calls until this morning.'

Savva laughed, 'You're an endearingly bad liar but don't apologise, as long as you're okay.'

'Did you have a good night?' asked Katianna, colouring now at being caught out and a little uncomfortable with how obvious it was her evening had ended.

'I did,' said Savva, beaming.

Katianna confused by his soppy grin eventually followed his gaze across the kitchen towards the sitting room and gasped, 'Sofia.'

Sofia clad in one of Savva's T-shirts, padded across to the kitchen in her bare feet. 'You dark horse you,' she said to Savva, and then, 'I'm so happy for you both.

'I'm so happy for you too,' echoed Sofia, nodding her head towards Polis who smiled widely. The women hugged again, their hugs tight and electric, congratulating each other.

'Who would have thought we'd both find love at the same time,' whispered Sofia to Katianna.

'It must have been written in the stars,' she answered.

Chapter 39

The house finally sold, at least on paper. And while Katianna half expected delays and complications, she focused instead on finalising the catering arrangements for the party with Sofia.

The courtyard garden twinkled with rows of firefly lights hanging from the rafters of the house and intertwined with the branches of the old olive tree, looking beautifully resplendent in the evening light. Bunting decorated the entrance and delicate white roses filled the huge terracotta pots. Tables ferried over from neighbours' gardens and Sofia's café were laden with mixed grazing platters the Greek Gods would be honoured to be served. Sofia had exceeded Katianna's expectations; the tables were displayed beautifully with fresh and dried fruit, homemade sweet and savoury pastries, meatballs, pots of olives and fresh earthy tomatoes, dips and fresh bread cut into chunks in keeping with traditional village fayre but all with a twist of modern-day Cyprus cuisine and Sofia's special touch.

It seemed like the entire village, from young to old, came through the gate and joined in the celebrations. The older generation marvelled at the old pottery in the kitchen and the reclaimed tiles above the stove, her *yiayia's* beautiful cover on the bed and the restored shutters.

Katianna enjoyed shining in the light directed at her; she chatted and laughed, she drank wine and nibbled at the delicious food so lovingly prepared by Sofia. She felt lucky and blessed to be surrounded by these incredibly warm and generous people. People who had welcomed her with open arms and she hugged Savva tight as she found herself suddenly overwhelmed.

'So, this is it. You've achieved what you set out to do and you're giving the village house the sendoff you promised. Your *yiayia* will be...'

'Disappointed,' said Katianna.

'I was going to say proud of the way you've renovated her house with such care and dedication,' said Savva, in earnest.

'It's all down to Polis' sensitivity. He's been... incredible,' said Katianna and she suddenly felt a little lightheaded.

'Just with the house?' asked Savva. 'I'd say judging by your wistful expression he's touched you there.' He put his hand over his heart in a mocking but kind gesture.

'You two look like you're having a moment,' said Sofia.

'Maybe,' Katianna said and as if shaking off her overwhelming emotions, she tilted her chin, took a deep breath, and reached out for each of their hands. 'Thank you, both. You've both become good friends and I'll miss you.'

'You'll be back. Polis will make sure of that,' said Savva.

'He will. He's a good man. I don't deserve him,' Katianna said, wiping a tear and in that moment the tinkle of a wind chime danced on the air and Katianna's hair stood up on the back of her arms. Inside she felt her heart racing; her *yiayia* was watching over her again, she was certain of it.

'You deserve everything good coming your way including a loving man who will be there for you,' said Sofia and she gave Katianna a squeeze.

'Talking about me again?' asked Polis, as he put his arm around Katianna's waist and pulled her close.

'You're the talk of the village – this house, Katianna...' said Sofia, laughing.

'And look at the turn out,' said Katianna. 'It's amazing.'

'I don't mean to burst your bubble but where there's food and drink, Cypriots will come running,' said Savva, draining his glass.

'Speech, speech,' someone called out and the entire courtyard filled with clapping and a merry cheer as all eyes turned on Katianna.

Katianna looked at Sofia who gave her a little nod of encouragement.

Suddenly self-conscious and filled with deep emotion, Katianna knew what was expected of her. Even though in her professional life she had addressed hundreds more people in venues across London, and even appeared as a guest speaker at the TedX conference last year in Hammersmith, this was different. This was something outside her comfort zone and she wanted so much to be a part of the community she had grown to love, to adore.

She coughed and everyone quietened, shifting the attention of everyone; an almost magical hush blanketing the twinkly courtyard. She addressed everyone in Greek, Sofia having helped her write a speech just in case.

Holding her speech in her hand, she unfolded the sheet of paper and began, 'I don't know where to begin really. Being back here after so many years seems surreal. *Yiayia* Anna was truly loved by you all, I see it in your faces when you talk about her, and I hear it in your voices.' She stopped and took a breath, keeping her emotions at bay. 'I want to say how much I've enjoyed being part of this amazing village again and I promise to come back. I know you'll gain so much from the well here, the well which was the subject of so many made up stories when I was little. I'm glad something good has come out of all this.' She paused, everyone clapped, cheered, and whistled.

'And of course, thank you to Polis for such an incredible job on the renovation, to Sofia for the amazing food—please don't leave until all the food and drink is gone—to my cousin, Savva for putting up with me and for insisting I come out to Cyprus in the first place.'

Polis leaned in and gave her a kiss, Savva hugged her and before she knew it, she was surrounded by happy faces and her cheeks were being kissed over and over to the most tremendously loud clapping and cheering.

Children jumped up from sitting cross-legged and chased each other around the restored well and tried to climb into the old stone oven perched at the far end of the little paved garden. Their parents continued to savour the food and nattered animatedly and smiled widely and, Katianna guessed, their hearts full of joy at the new natural water supply afforded by the well. Her *yiayia's* memory would live on in all the villager's minds for a long time to come.

She took a step back, hanging in the shadows of the kitchen door. She looked out into the crowded courtyard, Polis' arms around her, and fought the tears welling inside her. This was a beautiful place and if things had been different, she would never have sold it but at least the new owner had promised to honour the traditional style of the house; something she had insisted upon even though it had meant turning down countless potential buyers.

She shook off a shiver and heard a tinkle behind her. She turned and looked over Polis' shoulders but saw no one. Bright light bounced off the old mirror hanging above the tiny fireplace and reflected around the kitchen. She was sure her *yiayia* was watching, sure she would be proud of her despite not holding onto the house.

***

Katianna giggled as Polis gently pushed her back into the courtyard and she waved off the last of her guests. The cascades of white roses, now wilting in the late evening heat, their heads drooping, seemed to be nodding in her direction.

'What a fabulous time we all had,' she breathed happily.

'It was wonderful my darling. You'll be the talk of the village for a long time.'

'I'm glad everyone enjoyed themselves. It felt good to be celebrating,' she said with a prick of tears stinging her eyes.

Polis coughed, clearing his throat, and looked her straight in the eyes, suddenly serious, stiff. His hands tightened into fists by his side.

'Is everything okay?'

'Katianna, I want all my days to be filled with family and friends but most of all with you. I want to be sure you're mine. Will you marry me?'

'What? Oh my gosh, Polis...'

'Don't think about it,' he interrupted. 'Just say the first word that comes into your head.'

'Yes,' she said, and he swept her into his arms and spun her around until they both almost collapsed from dizziness.

He put her back down gently and she dabbed at the smudges of happy, teary makeup around her eyes. He stroked her cheeks burnished by the late sun. He felt for something in his back pocket; all the time holding her gaze with his. He took Katianna's hand in his and placed a gold band in her palm. A red ribbon tied around a gold ring with three diamonds set into it lengthways. The jewels sparkled, reflecting the autumn sunlight, like beams of magical light.

'This is beautiful,' gasped Katianna. 'How did you know I'd say yes?'

'I didn't,' he laughed taking the ring, still attached to the ribbon, and slipping it onto her finger. 'All I had was hope.'

She stared at the ring on her finger and wiping her tears she hugged Polis tight again. Not wanting to let him go. As she pulled away, she held out her hand, 'We're getting married,' she yelled, her eyes gleaming; an outpouring of emotion like fireworks filled the air and inside her a fluttering tightened her stomach.

Katianna spent the next few minutes looking from her ring to Polis and back again until almost dizzy with the pure adrenaline of it all.

Chapter 40

The flight back to London felt surreal after the overwhelming excitement of Polis' proposal and Katianna, despite paperwork sprawled out in front of her, did little reading or concentrating, barely marking any paragraphs in the margins with pencil. The four and a half hours seemed to drag; the imagined second hand on a clock deliberately in her head.

She grabbed a taxi straight from the airport to the office and summoned Angie within a few minutes of dumping her luggage and kicking off her heels.

'Welcome back,' she said and then, 'Oh my God. You're engaged,' she screamed as she ran round the desk and hugged Katianna.

'I am,' beamed Katianna, 'and this is going to be our most celebratory year ever.'

She filled Angie in on her few days, not skimming over any of the details like she usually did with anything pertaining to her personal life, all the while admiring her glittering engagement ring.

Angie ordered them a take-out lunch, on her, to mark Katianna's good news. She liked the relaxed Katianna and took advantage of the rare situation, saying, 'Don't rush back to your to-do list, indulge yourself, enjoy the moment.'

'I certainly did that,' she winked, dissolving into laughter. 'Now, what's been happening here?'

'Everything's in place for next year. I had a brief chat with everyone to clarify where we are going with this and how each of their areas of responsibility fit into the company's new structure and organisation,' said Angie.

'Thank you. You've certainly taken this role and made it your own,' said Katianna as she dipped her warm pitta bread into a pot of fresh coriander *houmous* from the deli.

'Thank you too for the opportunity. For trusting me.'

'The main thing is that it'll work and is sustainable,' said Katianna.

'We can do bi-weekly Zoom meetings to go over figures, include John too. That way we can stay on top of everything. I think working pro-actively as opposed to reactively is the way forward.'

'You're an absolute asset. And keeping John in the loop makes sense despite his faux pas. But he's shown nothing but regret over his mismanagement, so all is forgiven.'

'Everything happens for a reason.'

'True and I'm so grateful for everything you're doing. And how's your mum doing?'

'She's okay. There are good days and not so good days. When she's having a good day it's like there's absolutely nothing wrong with her, but the bad days are getting worse and coming more frequently.'

'I'm sorry.'

'All I can do is be there for her. I've got a fabulous girl, local, and she's been dropping by most days which allows me to work. We've come to an arrangement so it's succeeding, at least for now.'

'And Jamie?'

'Ticking along really well.'

'Anything you need, just ask. And thanks again for looking after things. Having you on board makes it all less stressful. You're the best person for the job.'

'Ooh, there's one more thing. A new offer and schedule have just been emailed across for filming. The proposal is for a Christmas show next year with filming in September.'

Later that same day, Katianna beamed; the stars were shining down on her and she felt like a ridiculously happy schoolgirl as her team celebrated her engagement during an impromptu drink's reception organised by Angie. It finally looked like things were working out.

***

The celebration felt like a lifetime ago and as Katianna, using all her powers of persuasion and business savvy worked on a strategy to keep all her staff happy and informed. The atmosphere and momentum at the office soon reached its peak again. The three newest recruits to the team were all in their early twenties, two living at home and one sharing a room with their girlfriend, so were grateful for the offer of a part-time six-month contract.

The agency had survived, and Katianna began to feel the effects of late nights juggling figures and problem-solving with Angie. John, four months into his recuperation was almost back to his previous levels of energy and focus but had not fully gained movement on one side of his upper body. His reduced role in the company was a welcome relief for him and he had thanked Katianna for keeping him on, not realising he would have been in the same position had he not suffered the TIA. But Katianna had taken advantage of the situation, turned it into a positive and the outcome was a win-win.

'Things are going well,' said Angie. 'We've got the investment from Vicky and there's nothing here that needs your personal attention.'

'I feel like I should be here. I shouldn't be walking away from the Godsend in the shape of Vicky's investors. I should be here to hold the reigns with you.'

'Go to the wedding, surprise Polis. He'd love you to be there. Don't disappoint him.'

'I've spent so much time out there already. I don't need to be there. I don't even know his cousin.'

'But he wants you there. It's what couples do, Kat. They support each other.'

'I've told him I'm not going. He'll get over it.'

'Why should he?' asked Angie gently.

'Weddings are huge out there. My best friend married a Cypriot and the wedding... well, let's just say it's the biggest most extravagant affair I've ever been to.'

'He won't even notice me missing.'

'Who are you kidding? Just go.'

'If it makes you feel better, I'll think about it tonight, sleep on it.'

'There's a flight out tomorrow night. You'll get in at two am. You'll easily make the wedding, without being jet-lagged, in the afternoon.'

'I suppose I could sleep on the flight out and be back on the same flight back that night.'

'You could,' said Angie, with a twinkle in her eye.

'You've become quite the mischievous little imp since dating Jamie,' said Katianna.

'Stop it.'

'Seriously though, having him to share the load must be a Godsend.'

'I didn't quite realise how much pressure I was under, and he is so accommodating and patient with me,' said Angie, almost swooning with emotion.

'He's good for you.'

'And Polis is good for you.'

They both sat, in silence, overlooking the new vista from the fourth floor where they had relocated the week before. Not as stunning, they had been spoilt with that from the twelfth floor, but thankfully something which still provided beautiful views across London. The move had been seamless; everyone had helped with the boxes.

The new space was already furnished in an almost identical way and so the only furniture they needed to move was four large filing cabinets which Katianna paid the caretakers to do for her. Her powers of persuasion benefitting all areas of her life.

'So have you decided?' asked Angie the following morning, as she dropped Katianna's coffee on her desk, turning the mug round so that the Cyprus image faced her.

'Very tactful,' said Katianna, smirking.

'I am.'

'I'm booked on the flight out tonight. Economy.'

'Yes!' Angie could not hide her happiness. 'You will have the best time.'

'It'll be an exhausting time.'

'But worth it,' Angie said with a twinkle.

'Go. I've work to do,' said Katianna, playfully and Angie skipped out of the office knowing Katianna would book her flight out to Cyprus. She was sure of it.

Chapter 41

Flying to Cyprus, quietly thanking Angie for persuading her to up and leave London, Katianna wished she could blink and already be in Cyprus; the four- and half-hour flight couldn't pass fast enough.

The following afternoon the service took place in the chapel of Omodos' mediaeval monastery; its tiny proportions forced many guests to wait outside for the bride and groom to make their exit.

Katianna, however, pushed her way in and sat in a pew at the back of the church. She wanted to surprise Polis. Wanted him to see she had made the effort to come to his cousin's wedding, despite insisting she was too busy to fly back, and it had taken a lot of persuasion to keep her trip a secret but the thrill of being present almost dissolved her into an ecstatic bout of joyous, nervous laughter and she was aware of a hot undignified swirling inside her. She put it down to being high on exhaustion, trying to ignore her insatiable arousal.

Thoughts came rushing at her and, for the first time in years, she dared to ponder her own wedding day and what it would be like. Goosebumps ran up her bare arms and she pulled her silk shawl over her shoulders. The natural masonry of the church's interior held the coolness of the stone until more guests piled in behind her.

A family lit their candles and pushed the tall slim tapers into the fast crowded and overflowing sand boxes. Others made the sign of the cross three times before kissing the heavily gilded icon of Mary hugging a baby Christ. Other icons resembled beautiful-veiled brides as embroidered Pipilla-lace mats, the technique and stitching famously associated with Omodos' most famous handicrafts, adorned the ancient images, or decorated the mounts of the icons. The mint of candles flickered a soft yellow light and the heat from the flames soon warmed the air, making it almost stifling if it not for the gentle waft of air entering via the open doors through which she took in the less sombre atmosphere.

Outside more guests chatted amicably as the October sunshine cast shafts of warm pinkish light through the low clouds sitting on the mountains, just hovering above the vineyards. Girls proud in their best dresses and boys awkward in their new shoes chased each other around the marble water fountain and under the monastery outer buildings' stone arches, the thousand-year-old laurel tree casting a shadow across their path. Their laughter rang through the church's entrance and only quietened for an instant, their parents directing admonishing glances at them. As quickly as they stopped running, they started again with renewed vigour when their parents' attention waned.

Katianna smiled in her happy place and for once wasn't thinking about work or the dating agency or the TV production company. Being in this holy place made her want to give everything up to God's universe and face what it mirrored back at her; she wondered whether this might be the right time to embrace whatever may be and trusted it would be for her good.

At the front of the church Polis, in his new suit and crisp white shirt, greeted family and hugged the bridesmaids and page boy. During their last conversation, the previous month he had animatedly filled Katianna in on having his suit made; all the details of his visits to the tailors and the many adjustments and alterations until it fit just right.

But on sharing her news of being unable to join him at the wedding Polis had displayed his disappointment with a terse goodbye, abruptly ending their call and they had not spoken since. Not properly. That was over a week ago. Katianna, swamped in making uncomfortable decisions inevitable to keep the business afloat and Polis avoiding any more confrontation, had given her the space she said she needed.

Katianna surveyed every part of him, taking in his stance, his expression, his demeanour; deep down she knew he would be all those things she had hoped for her in a husband and more. It was plain to see. He already supported her independence, celebrated her achievements as genuinely as she did his. He would be there to share her worries, stresses and to celebrate the good times too. And she hoped there would be many celebratory moments to enjoy.

Katianna listened carefully to the service, absorbing the atmosphere, tuning into the words of the priest: *you shall see the good things of Jerusalem all the days of your life... now being joined to one another... be granted unto them the happiness of abundant fertility... love for one another in a bond of peace... offspring long-lived... worthy to see their children's children... fill their houses with bountiful food...*

At the end of the ceremony, the bride and groom walked the few steps back up the narrow aisle to the chapel doors. Polis followed. Katianna stood tall, waiting for him to notice her. Her heart raced. She wanted to run to him but resisted. Holding out for the moment he would notice her. He paused. *Had he noticed her?* Her smile, full of so much happiness, faded, wilted like the water-starved flowers adorning the pew-ends. He searched the sea of faces in the first few rows of pews and with a full smile, which reached the crinkles at the corners of his eyes, took the hand of a tall woman who leaned in to kiss him.

Tears filled Katianna's eyes. *It hasn't taken him long to move on. What was I thinking?*

She stepped back into the recess, the long shadows camouflaging her. She didn't want him to see her so vulnerable, breaking like glass.

She walked out into the church's open courtyard, blindly fighting her tears and the overwhelming feeling she was going to pass out, her breaths short, filled with panic and shock.

Through her tears she watched the scene unfold, surprised at what she noticed; a vast number of people crowded round the emerging couple, throwing rice in handfuls at the bride and groom, a small child played a wooden flute which sent notes high into the air like majestic butterflies while others pushed forward to congratulate the happy couple. Mobile phones held in the air caught the happy couple's various poses as they patiently stood for photos with family, friends, and their parents. The official photographer yelled out his instructions for various shots he wanted to take and ushered everyone into position pointing to them from behind his tripod.

The guests began to disperse making their way on foot to the main square which was set up for the wedding reception.

Katianna watched Polis, through tear-stained eyes. The woman laughed, leaning into him, holding his hand, natural warmth seemed to emanate between them. Was this the woman Savva had mentioned to her? Was she the one who had got away? She looked like she was back to stay. Katianna's heart splintered into a thousand pieces.

Katianna searched the crowd for Savva. She found him and faking a headache asked him to walk her home.

'I need to lie down,' she said. 'Please, Savva.'

***

Three hours later, Katianna wandered around Larnaca Airport.

'Where are you?' Katianna could hear Savva breathing heavily down the phone.

'I caught an early cab to the airport.'

'I thought you weren't feeling well.'

'I couldn't stay.'

'Why? Polis said he didn't see you.'

'But I saw him.'

'What do you mean? What's going on?' asked Savva. 'What are you not telling me?'

'I saw him,' she blurted out. 'And her. The woman he was with.'

'Daphne?'

'All over each other.'

'Don't be ridiculous.'

'Don't cover for him. I saw them with my own eyes,' she said, choking back the tears.

'She's his cousin from America. She flew over for the wedding.'

'His cousin?'

'You didn't think she was his girlfriend, did you?'

'Omg. I need to talk to Polis. I've ruined everything. I've lost him,' she said, her frustration falling in big wet drops down her cheeks.

But the final call for her flight back to London forced her to board her flight home. She waited for a call from Polis hoping she could salvage the mess she had created through her own self-doubt and suspicious mind. The call she prayed for did not come.

Chapter 42

Back in London, Katianna couldn't shake off the feeling she had made the biggest mistake of her adult life. She sat at her desk, scrolling through her emails, opening, and closing them, unable to concentrate one minute and then throwing herself into work with such ferocity she no longer distinguished which day of the week it was or what time of day.

It had been a week since the wedding. The third "gate," Wedding-gate, as Angie called it and despite the turmoil of ruining what she had with Polis, Katianna had come to a decision. She was going to move her business to Cyprus. Why hadn't she thought of it before? She realised how her own stubbornness, having only ever had herself to rely on, had prevented her from taking Savva's previous suggestion about relocation seriously; that and her blinkered determination to keep things the same. But they weren't the same anymore and she knew she wanted to be in Cyprus, whether she sorted things out with Polis or not. Her outlook had changed. Her ambition had shifted.

All she needed was a base. Technology linked everything and everyone and with the support of HR she had been able to find a fair and workable solution. The staff would go self-employed, and work with *Under the Setting Sun* on a rolling contract. The only thing she had to work out was how to buy back her *yiayia's* house because as luck would have it the sale went through.

She needed to speak to Polis and hoped he had switched his phone back on. So far, every call she made to him had gone unanswered, his phone dead. She had considered emailing him but that felt too desperate and there was still a little stubborn nodule of pride prodding at her.

She felt a thrilling anxiety mixed with excitement finally deciding to seize her destiny and create the outcome she wanted. She felt a tingle at the base of her neck. She had the first seeds of a plan and as the seeds unfurled, she hoped it would work, believed more than ever it was the right decision.

***

Two weeks later, counting down the days till the week before Christmas, Katianna looked forward to Polis coming to London. He had gracefully accepted her invitation, and grovelling apology for jumping to conclusions, though she knew she had hurt his feelings, dented his integrity and behaved like a spoilt child.

She had a lot to recompense, and her mind overflowed with the places she wanted to take him and the sights they would see together. She fantasised about the moments they would share. Filled with fortitude, and a girl-going-on-her-first-date kind of elation, she planned their time together meticulously. Nothing could go wrong.

In the office Katianna spent her days oscillating between manic work-based decision-making and tirelessly working all day without a break to sitting at her desk day dreaming, her thoughts imagining Polis in her arms.

'You're going to have the best Christmas,' said Angie.

Katianna uncharacteristically marked off another day in her diary with a red heart; her fingers gently running over the numbered pages counting down the days until his arrival.

Angie had bustled in with the sheet of heart-shaped stickers one morning. Katianna had secretly loved the idea, the teenage romance of it, but publicly she laughed, fobbing it off as too sentimental.

'I hope so. It's a shame he can't be here for Christmas but at least we'll get some time together during the festive season.'

'London's so romantic with all the lights and Christmas trees, carol singers and choirs,' she said, placing a bottle of bubbly and two glasses on Katianna's desk.

'I hope so,' said Katianna, a moment of doubt making her wobbly.

'It'll be amazing. Who are you kidding?'

'And you are too. How did your suggestion go with Jamie?'

'He loved it and so did our mums,' Angie said, while carefully popping the cork. 'So, the four us will be spending Christmas Day together at a local boutique hotel just in case Mum gets confused or we need to get her home.'

'That's perfect, Angie. I'm so happy for you. Jamie's a lucky man.'

'And I'm a lucky woman,' she said and pouring out the champagne they clinked their glasses together in a celebratory toast.

It felt as though the last few months had mellowed Katianna in so many ways, at work, at home, with Polis. She had found a new strength in having someone by her side, someone to stand in her corner. She had accepted his nurturing side, rejecting what she once would have thought of as mollycoddling and she felt like his equal. She relished the sound of his voice, their talking long into the night, the simplicity, the security, and realised she had what thousands of other people her age had, and she liked it. She liked it a great deal. She liked the way Polis was willing to focus on her and make her shine, not worrying about dimming his own light, glorying in her light with her.

She embraced her exhaustion, physical and mental, looking forward to the end of the day and meeting him at the airport, a smile playing on her lips despite her jittery fatigue.

Chapter 43

The snow fell. A wild flurry of snowflakes danced and melted against the office window. Within half an hour the snowy ground and white-dusted roofs created a picturesque Dickensian London; lights twinkled, the settled snow glittered, bright and powdery, and pedestrian footprints dotted the pavements below like a tiny winter pin-prick scene on a sheet of white paper.

Katianna fidgeted, brushed a strand of hair from her face, browsed through her mail, not really reading any of it and moving it from one pile to another back and forth from one side of her desk to the other. Polis was arriving in five hours. In five hours, he would be here, and she would be in his arms. A tingle zapped through her as she pictured him wrapping his strong arms around her.

She took out her compact and patted her face with powder to abate its sweaty sheen and touched up her eyes. She finished off with a red outline around her lips and carefully filled it with her ruby lipstick. Pressing her lips together she surveyed herself in the tiny mirror, noticing the tiny fine-line fans around her eyes and a blemish on her chin. She patted some more powder over the mark, concealing it. If only it was as easy to conceal her bubbling emotions.

The rest of the afternoon dragged painfully like a piece of chalk across a board and finally she decided to head out to the airport. She could have a coffee if she were too early for his arrival.

Katianna tightened her woolen coat's belt and pulled up the collar against the snowy chill. She looked in all directions for a taxi but the two she spotted drove by ignoring her waving hand. She continued walking, crossed at the lights, hoping to catch one further along but at almost five o'clock and still nowhere she knew she should have booked a cab. Just as she turned to go back to the office a taxi appeared, and she quickly hailed it to a stop. Just as she closed the door, she glanced up and through the cab's window saw Angie; her shoulders hunched, her usual upright stance amiss, making her smaller and more vulnerable than ever.

'Wait here for me,' she told the driver. 'I'll be one minute.' Katianna rushed over to her, aware her feet slid across the snowy street precariously. 'What's the matter?' she asked Angie, grabbing her by the arm, disorientated by the fear welling inside her.

'It's Mum. She's had some sort of accident... a car... I'm not sure...' Tears streaked her rosy cheeks and bubbles of snot popped from her nose.

'Oh my, is she in hospital?

'She's with a neighbour. I need to get to her but can't think straight. The world feels off kilter.'

'Don't worry. I'll come with you... I've got a cab waiting.'

'No... you've got to get to the airport.'

'I've got plenty of time. And if I'm late Polis will wait for me.'

They sprinted to the cab double parked across the road, traffic already building up with the heavy fall of snow. A bus had stopped in the middle lane, its hazard-warning indicators flashing; the road too hazardous for it to continue.

Katianna waved her apology to a car as it slammed its brakes to avoid hitting her and Angie. The narrow miss added more havoc to the rush hour traffic.

'Here,' Katianna said, handing her a tissue once in the waiting vehicle. 'She'll be fine. If she's with a neighbour she can't be hurt, at least not seriously.'

Angie nodded unable to speak.

Forty minutes later, Angie was already opening the door before the taxi had even come to a standstill outside a boldly illuminated semi. The snowy pavements were already inches thick with fresh snowdrifts and the heavy sky threatened a blizzard as the snowflakes swayed in an angry whirl on the blustery wind.

Angie navigated the steep decline of the path and pushed through the neighbour's gate, tottering in her high heels. Katianna, close behind, grabbed Angie by the sleeve and just managed to stop Angie from toppling on the slippery slope and into a row of three LED white reindeer.

In the front room Christmas decorations of varying sizes and colours and styles choked every surface. Angie's mum sat by the gas fire; her legs wrapped in a knitted festive blanket of so many clashing colours it almost made Katianna dizzy.

'Mum. What happened?' asked Angie, her voice gentle and full of love as she knelt beside her, her handbag discarded on the floor next to a miniature blow-up Santa and his sleigh.

'Nothing my darling, I'm having a nice cup of tea with... with...' she didn't finish her sentence, the name of her neighbour evading her fading memory.

'Janice said you had an accident,' she looked to Janice for confirmation.

'She walked out behind a car. I was just getting back with the last of my Christmas shopping,' said Janice. 'It was reversing into a parking space. I guess the snow flurry made visibility difficult. I saw her fall.'

'Oh, Mum,' said Angie.

'But I don't think there's any lasting damage. She may be a bit sore, but the bruising will fade in a couple of days. She's scuffed her hands and knees quite badly, but I've smoothed a little antiseptic across the cuts.' She turned to Angie's mum. 'And you're fine aren't you, my love?'

'Lovely decorations... I must ask my daughter to help me with mine,' Angie's mum said.

Angie got up off the floor and walked out to the kitchen, biting on her lower lip to stop the tears. Katianna followed her into the kitchen and Janice came bustling in after them.

'She's not even acknowledging me. She's talking about me as if I'm not here.'

'I'll put the kettle on. She's fine Angie. A bit confused. The gentleman was most apologetic and left all his details in case you wanted to speak to him.'

'Speak to him? I'm going to throttle him.'

'That's not a clever idea when you're emotional and tired, Angie. Wait until morning. The main thing is your mum's conscious and seems quite happy. Go and sit with her. We'll make the tea,' said Katianna.

Angie left the two women to make the hot drinks. She went back into the sitting room and her gentle voice could be heard as she cooed, 'I love you, Mum.'

Two cups of tea later, and overindulgence in home-baked shortbreads, mince pies and dried-fig balls, Katianna kissed everyone good night and ran out to her waiting cab; the impatient hooting of the driver reverberating across the silence of the little cul-de-sac and as she settled back into the taxi she knew she had found something good in Angie; a mutual friendship filled with love and respect and, despite being pulled into the harrowing situation, she was grateful.

Chapter 44

The busy concourse leading to the airport building, thankfully already gritted, crunched under Katianna's shoes with every hurried step. She was late but knew Polis was still waiting for her; they had spoken briefly during her taxi ride over.

As she neared the arrivals area a ball of anxiety began to unwind like a ball of wool in her chest. She slowed to calm her beating heart and then saw him in the distance; recognising the back of his head her heart gave a little leap and, as if sensing her approach, Polis turned and fixed his eyes on her.

His arms around her felt surreal and she pushed into him as if wanting to verify his realness, his being there. Lost in the moment, they kissed, dithered, and then kissed again, deeper this time.

'So good to see you,' he gasped, swallowing her in gulps, hugging her tight.

'You too and sorry I'm late. There was an incident with Angie, and I just couldn't let her deal with it alone.' Katianna took in Polis' travel-creased face. His woody smell lingered on her coat and on her skin from pressing into each other, pouring into each other and she didn't realise she was crying, with joy, until she tasted the trickle of her salty tears.

'It's fine. I passed through customs not even half an hour ago. And you're here now.'

Katianna wondered what Polis would make of her apartment; a complete contrast in style and ambiance to her *yiayia's* house in the village.

Katianna observed him from a distance; he unwound his scarf and unbuttoned his jacket. Laying it neatly on the back of the sofa he walked to the window.

'You weren't wrong when you said you had a magnificent view,' he said.

After a few seconds he turned around and beckoned Katianna over. He took her hands in his and leaning close to her breathed into her ear, 'This is what I've been waiting for.' She buried her face into his neck, feeling the softness of his ears against her head.

They kissed again, this time any inhibitions pushed to the side, no one watching, in their own private world, and within minutes they were tearing at each other's clothes like hormonal teenagers discarding their uniforms in celebration at reaching the end of another school year. They dropped their clothes in heaps, leaving a trail across the living room, as Katianna led him to the bedroom. Katianna knocked into the sideboard in the hallway and winced. She bumped her shoulder into the door frame as they pushed into the bedroom, her excitement dulling the pain.

They collapsed onto the bed, explored each other with a raw passion and an ignited desire so full they tore at each other; hands, tongues, fingers, teeth, lips. Katianna drank in his heat, and it changed her whole body. She breathed in his scent, his evident excitement; she knew he felt the charge of electricity between them. She picked up the remote and the blinds closed over the bedroom windows. They tussled, animal-like hungry, desperate for each other.

The next hour passed in a haze of beautiful indulgence and a sexual tension which sent Katianna to the edge of somewhere she had never been and as they violently released their longing, she screamed his name. They came, together; Katianna felt ethereal, ecstatic, eternal.

***

Katianna picked up Polis' jacket and tucked his scarf inside the sleeve. 'If you need your jacket it's hanging in the hallway,' she called to him, smiling at the simple domesticity of her behaviour. She shook her hair out of the towel turbaned around it and ran her fingers through the wet strands.

Her white tightly belted robe accentuated her full hour-glass figure, and she could feel Polis surveying her from behind. She turned to face him as he padded barefoot to her, wearing a pair of jogging bottoms and a T-shirt. A shiver ran through her as she surveyed his shoulders straining across the cotton fabric as he stretched in a yawn, the dark hair on his belly flipping her tummy.

'Nice shower?' she asked.

'It's a great shower. It's got such a lot of power. All that water.'

'The water rates are astronomical but at least I get my money's worth,' she smiled as she took two mugs from the glass fronted cabinet and put them on the granite worktop.

'Has Savva told you how ecstatic the villagers continue to be about the well and its water supply? You're a hero for the second time,' he laughed.

'The magical well. I still can't believe it.'

He wrapped his arms around her waist from behind; pulling her damp hair to one side he nuzzled her neck and grazed her skin gently with his chin and then, turning her round, his lips found hers. A shiver curled its way inside her; a different level of intimacy existed between them, and it ping-ponged back and forth making her giddy. She weakened in his arms, letting him carry the weight of her.

'I've got the best four days planned for us,' she said.

'I've got everything I need to make them the best right here in front of me,' he said, as he twirled a lock round his finger.

And with a note of desperation, she said, 'I can't believe I nearly lost you.'

'If it hadn't been for your savage stubbornness, you might just have,' he teased and then more serious, 'If it's any consolation I thought about you the whole time, wished you'd made it to the wedding. It was quite by chance Savva mentioned you putting two and two together and making two million! But my phone was playing up and it took a few days to get it replaced. I didn't see your messages and then, when I finally did, wanted to give you some space.'

'Proof surprises don't always work out how we imagine.' She smiled weakly and in that second, he too looked vulnerable, unsure of himself and Katianna knew. Knew she loved him. Knew he loved her back.

Chapter 45

The first night of Polis' London visit they hibernated in Katianna's flat and ordered food from the local pizzeria. Polis fed her pizza and pieces of mozzarella drizzled in olive oil and balsamic, while she slipped salty anchovies and slices of vine-ripened baby tomatoes into his mouth. They shared a pot of salted caramel ice-cream and laughed at the way he pulled a face with every spoonful.

'Who puts salt into an ice-cream?' he complained each time she pushed another dessertspoonful between his lips.

'It's trendy… it's one of those fads.'

'Sugar and salt? It's a heart attack in a tub,' he argued through his laughter. 'Give me pistachio or vanilla.'

Katianna made a mental note. There was so much she still needed to learn about him, that they both didn't know about each other.

'I think we're going to have a lot of fun together, you, me and this big city of mine.'

'A toast to fun, and love in London,' he said.

They clinked their glasses and Katianna drained her half glass of red in one swallow. She breathed in the air as if wanting to swallow the words which hung between them like the tinkle of a Christmas bell.

After eating Polis made himself useful; Katianna secretly liked how he loaded the dishwasher and happy he was someone who didn't divide chores into women's work and men's work like so many Greek Cypriots still did. He emptied the last of the wine, sharing it between their two glasses and Katianna snuggled into him on the couch. She liked the way her body moulded into his, smooth like clay and soft like butter in all the right places.

'So, what do you have planned for me?'

'Trafalgar Square, The London Eye, The British Museum and of course Carnaby Street and Fortnum and Mason and Simpsons, lunch at Claridges, dinner at The Savoy…' she trailed off. He looked at her as if seeing her for the first time.

'I like this organised, knowledgeable, confident side to you… the masterful side.'

'Masterful?'

'Yes.'

'So would you like to see more of my masterful side?' she hiccupped.

'Oh, yes,' he said, and she screamed as he tickled her and pulled her closer, kissing her deep.

'This is the famous Trafalgar Square,' he said, looking at the stone lions bathed in a frosty-ice coating. 'They don't look as big as I always imagined, or as ferocious. Their backs don't look right,' he said, gazing at one of the iconic brass statues.

'Ha! You're good. The lion's back should be concave when lying down and not convex. It's a design mistake.'

'I can see that,' he said.

'You can?'

'In truth I read it in my guidebook.'

'I love that about you. You always seem to be learning, lapping up new things. And your attention to detail was so thorough when we met to discuss the refurbishment of the house that I intuitively knew you would be the right person for the job,' she said.

He pulled her further across the square, slipping and almost losing her balance, he held onto her, keeping her upright. She laughed and he noticed the tinge of red across her cheeks deepen as she shied away from him.

They wandered around taking photos for another twenty minutes, Nelson's Column silhouetted against the bluest winter sky. They spied the tiny police box on the southeast corner of the square and roped in a tourist, hunched over from the bulky weight of his backpack, to take a photo of them. They posed together, awkward in their big coats and scarves but smiling all the same.

Chapter 46

Within a week, Katianna flew out to Cyprus to be with Polis, unable to keep apart from him. She woke up in Polis' bedroom which was unusually light and matched Katianna's mood; a floating-on-air-lovey-dovey mood. She carefully extricated herself from under Polis' arm; he stirred but continued to sleep soundly. Slipping on one of his jumpers Katianna ambled to the kitchen, his kitchen.

She turned on the radio and listened to the morning mix of old Greek ballads and love songs. Love was all around her and she swayed a little to the rhythms and hummed along to the melodies.

She propped up her mobile on the counter in front of her and furrowed her brow in concentration. She cracked four eggs into a bowl, added a splash of milk, and a dash of seasoning and whisked until super fluffy, going through the steps of Sofia's online cookery video. The knob of butter melted, sizzling in the old copper pan. She poured in the egg mixture, threw in grated halloumi, and sliced tomatoes just before the liquid set, resulting in the perfect omelette.

She messed around with his coffee machine until it finally bubbled and gurgled to attention, poured coffee into two of the biggest cups she could find and slid four thick slices of sesame-topped *koulouri* under the grill. Just as the bread browned, Polis padded out of the bedroom in a T-shirt and his boxer shorts. She turned and came face to face with his dark eyes staring at her.

'Good morning,' he said, kissing her.

'Good morning,' she said as she picked at the toast crumbs on the worktop, unable to stop her flow of laughter.

'What's so funny?'

'Absolutely nothing. This is happy laughing. Pure, blissful, happy laughing.'

'Making breakfast makes you happy?' he teased.

'Making breakfast for us makes me happy.'

They carried everything over to the verandah and sat together; totally comfortable in each other's company; the old chairs groaning as if in protest under the weight of them, an old plough looking on as if proud of them both, sharing its enduring strength and longevity.

'You can cook,' he said, as he took another gulp of coffee.

'You can't call this cooking. Cooking is what I did with Sofia. She taught me a lot and one of the recipes was my *yiayia's,* such a wonderful discovery.' She smiled, her heart thumping in her chest, aware of a flush across her cheeks. It had felt good to be cooking with Sofia.

He leaned close to her and tucked a strand of hair behind her ear. He cupped the side of her face in his big strong hand, rough but full of gentleness. 'You're beautiful Katianna.' He reached for her hand and beckoned her to sit in his lap. She didn't make him wait long for a response; Katianna's body arched towards him and kissing him back she almost ran out of air as she swallowed him.

There on the verandah, in the shadow of an orange tree, quickly forgetting the cold against their skin, their lovemaking found a different rhythm, their bodies instinctively knowing, listening to each other and, as if playing in tune with each other's, found a momentum which united them in a blissful peak. Within minutes, she sat moulded into his chest satisfied; he wrapped his arms around her adjusting the jumper to cover her bare shoulder. They didn't say anything. They didn't have to. Their hearts beat fast, their breathing erratic. Katianna opened her eyes after a few seconds and took in the image of her and Polis reflected in the sliding door behind them. This was real and she was not in as much control as she thought. But she didn't care.

A few hours later the snow had settled thick and hard across the

Troodos Mountain tops and their feet sloshed through the melted snow as it trickled across the hardened ground. Katianna's mind drifted to London; it had snowed again there, and the news had been full of busy clips: delivery vans, taxis and cars, couriers on motorcycles and cyclists who, despite the dangerously treacherous conditions, seemed to be relentlessly getting on with their day's business.

Sitting quietly, Katianna dissolved into the sights and sounds of London as they flooded her mind; the brightly painted buildings along Camden high street, the beautiful town houses of Swiss Cottage, the red brick monstrosities built in the 70s by the council, decrepit three and four-storey buildings in Islington; all dusted, she knew, with a powdery layer of snow.

'Different from London but surprisingly pretty all the same,' she said, taking in the tall snow-dusted pines, the icy protruding roots like gnarled fingers and the songbird filling the icy air with a happiness she felt oozing from deep inside of her.

It was only just noon and the weather conditions no doubt kept many from venturing out onto the icy roads. Katianna's scarf flew across her face in the icy wind as the gust threatened to pull if from her. Katianna knew her nose and cheeks were, within minutes, red from the bite of winter. She held her hands in front of her face, blew into them to warm her, and imagined her ice-blue lips thawing to pink again. Polis pulled off his woolen gloves and slipped them over her hands.

Later that same day, the warmth of the flames from an oil drum crackled as the chestnuts browned and prickled her cold face. Katianna sneezed as she pulled her coat tighter. The sound of the spitting echoed across the relative buzz of the people lining up behind them.

'You look miles away,' Katianna said to Polis.

'Memories... they creep up on you when you least expect them.'

'Good ones?'

'Stories of old, Christmas traditions, the *kallikantzaroi.*'

'Oh, yes,' she giggled.

Polis pulled her close, his arm tight around her waist and Katianna fought off more than a spark of fire growing within her. She thought about Polis and how equally comfortable he was with long-ago traditions and modern-day culture, how he voiced his thoughts openly and with no inhibitions. She liked that about him. It was a strength. It was a unique thread which connected her to him, and she had only just realised what a strong and endearing characteristic it was.

'Your *yiayia* must have spoken about the little elves who pop out of nowhere between Christmas and Epiphany to cause havoc. Old traditional tales but I cling onto them all the same.'

'There's something about traditions and being here which, I like. And which haven't entered my thoughts for a long time.'

Chapter 47

'I didn't realise Cyprus twinkled quite as much as it does this time of year, it's like a dreamy picture-book illustration. It's breathtaking despite the cold.'

'You're not missing your festive London streets and crowded shop floors?' mocked Polis.

'Not much. It's beautiful here. I underestimated it.'

And as Katianna looked across at Polis, she knew that it wouldn't matter where she was, if she was with him, it would all be right in the end. Perhaps her fairytale ending was closer than she thought. And in that moment a whole new dimension revealed itself to her; her past and her present had merged, and she revelled in the enchanted feeling of it.

The restaurant, though sectioned in half and its huge all-round balcony closed for winter, was magical with just enough decorations to bring home the feel of Christmas. Holly twigs and dried orange segments, little bundles of cinnamon sticks and red velvet bows adorned the huge open fireplace; its heavy wooden surround varnished to a high shine, reflecting the twinkling fairy lights draped over it. The huge mirror above it reflected the glowing light of an antique chandelier and mirrored its hundreds of clear crystal drops.

The waiter appeared and handed them each a menu. He laid the wine menu on the table beside Polis and disappeared. Within minutes he re-appeared with a *tsestos*, colourful-woven basket, of warmed bread and two bottles of water, one sparkling and one still.

Once the waiter had taken their food order, Polis took Katianna's hands in his and held them across the table, gently massaging her palms with his thumbs. She felt the tingle make its way through her and for a moment allowed herself to be lost in it, that warm feeling.

'It's been another wonderful day,' said Polis.

'It has though the snow has ruined my boots,' she groaned.

'We can buy new boots.'

Something in the simplicity of his statement made her heart burst. She leaned over and gave him a kiss. Aware the other diners, locals with their families, were staring she threw caution to the wind, a new daring in her revealing itself, and gave him a second kiss.

'Guess that was the right thing to say,' he said.

'It was and I'm so glad to be here, with you. It's been a wonderful couple of days.'

'And the next two will be too. Let's make a toast,' he said, raising his wine glass, 'to us and the magic of Christmas in Cyprus.'

'And to my *yiayia*, for bringing us together. May God rest her soul.'

Katianna clinked her glass against his and the sharp ringing filled the air above the low hum of conversation around them. She settled back in her chair and recognised the happiness which filled her. She was content and this man, though not here for long, had already become a part of her, her thoughts, her actions, her reactions, and her plans for the future. Where this would take her, she didn't know but she was at last, after all this time, willing to try and see.

Katianna added a sprinkling of pepper to her *avgolemoni soup.* The aroma of chicken and lemons filled her senses and her stomach rumbled with her first spoonful.

'Absolutely delicious,' she said, licking her lips. 'I bet if Sofia was here, she would have something to say. She's so creative with her cooking. Her skills are amazing. She adds a little Sofia twist to all her dishes.'

'She certainly does and I'm sure her business is doing increasingly well now that she's a regular guest on *Cook with Athena.*'

'I'm so pleased for her. She's a natural in front of the camera,' said

Katianna between spoonfuls.

'She deserves the success. She works too hard though I think Savva's taking up some of her time now.'

'I'm glad. I've realised how much I sacrificed to make the dating agency a success and its time I can never get back.'

'Do you regret it?'

'No, not at all. It's been a phenomenal achievement, despite the financial issues which need to be ironed out. But I've brought so many people together and brought happiness to them which in turn has also made me happy.'

'And now you've met me?'

'And now I've met you I'm even happier.' Katianna rested her spoon having finished her soup and dabbed at her mouth with her linen napkin suddenly embarrassed by her open proclamation. She peered at Polis from under her long dark lashes and saw the smile playing around his lips. They were both happy... but how long would it last?

The waiter cleared their plates and placed their main courses in front of them. 'For you, beef moussaka and roasted vegetables.'

'Delicious. Thank you,' said Katianna.

'Dear Polis, sea bass with fried potatoes and *bourgouri. Kalin orexi*,' said the waiter as he topped their wine glasses and edged away from the table.

Katianna finally pushed back her chair slightly and crossed one leg over the other, folded her napkin across her lap. She sipped at the strong cup of Cypriot coffee, its aroma rich and dark. Dessert had filled her to the brim; the milky custard and cracker dessert tasted divine. She felt a little giddy and hoped the coffee settled her. It had been a long day albeit a good day and she again had enjoyed Polis' company. He was generous in his conversation, gentle in his thoughts and seeing more of his social side pleased her. He was someone she would happily spend more time with but again wasn't ready to commit to anything big in terms of where they would live and how it would work out in the long term.

The bitter cold, as they stepped out into the road, pushed drifts of flurrying snow around her face and bit at Katianna's skin. It found its way under her collar. She pulled her scarf tighter. She shivered and Polis put his arm around her. 'Come on let's get you home,' he said.

'Home,' she said and felt the happiest she had ever been.

Chapter 48

'You said no work until after New Year,' said Polis, catching Katianna at her laptop early in the morning. They had spent the night in her *yiayia's* house.

'I couldn't sleep any longer. I'm not used to sharing a bed with someone… not that I'm complaining.'

Polis hesitated, 'I'm sorry you're not sleeping properly with me. I guess we both have some adapting to do.'

'It's not you. It's everything. The house. The way it makes me feel. The way you make me feel. And you're right. It's about adapting.'

'And what else can you do about the house?'

'John's still pushing me to honour the sale despite the decisions I've made about running the business remotely, says we still need the injection of funds. But I just can't bring myself to tell him I want it back. The buyer's his sister and, though she's helped me with so much already, I'm not sure I want to let go of it. It's the last tangible ancestral link I have connecting me to my roots, my *yiayia*. Letting go feels so final. Like the end of something and if I'm going to make a life here there's nowhere else, I'd rather set up home.' She slammed shut her laptop. 'I'm stuck between Aphrodite's Rock and the Troodos mountains.' Polis gave her a quizzical look. 'Sorry but you know what I mean. The money from the filming won't be paid out till after the TV series has aired. I can't wait that long. What other choice do I have?'

'There's always a choice,' Polis said gently.

'I've spent ten years building a business. It's taken so much of me, too many hours and days.' She emailed John and followed with a quick text before she could change her mind. 'I'll call the solicitor and tell him I'm ready.'

Polis looked over at her and without saying anything pulled her close. 'All will work out the way it should. Trust me,' he said. She looked past his shoulder to the distant landscape through the icy windows; tiny, crystallised snowflakes clung to the window, and she felt him shiver. 'Let's have a coffee and some of those Scottish cookies you keep going on about.'

'For breakfast?' giggled Katianna.

Polis opened drawers and cutlery clanged on the old granite work surface. She liked the way he moved, and his gaze flitted from what he was doing back to her constantly. He filled a space which, until now, she hadn't realised was even there. It was Polis-shaped and no one else could fill it before without making her feel claustrophobic.

She wondered how long it would take to get used to him sleeping with her. She remembered how so many of her more mature clients had found this the most difficult aspect of having a partner to adapt to; having another person in their space when they were used to sharing it intimately with no one for so long.

Katianna snuggled on the over-stuffed, wood-framed couch he had rescued from being thrown out. She listened as Polis poured the coffee. When she heard the clash of the grill pan and the scent of bread warming under the grill, she realised he had changed his mind about eating shortbread for breakfast.

'Breakfast is ready,' he smiled.

He placed the bamboo tray, with the map of Cyprus on it, in front of her and opened the pot of honey and sliced the creamy feta cheese, which fell in crumbly slabs onto the plate. Katianna stretched and he leaned in to kiss her nose.

'I'm going to get used to you and wonder why I have no breakfast waiting for me in the mornings back in London…' Her voice trailed away, and she bit her bottom lip forcing back the tears which threatened to come. She shook herself out of the melancholy which suddenly draped her shoulders like the wings of a raven and sneezed.

'Maybe you won't have to. Maybe we can work something out.' He waited, holding his breath in anticipation of her response. Her shoulders perked up and her eyes widened.

'What are you saying?' She sneezed again and blew into a tissue.

'Bless you. I'm saying that maybe it won't always be like this.'

'Don't say things just to placate me or make me feel better Polis, that's not fair,' she mumbled through a mouthful.

'I wouldn't do that. I promise. But I have a plan and if it works out you will be happy. We both will.' He spread the honey onto his toasted bread and took a bite. 'Reminds me of my own dear grandmother. She used to spread her honey generously.'

'The good old days had their best bits too... happy memories.' Katianna's mobile vibrated next to her on the couch. She glanced at it ready to ignore the call but saw Angie's name flash across the screen. 'Angie, what's up?'

'I know you're not here but I'm not in the office either.'

'Is everything okay?'

'I've been at the hospital. Mum collapsed a couple of days ago, they thought it was pneumonia.'

'I'm so sorry. What's happening?'

'She's out of ICU and hopefully home tomorrow.'

'Keep in touch and I'm so sorry. Send her my love.' She ended the call and looked at Polis. 'I hope this isn't a sign of how the rest of the day is going to go...'

'What sorry... I'm just checking a couple of things here that can't wait... do you mind if I use your laptop?'

'No sure, go ahead.'

'Emailing on this tiny phone keypad is ridiculous with my clumsy fingers and going to the office will take too long with the ice on the roads. The snow has been swept down from the mountains with those ferocious winds.'

'I'm going to take a hot shower. I'm feeling chilly.'

In the tiny bathroom with the stone shower tray and brass spray head, Katianna fought against an uncomfortable feeling. For what did Polis need the laptop? It was the first time he had mentioned work since her arrival, and it discombobulated her. She hoped there was nothing about to explode which would spoil their last few days. So far, their time together had been unblemished; Polis the perfect partner. She hoped it wasn't just what they called the honeymoon period.

Showered and dressed, she pulled the bedroom door open, slipping her jumper over her head. She heard him talking in a hushed voice; she hesitated and stayed where she was, listening.

'I'm sure, yes… of course I'm going to pay you your cut. That's what we agreed and I'm a man of my word.' She peered into the sitting room and watched his posture go from relaxed to stiff and rigid. 'No, no, I'm not going to mention anything to her. I need to be sure it's happened.'

She shivered and leaned onto the door jamb for support. The words I'm not going to mention anything to her flooding her with memories of her ex and the carnage his lies and cheating left behind him. What was he referring to? What was he not ready to tell? Suddenly the room spun. Polis' voice came in and out of earshot, evasive murmurings of my love, my love and she lost focus. She felt the colour drain from her face and blacked out.

Chapter 49

'Katianna, Katianna...' Polis gently splashed a little water on her face. He propped her head up with his hand. 'Please wake up...'

'What?' she said, as Polis face, close to hers, came in and out of focus.

'You fainted, my darling. I don't think you've banged your head.'

She leaned into him, and he pulled her to her feet careful not to rush her. He guided her over to the lumpy old couch, she slumped into it like a rag doll. 'I heard you speaking... what's going on?'

'Nothing. Nothing at all. Let me bring you a glass of water.'

'Don't fob me off, Polis. I know you're hiding something,' she said and burst into tears.

'Don't cry my love.'

'That's two things gone wrong. They come in threes...'

'Now's not the time for this. We can talk when you've stopped shaking,' he said, handing her the glass.

'I'm fine, Polis.' Katianna took a couple of sips and pushed back into the cushions behind her. 'Now... tell me... please.'

'I didn't want to tell you like this. You know how much I love you, don't you?'

'Tell me what?' Her eyes shone fiercely, and Polis took in a deep breath before speaking again.

'I'm selling sixty-five percent of my building business. I'll be a silent partner from now on.'

'You are? Why?'

'I own three holiday lets. Cyprus is an all-year-round destination, so my income is stable.'

'What are you saying?'

'I'm planning on living my life with you. We're going to be married. It makes sense.'

'And?'

'Well, that's the other bit. I have another surprise for you. Two surprises.'

'There's more?'

'I've used the money from the business to re-invest in a property.'

'To expand your property portfolio?'

'Not exactly.'

'I don't understand?'

'I've bought back your *yiayia's* house for you.'

'The village house?'

'Yes.'

'Why would you do that?'

'For you. You wanted it.'

'Don't make this about me and what I want. You've done what?' Katianna's eyes widened in disbelief. 'You have waltzed in and bought my *yiayia's* house without discussing it?'

'No, it's not like that. I've got you back the house and saved your business at the same time,' Polis said, stepping back, stunned at her reaction.

'And I'm supposed to be grateful?'

'Not grateful. I wanted to show you how much I care.'

'Oh, my goodness. You don't know me at all. You don't know what you've done.' Katianna became hysterical.

'Please, my darling. I thought you'd be happy.'

'Happy? To be indebted to you?'

'No. I love you. There's no debt. I've done it to help you,' Polis said.

'To keep me here in Cyprus more like. To keep me under your thumb.'

'Katianna, please...'

234

'I don't need your help. I never asked for it.' She tugged at her engagement ring and with one last twist she pulled it off and threw it at him.

Polis, started to say something but the words came out mumbled. He grabbed his jacket and left as she screamed, 'Get out, get out. Go.'

Tears streamed down her face; serendipity had been her magical, guardian angel of luck one minute and her cloak of darkness the next.

She could not face him. He had deceived her. Lied to her. She threw her belongings into her suitcase, texted a quick message to Savva and Sofia using a work emergency as an excuse for leaving so suddenly.

Sobbing, she locked up the village house, for the last time, and left without glancing back.

Chapter 50

London was bitterly cold. Colder than her mood and colder than Cyprus had been which annoyed her. She FaceTimed with Sofia and flooded with angry, hot tears which she couldn't stop or wanted to stop.

'How dare he!' she blasted, telling Sofia the real reason for her rushed departure.

'He did it out of love. Love for you and for what he thought you had together.'

'How could I have been so blind to what he was up to. Men!'

'Polis is an honest man. His reputation in business is unflawed.'

'This isn't business. This is personal,' said Katianna, thumping her fist into one of the sofa cushions.

'It is personal, yes. But it's not underhand.'

'He could have discussed it. I didn't need rescuing. I told him about the predicament I was in because I thought that's what couples did. Shared their good times and their problems.'

'He wanted to help you.'

'Without discussing it. Going behind my back. That's sneaky. Manipulative.'

'Look, he's not your ex. He was trying to do something nice for you.'

'I don't need nice. I need open, honest, and kind.'

'And what he did isn't kind?' Katianna picked up on Sofia's

exasperation.

Katianna tipped back her glass of wine and swallowed. 'I'm tired and I've got an early meeting with the bank tomorrow,' she said, but she was embarrassed to hear her own stubborn hostility.

***

For the next few days Katianna worked on auto pilot, ignoring the usually magical few days before Christmas. She immersed herself into her business and coincidentally received a nomination for Most Driven Femalepreneur run by Cosmopolitan Magazine. She didn't feel any pride or worthy of the award though it went some way to reminding her of her success. The award ceremony came and went. The usual excitement surrounding her attendance was faded, flat; she admitted how tired and fed up she felt.

John was unable to keep up with Katianna's demands, her irrational thoughts, her stubborn single-mindedness, and he recognised Katianna's new-found energy as a way of controlling the business and her future. Vicky came through with alternate silent investors and Katianna rewarded her with a sumly commission which was worth every penny. She did not mention her *yiayia's* house too incensed by the situation to talk about it. Katianna longed to be back in control, but sensed she was a long way from being at the helm of her ship again.

But Savva, Sofia and Angie knew her manic energy was a way of avoiding her true feelings for Polis; Katianna steered away from any conversation which wasn't about the business and its planned relocation. That was one thing she had no doubts about. She joined in the Christmas office party reluctantly and persuaded by Angie and coaxed by the bottle and a half of Chardonnay, sang her heart out on the karaoke with Angie and John.

Eventually, two days before New Year's Eve sitting at home with a bottle of her once-favourite Merlot – the delicious Cyprus *Oikade* having won over her taste buds – and a takeaway meal for one, Katianna finally gave in to Polis' incessant calls and messages, accepting his call at midnight.

'Katianna,' he breathed, 'you picked up.'

'I did.'

'How are you?'

'I'm good, thanks. Busy. Working,' she lied, taking another slug of wine.

'I signed the papers transferring the deeds to the village house back to you today.'

'And you're telling me because?'

'I was hoping we could start over. Go back to how things were before.'

'Before you were an absolute pig.' She heard Polis sigh, knew she was being unreasonable, a grouch, but she could not stop herself.

'Before I misread the situation. Before I made the biggest mistake of my life.'

'Is that an apology?' she asked.

'It is, yes.'

'It's too late.'

'I want you back. I want there to be an us again.'

'I can't go back.'

'I really am sorry,' Polis said and hung up.

She fell asleep on the couch and woke almost three hours later; she sat up fighting the disorientation she felt and rubbing her eyes. She went over her conversation with Polis.

In life you have to take other's good intentions as just that or you'll forever be pushing them away. Her Mum's words whenever she spoke about Katianna's dad whisking her off to England. Her mum and dad, the inextricable couple. She understood, finally, what her mum had meant, what she had been referring to.

She knew what she had to do.

Chapter 51

Katianna would never have dreamed of spending New Year's Eve in Cyprus, in her own village house. Life was the best it could be, and she flitted from room to room humming a tune out loud, her steps light and her heart lighter still. Chatter and laughter filled the village house with life again. Through the shutter-framed windows, the old olive tree twinkled adorned with Christmas lights.

Finally, taking her seat around the table Katianna felt herself close to tears as she took in the activity around her. Sofia placed a footed bowl, filled with light pastry cases oozing with a cinnamon and vanilla cream laced with brandy, in the centre of the table which added a magnificent twist to what would still have been a deliciously festive feast.

Savva poured the wine and Angie finished laying the table. Jamie, a secret expert baker, took the most beautiful crispy fig-filled mince pies out of the oven.

'This all smells delicious,' said Katianna and she breathed in the festive aroma of sweet figs and cinnamon.

'Looks like a master bake off,' laughed Sofia.

'Now that's an idea,' said Jamie.

They all sat around the table, each chair a proud testament to the Phini chair project. The fire spat and snapped in the stone hearth and Katianna felt the tears stinging for a moment. She fingered the edge of her *yiayia's* blanket hanging on the back of the chair before taking her seat.

'That roaring fire will definitely keep the *kallikantzaroi* away,' said Polis and, noticing Angie's and Jamie's confused expressions, he explained the old folk story about the mischievous little imps and their efforts to spoil the days between Christmas and Epiphany by climbing down the open chimneys.

They made a toast and laughed at the tale, smiling as they tucked into their fayre, hardly talking for not wanting to miss even a single sensational taste across their tongues.

'I would never have imagined us all here celebrating New Year in Cyprus.'

'Neither would I,' said Angie, leaning into Jamie for a kiss.

'And us too,' said John, leaning in and hugging Vicky.

'And I'm so happy you're all here,' said Katianna, 'and thank you Vicky for all your support, on both sides of the water. It's good to have you on board and I know John is grateful too, even if he pretends, he isn't.'

'No more sibling rivalry,' Vicky teased. 'We're sweet.'

'And we're grateful too. To have you here,' said Sofia to Katianna and Katianna caught the slightest shift in Sofia's posture as she moved her hand to grip Savva's under the table.

'To friends,' said Savva, with a twinkle in his eye which Katianna knew sparkled for Sofia.

'To us,' said Polis and he clinked his glass against Katianna's. Katianna's engagement ring, rightfully back in her possession, gleamed in the candlelight. Polis squeezed her hand and leaned in to kiss her.

She thanked her lucky stars for bringing Polis back to her; he had come into her life to teach her how to move from the shadows of a long-faded love and into the light of a new-found love full of passion.

'To the village house,' said Katianna and she fought the tears in her eyes as her heart filled with a wondrous spirit she had not felt or allowed herself to feel for a long time. She was home. Surrounded by love and people who loved her. The tiny tinkle of a wind chime floated through the air and Katianna knew her *yiayia* and the magic of the village house had made it all possible. 'To new beginnings, *yiayia,*' she whispered.

THE END

References & Notes

Commandaria:

This is a sweet wine which has the richness of caramel too and is mostly enjoyed as an after-dinner drink or with a chocolate dessert.

The wine is made from two local grapes, the blue grape *mavro* blue and the white *xynisteri*. The grapes are grown on the southern slopes of the Troodos Mounatains, about 30 km north of Limassol, in poor volcanic soils. There are only fourteen villages entitled to make Commandaria.

The grapes are picked very ripe, even overripe, and thus are very rich in sugar. They are dried in the sun for up to two weeks to further increase the sugar content. Following the drying process, the grapes are pressed and undergo a long fermentation for up to three months. Sometimes the winemaker may fortify this with grape spirit, but it is not mandatory. After being aged in oak barrels for at least two years the alcohol content is between 15% and 20%.

Visit www.forbes.com for more details.

Hypnos & Pasithea:

Hypnos is the Greek god of Sleep and was married to the youngest of the

Graces, Pasithea, a deity of hallucination or relaxation, depending upon interpretation.

Visit www.greekmyths-greekmythology.com to read more.

Kallikantzaroi:

These small underworld creatures resemble trolls, elves, or goblins. Many believed that if they made their way into your home, they would steal your food, hide your tools and other personal belongings, ruin your furniture, and make a mess. Some feared them while others believed they were simply a bunch of tricksters. They were most talked about at Christmas when they would come out to play and according to Greek Orthodox tradition would appear between the 25th December and the 6th January. This period, known as the twelve days of Christmas, was when they were allowed to roam freely. On the day of the Theophany, known as Epiphany in the west, the kallikantzaroi would run back to the nearest caves, tunnels, and knotholes, and reenter the underworld.

Visit www.helinika.com for more details.

Moonstruck, poem by Angelos Sikelianos:

Angelos Sikelianos was born on March 28, 1884.

He was a Greek lyric poet and playwright. His themes include Greek history, religious symbolism as well as universal harmony in poems such as The Moonstruck.

More details can be found at www.tumgir.com

Oenou Yi Wine:

On the surrounding hillsides of Omodos, embracing the wine-producing estate of Vassiliades, "Oenou Yi", you will find the beautifully aliened vineyards that lay amphitheatrically.

The contemporary winery "Oenou Yi" combines high technology equipment and the ideal practices for best quality winemaking to successfully govern the vineyards. Learn more about their beautiful vineyards and wines here:

www.oenouyi.wine

Phini Chair:

The famous wooden chair associated with village life and traditional establishments across Cyprus derives its name from the Phini Village, of approximately 300 inhabitants, next to the springs of the River Diarizos on the Troodos Mountains. Dio dio Handicraft collective aims to ensure the craftsmanship and knowledge continues.

More can be found on their website www.diddiohandmade. wordpress.com

Pipilla lace:

"Pipilla" is a delicate handmade lace, made only by using a needle and thread, which create tightly or lightly tied knots known as "velonokombos". According to oral tradition, it is believed that "pipila" is of byzantine origin.

Visit www.cyprusisland.net and www.unesco.org.cy for more information.

Tatsia dance:

Can also be written as tacha and datsia or dacha. A dance performed in social gatherings and at weddings. It demonstrates the agility of the dancer - a man - as well as his skill to balance glasses filled with wine centrifugally turned in a circular sieve.

Visit www.kypros.org to learn more.

A personal note on the words *"Not the North"*, Chapter 10, from the author:

For those readers who might not be familiar with Cyprus history the northern part of the island is illegally occupied by Turkey who invaded the country in 1974. Turkish armed forces still occupy the north, splitting the country into two halves, as well as making Nicosia, the country's capital, the only divided capital in the world. For me, and my family, and thousands of Greek Cypriot and Turkish Cypriot people, this remains a desperately sad and painful situation. I have crossed the border, going from south to north, and found it all too surreal and upsetting to see Greek signage obliterated and replaced with Turkish writing on village signs and street names. Whole villages have remained abandoned, sitting like ghost grounds in half a century of dust and grime, churches and cathedrals have been desecrated. Many Greek and Turkish Cypriots are still fighting and campaigning for a peaceful, unified country.

For anyone wishing to learn more, there are many sites across the internet and a number of good books which will provide the background and knowledge on the history of Cyprus and the unfortunate situation which means a part of Cyprus still remains illegally occupied 48 years on.

Acknowledgements

I am deeply grateful to the team at Kingsley Publishers for all their support, abiding faith in my writing and professionalism in bringing this book to market.

Thank you to my mum and dad with whom I took my first ever trip to Omodos; it ignited my passion to write this story.

Thank you to my wonderful writing buddies who guided me forward with their thoughtful and detailed feedback and excellent advice from when the book began this journey in its rawest form. Warmest thanks to Judith Crosland who read my chapters over and over with a keen eye and incredibly useful advice. Also, my beta reader team – Lia Seaward, Maria Amoss, Thoula Bofilatos, Julianna Kotlinski and Vicki Powell – who gave wholeheartedly and generously of their time and who prompted me to make the story even better with their notes, questions, and probing inquisitiveness.

To Nadia Marks for her beautiful front cover endorsement; forever grateful to you.

To Alan Reynolds, my partner in everything and my biggest fan, my constant always and forever friend, you're the best.

About the Author

Born in London to Greek Cypriot parents, Soulla Christodoulou was the first in her family to go to university and later retrained to become a teacher.

Her novels, Broken Pieces of Tomorrow and The Summer Will Come are available on Amazon alongside Alexander and Maria which was nominated for the RSL Ondaatje Prize 2021.

The Summer Will Come, a book club read in the Year of Learning Festival 2019, is currently under contract for translation into Greek and earmarked as a book to movie project.

Soulla is happiest writing in her pretty garden Writing Room and drinking tea infused with cinnamon sticks and cloves.

Connect with Soulla on her website
https://www.soulla-author.com/
Instagram: @soullasays
Twitter: @schristodoulou2
She loves to hear from her readers.

Lightning Source UK Ltd.
Milton Keynes UK
UKHW041448230223
417521UK00001B/28